A light boat, sailing across a broad bay, with the tops of ancient sky-scrapers deep below. Our western North American world, hundreds and then thousands of years into the future. Dozens of remarkable stories, in the unfolding ecologies of post collapse, post climate change. Civilizations and technologies die or are lost, but human ingenuity—families, tribes, and villages, the musicians, shamans, philosophers, and people of power—live on.

 — Gary Snyder, poet, *Mountains and Rivers Without End*

Utterly fascinating and alternately horrifying and deeply moving.

 — Gayle Wattawa, ed., *Inlandia: A Literary Journey Through California's Inland Empire*

The Great Bay is an extraordinary book that thrives at the intersection of dystopian imagination and planet-scale history. Its tale of how humankind rediscovers what matters after an all-too-imaginable global disaster is informed by Pendell's knowledge of anthropology, botany, Buddhism, and the place we call California, but it is not bur-dened by these things. Instead, it soars into its own particular dream-time, flickering at the edge of familiarity like a newly met friend you're supposed to know, populated by archetypal characters who have populated literature since before there was literature. A wise, cunning, and important book.

 — Steve Silberman, contributing editor, *Wired*

THE GREAT BAY

CHRONICLES OF THE COLLAPSE

a novel

DALE PENDELL

North Atlantic Books
Berkeley, California

Published by
North Atlantic Books
Berkeley, California

Cover art by Paul Honatke
Cover and book design by Brad Greene
Printed in Canada

The Great Bay: Chronicles of the Collapse is sponsored and published by the Society for the Study of Native Arts and Sciences (dba North Atlantic Books), an educational nonprofit based in Berkeley, California, that collaborates with partners to develop cross-cultural perspectives, nurture holistic views of art, science, the humanities, and healing, and seed personal and global transformation by publishing work on the relationship of body, spirit, and nature.

North Atlantic Books' publications are available through most bookstores. For further information, visit our website at www.northatlanticbooks.com or call 800-733-3000.

Library of Congress Cataloging-in-Publication Data

Pendell, Dale, 1947–
    The great bay : chronicles of the collapse : a novel / Dale Pendell.
        p. cm.
    ISBN 978-1-55643-895-0 (hardcover)
    ISBN 978-1-62317-402-6 (paperback)
    1. Global warming—Fiction. 2. California—Fiction. I. Title.
    PS3616.E538G74 2010
    813'.6—dc22   2010003856

1 2 3 4 5 6 7 8 9 MARQUIS 24 23 22 21 20 19 18

Printed on 100% recycled paper

TABLE OF CONTENTS

The First Decade of the Collapse, 2021–2030

The Second Decade, 2031–2040

The Third Through the Fifth Decades, 2041–2070

Humboldt Bay

Sleepy Hollow

Winnemucca

Paradise

Battle Mountain

Donner Pass

Wheatland

San
Francisco

Tracy

Modesto

Salinas
Bay

Kearsarge
Pass

Bakersfield

Fort Tejon

Chemehuevi
Valley

Palos Verdes Island

Capistrano

San Gorgonio
Pass

San Diego

The Second Half-Century, 2071–2120

The Second Century, 2121–2220

The Third Century, 2221–2320

The Fourth and the Fifth Centuries, 2321–2520

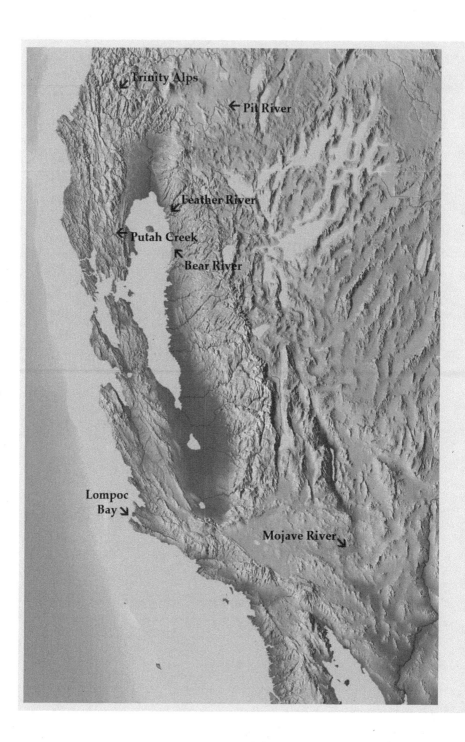

The Sixth Through the Tenth Centuries, 2521–3020

The Second Thousand Years, 3021–4020

The Third Through the Fifth Millennia, 4021–7020

The Sixth Through the Tenth Millennia, 7021–12020

The Far Millennia, Beginning Ten Thousand Years After the Collapse

Pre-Flood Cemetery Discovered

The graves were laid out in a precisely geometrical grid, covering many acres, and are believed to be at least twenty thousand years old.

"They were more like beads than people," in the opinion of Philosopher Jantz, who described evidence of a highly regimented society. "They were sophisticated technologically, and clearly were familiar with the Third Circle," said Jantz, "but they seem to have been hypnotized by the Forms, and to have mistaken the Interdimensional Constants for reality."

Believed to be the last issue of the New York Times, *dated August 18, 2021, from the papers of Janet Conway, Archives of the Scholar's Guild, Berkeley.*

*** August 18, 2021 ***

PRESIDENT CALLS FOR CALM

In a recorded message released by General Springman, the President today called for calm.

———

All Reservists to Report

Police Fire on Looters

Gasoline Trucks Hijacked

———

STOCK TRADING CONTINUES DESPITE OFFICIAL CLOSURE

General Springman, speaking for the President, ordered all banks closed for the duration of the emergency.

———

Chinese Exchanges Open

Gold at $6,000 per Ounce

Futures Collapse

"It's hardly surprising," according to Morris Feingold, CEO of FGGS Associates. "The future looks pretty dicey."

Pawn Shops Doing Brisk Business in NY

———

OFFICIALS FEAR BLACKOUT MAY SPREAD

Large parts of the West are without power for the third day. Spokesmen for the Energy Conglomerate complain of lack of workers.

———

Private Militias Struggle to Maintain Order

Health Officials Recommend Boiling Drinking Water

Government Scientists Still Hopeful for Vaccine

———

The First Decade
of the Collapse
2021–2030

For a while they buried the bodies in mass graves with bulldozers. The National Guard had been deployed since the imposition of martial law. When the disease spread and the bodies became too many, they just burned them in houses, sometimes a whole block at a time. The electricity failed in August. In a week the gasoline supplies ran out and the smell of carrion in the cities was overpowering. Corpses lined the streets where people had carried them out of their houses and apartments, while there were still enough people who wanted to do that. Occasional helicopters flew over the cities telling people to stay in their homes. Nobody had any better idea. Dogs ate at the corpses and some people shot at the dogs; others, in frustration, shot at the helicopters.

2021 had been the hottest summer on record, even topping 2020. The power grid had been stretched to the breaking point for weeks. The "strategic oil reserves" had been depleted the year before—an election year—though the election was never held. The government had imposed rationing, though it didn't extend to private jets or to the air force. The stock market closed. Paper wealth disappeared overnight.

1

The disease struck the National Guard as hard as everyone else in the cities. Actually, the guardsmen stayed on the job longer than the corporate security armies protecting the wealthy suburbs, who equaled them in numbers. The guardsmen had a sense, at least a little sense, of legitimacy and loyalty to a cause beyond themselves. In the twenty-first century no one looked upon the corporation as the East India Company, as the spearhead of progress for whom the noble were willing to die. Nonetheless, by the end of August most of the guardsmen had deserted to escape the cities or to try to find their families.

One by one the power plants went dark, another kind of funeral pyre with no one to light it and keep it burning.

Nobody agreed on the precise nature of the pandemic. The government blamed an Asian influenza. Doctors said it was a new kind of chicken pox, or smallpox. There was a rumor that the disease was an army bug, a genetically engineered biological weapon that had back-fired, perhaps brought back by soldiers returning from the oil fields in Central Asia. The disease certainly spread with an engineered efficiency—two hundred million died in the United States in the first month.

Most agreed the power outage started in the Southwest, and that the blackout had spread from there.

In California the pumping stations went down. Los Angeles was without water, as was San Diego and most other large cities. The pandemic showed no signs of abating. People were still getting sick. The cities were the worst. Dysentery was widespread. There were rumors of typhus. Nobody wanted to risk infection. Nobody wanted to be around other people. In Central California the owner of a forty thousand acre ranch tried to protect the sovereignty of private property by shooting two trespassers and was killed by the third.

By October the population of the United States was about fifty million. Many had survived the disease, if crippled or blinded—but the disruption was complete. People camped out in the country, alone, or in small groups. Sometimes whole families had escaped the infection; sometimes whole families had died together. Mostly, the world had become widows, widowers, and orphans.

There were no workers. Small groups of police operated as armed bands for their own benefit, pillaging and killing those who resisted. Regiments of the regular army were still functioning, but without electricity or fuel they had no clear objective. They couldn't find the people needed to bring back the power grid. Central leadership disintegrated, or was ignored. Entire regiments went AWOL.

Rumors of a refugee camp at the Vandenberg Air Force Base sparked a mass emigration from Santa Maria, thousands streaming twenty-five miles down Highway One through Casmalia onto the base. A colonel ordered his command to fire on the crowds to keep them out. No one obeyed his orders. The crowds swamped the base and refused to leave. After ten days they were too weak to leave.

In Lompoc two hundred forgotten prisoners in lockdown died in their cells. In other prisons it was worse.

Nuclear ships of the world's navies cruised around the world, looking for a safe place to go. No one knew how the disease got onto the ships. Some suspected mosquitoes.

In Texas, the few surviving workers at a large game reserve

released the animals, rather than watch them starve. Most of them starved anyway. Thousands of large cats were released—there were more tigers in Texas than in the wild—but most of them were too inbred to be able to feed themselves.

The disease moved around the world, mutated, and went around again. Communities at high elevations seemed to escape the worst of the disease, but they couldn't escape the shortages. Many died in the winter. The next summer the disease came through again, more sporadically if with no less virulence. In the United States, as much as that still existed by the autumn of 2022, the population was about fifteen million.

Groups began to form, and communities. Armed gangs would take over warehouses of food or other supplies, until some other armed gang took it away from them. There was no harvest in the fall of 2022—no one had planted anything. That winter the survivors ate up whatever was left of the stored food, and any odd- or even-toed ungulates they could find, and dogs and cats, and sometimes each other. Fishermen did better than many others—at least those with skiffs that could be rowed.

Vigilance committees formed. Sometimes there were trials.

Occasionally someone would find a stash of gasoline or diesel. There were still untapped gas tanks in abandoned vehicles and depots and buried tanks. The problem was that if you got too much, others would try to take it away from you. By the spring of 2023, those with any sense, and there were many, planted gardens. In the summer the disease made one more attack, but its virulence was somewhat attenuated. Children and those already weakened by malnutrition suffered the worst.

People who knew how to do things found each other. One

group boot-strapped some hydroelectric power from a small dam on the Feather River, hoping to build off the local grid to gradually reconstruct an infrastructure. In the mountains anyone with gasoline saved it for their generators and the chainsaw, and then just for the chainsaw.

In Richmond, experienced workers were trying to get a refinery operating, but it was always catch-22: "We need gasoline, so that we can make some gasoline." Some were saying that steam engines made more sense, but there weren't any steam engines. Food was a bigger and bigger problem. Urban fires were common and they burned until they burned themselves out.

People were working together because they wanted to help and because that's what people do. No one worked for money because nobody cared about money. What there was there was lots of and it was free. What was scarce had to be bartered for with something else that was scarce. Paper currency was useful only for fires. In Oroville a turbine failed and the incipient electrical grid once again went black.

2022 and 2023 were the Hunger Years. People can endure near starvation for long periods of time while awaiting rescue or deliverance. But there were no deliverers, no rescuers— there were no relief expeditions. People starved, quietly, and died quietly, and, like any animal who starves to death, with the dignity of acceptance.

In the autumn of 2023 some people in California were smart enough to gather acorns. In many parts of the world starvation was widespread. The last resort, the eating of the dead, became common. In some places no one survived who had not consumed the forbidden flesh. By spring of 2024 the population of the U.S. was eight million and still declining. People lost faith that the system of the old world would ever return and began to plan for the next year's winter.

There were plenty of firearms and weaponry for everyone and everyone was armed, but the roving armed gangs had mostly self-destructed—there was nothing left to steal. A lot of rural people were sorry they had eaten their horses. That fall the salmon were plentiful all up and down the west coast. Ships with sails were making a comeback. Acoustic music was all the rage.

Rural communities banded together for self-defense. The cities were ghost towns. Local governments took on an astonishing array of forms: democracies, consensus confederations, fiefdoms, bandit armies.

Maybe because Californians were more used to eccentric religious cults than the rest of the country, the wave of revivalism and zealotry that followed the pestilence was less virulent there. In Texas religious warfare involved firearms. There were lynchings in the South. Jews were killed. In the impoverished hills of New Hampshire and Vermont the petty small town bigotries and envies and animosities, never far beneath the surface, burst forth with an old-fashioned stoning. Mostly, though, pragmatism won out and the witches were needed as doctors.

In California, if anything, the sheer variety and diversity of the cults discouraged lethal rivalries. There were fundamentalist cults, Pentecostal cults—even the Methodists returned to the tents. There were antinomian Ranters, free-love Diggers, and all manner of communes: Eastern, New Age, prophetic, and libertine. There were pagan earth cults, death cults, Gnostic cults, Goddess cults, tantric cults. There was a cult that believed ingesting hallucinogenic mushrooms conferred immunity to the "White Plague." There was an all-women's collective in Santa Cruz. Penitentes returned, hemp-smoking saddhus carrying heavy crosses to the glorious apocalyptic wedding of Jesus and Kali.

Christians who had been expecting the Rapture set new dates. The dates passed and they set new dates. Those dates passed and the groups split, and split again. Hundreds of new and revived heresies appeared: Arians who denied the Trinity, Cainites who preached that God was evil, New Cathars practicing *coitus reservatus,* Monophysites denying the humanity of Christ, Swedenborgians with their angels. Several Jewish millenarian sects appeared and flourished, devoted to asceticism and constant prayer.

A charismatic preacher in Hollywood received a vision that the Second Coming could be achieved only by destroying everything that was left of the sinful world before the Collapse. His powers of oration were able to pull together a band of several hundred desperate souls who burned books and warehouses throughout Los Angeles. The libraries at UCLA were ransacked. The group moved through Cahuenga Pass and started fires in the San Fernando Valley, scavenging food as they went. After several months the group dispersed, but like groups appeared around the country for another decade.

In 2025, on a rural commune in the Sacramento Valley, someone heard a short wave broadcast in an unknown language from some part of the world that still had a functioning infrastructure. Someone else heard a call from a Russian submarine. Otherwise, all the news was local. Two more years passed and the population began to stabilize at about four million, 1/80th of what it had been five years before. About a quarter of the children were still being taught to read by their parents, but fewer and fewer young people showed any interest. Snaring rabbits and small rodents was a popular pastime.

A clever machinist was building steam engines from old oil barrels and salvaged pistons. Somebody made a hot air balloon. Distillation was common wherever people could grow corn. Mechanics who remembered carburetors adapted some engines to ethanol. Old tractors that could be converted became precious, as did antique automobiles. Groups of youths would make forays into the cities to hunt rats. No one knew what the rats ate.

Ships occasionally arrived on the east coast from Europe, vainly hoping that things might be better in America. The pandemic had spread across Europe as had the Black Plague, but at jet speed and with a designed lethality. Mortality in the cities had been over ninety percent.

But the Collapse had been piecemeal in Europe—some pockets survived with a functioning infrastructure for over a year. France kept their nuclear generators going for months. But no oil or coal was moving anywhere, and by 2023 even the frugal ran out of fuel and had to turn off their lights. Much of Northern Europe could have survived on coal, if they'd had any food. But they didn't. Eastern Europe might have acceded to some cultural dominance—they had the most farmers who could function without machinery—had they not started fighting each other. Around the Mediterranean the coastal fishing peoples avoided the worst of the famines.

The pandemic kept bouncing across Europe and Asia like a wave in a box. High density areas were hit the worst. Depopulation of the lowlands of China was almost complete. In India, isolated rural communities did better than the cities. Lapps survived as well as anyone. And Chukchis.

Africans, like everyone else, died in heaps. It wasn't a fast enough decline to save the chimpanzees, or the gorillas, but it was enough to save the elephants, and the antelope, at least for a while. In South America the highest survival rate was in the Amazon.

అ అ అ

Amanda

Santa Monica, 2021
from Janet Conway's Stories of the Collapse
Archives of the Scholar's Guild, Berkeley

When Amanda's mother got sick at the end of September she ordered Amanda out of the house. She told her to go to her father's and not to come back. When Amanda started to complain that she wasn't sure she knew the way, that it was too far, her mother had screamed at her not to come any closer.

Amanda left the house and walked down 14th Street by habit to her junior high school and walked through the playground. There was no one there and she continued down 16th to Wilshire Boulevard. She could see a few people walking around on Wilshire and she walked another block to Arizona Avenue. There were no cars moving on the streets. Anyone with a car had left.

She started up Arizona toward West L.A. There were bodies on the sidewalk on every block and swarms of buzzing flies, so she stayed in the center of the street. Some of the bodies were wrapped in sheets; others were bloated with grotesque expressions. After thirty blocks she finally came to the hospital of the Veterans Administration and she could see crowds of people milling around on the lawn, so she walked over to Ohio Avenue to avoid them. She crossed under the San Diego Freeway, and in another mile found her father's apartment house. It was mid-afternoon.

The door was unlocked and she went in. She called but there was nobody there. Amanda was very hungry by that time so without thinking she opened the refrigerator. The smell of rotten food almost made her throw up. She went in and lay down on her father's bed, which was unmade, and cried. When she woke up it was almost dark. She picked out a can of soup from the cupboard. The can opener was electric and didn't work, but it did make a small cut in the top of the can, which she was then able to make bigger with a kitchen knife until she was able to eat the soup from the can, cold.

She stayed in the apartment for two days until there was no more food and then went out. She tried the door of the apartment next door but it was locked. One of the downstairs apartments was open and Amanda went in and called hello. There was a bad smell in the house. No one answered and Amanda poked her head around a hallway into the bedroom. There was a corpse on the bed and the stench was overpowering. Clusters of thick-stemmed orange mushrooms were growing from the nostrils and ear canals. Amanda ran out. She decided to find a store and walked into Westwood. There was smoke in the sky.

In downtown Westwood she found a supermarket with all of its windows broken and went in. There were a few other people in the store but they didn't pay any attention to her. She took several plastic bags, filled them with cans of food and a bag of potato chips and some bottles of water. There was another girl her age getting water and Amanda said hello. The girl said her name was Inez.

Inez asked Amanda if she had any parents and Amanda said that she didn't know where they were. "What about you? Do you have any parents?"

"My mother died. My father lives in Oxnard."

"What are you going to do?"

"I'm going to go to Oxnard. Do you want to go with me?"

Amanda said no, and the girls went outside onto the street. A crowd of people was running down the street breaking windows and starting fires. A man spotted them and came out of the crowd and asked them if they were orphans. When the girls didn't answer the man told them to come with him, that he would take care of them. Amanda told the man that they couldn't because they were going to Oxnard. The man tried to grab them but the girls ran off.

The man called after them that they would be damned if they didn't become children of Christ, but at that moment the crowd began chanting "On to Century City," and the man turned back and rejoined the crowd.

The girls ran two blocks and then stopped to catch their breath on a small lawn. Amanda opened the potato chips and they both ate them, and drank a lot of water. They decided that they would be best friends. Amanda asked where Oxnard was.

"It's up the coast," Inez answered, "by Ventura."

Amanda knew where Ventura was. Amanda said they should stop

and get day packs at the surplus store in Santa Monica. "And more water. And a can opener."

Inez said she had some tortillas, that they were all moldy but that they could scrape the mold off.

They both felt better when they got to the ocean. Near Topanga they went into a convenience store but it was almost empty. They walked another mile to the entrance of the canyon and looked for a place to camp on the beach. There were men along the beach with fishing poles. One of them, in a cowboy hat, walked up the beach toward them. He addressed them as "ladies" and asked them if they wanted some fish.

The girls said yes and the cowboy man suggested that they come to his camp and he'd fix them dinner. The girls went. The camp was a lean-to with a fire pit and a few pots and pans and some blankets. The man said that he had a house up Topanga Canyon but that mostly he was camping down here at the beach. The cowboy's name was Philip and all the other fishermen on the beach seemed to know him. One of them came by and talked about going out in a boat.

The fish didn't look very good. They were small and bony but they ate them all, along with some beans that seemed undercooked. The cowboy told Amanda that she reminded him of his daughter. Amanda thought that he was the kindest man she had ever known.

The cowboy wasn't really a cowboy. He said he was a poet from England and he kept the campfire burning after it got dark and he told stories. A couple came down the beach and asked if they could camp there and the cowboy told them yes and gave them the rest of the beans. He gave Amanda and Inez a blanket to share.

In the morning the cowboy said he had to go up canyon for some supplies, but that the girls were welcome to stay there if they wanted to and that he would teach them how to fish. Amanda thought that might be a good idea but Inez wanted to keep going on to Oxnard and they said goodbye.

Three miles up the coast the girls heard a dog barking in a house off the highway. They opened the front door and went in to see what was happening. There was a small dog inside that was very friendly and very hungry. They found dog food for the dog and fed him and the dog followed them.

There were other people walking up Pacific Coast Highway and lines of abandoned cars at every gas station. Amanda and Inez fell in with a Mexican couple. Inez talked to them in Spanish and the man talked some with Amanda in English. They ate lunch together in a gated community above the highway and refilled their water bottles from the swimming pool at the Recreation Center. The man's name was Tony. Tony Romero. The woman was Cecilia.

When they were walking again Amanda realized that the dog was missing and started crying. Inez didn't say anything. Amanda thought that they should go back. The man said no, that they must not do that. That night they camped on the beach near Paradise Cove. The man built a fire and went off for a while and came back with meat on skewers. He said it was a rabbit that had been killed by a car.

The next day they reached Pt. Nicholas below the county line and wandered into a gated community on the point. There were signs that said "No Trespassing" and "No Surfing." Tony shouted and they heard a man answer from a huge house on the cul-de-sac. There was a very large sign on the lawn in front of the house that said "Proud to be an American." They went in and found a man lying on a large leather couch. His face and arms were pock-marked from the disease. The man asked them if they had any food. The man had been crippled by the pox and couldn't walk without a pole or a table to keep him balanced. Tony said he was sorry but Amanda gave him all of her food except for two cans of corned beef hash. They filled their water bottles at the man's swimming pool and filled some buckets for the man and brought them in before they left. As they walked on that next day they passed people walking the other direction, toward Santa Monica. They were looking for relatives. There were more and more abandoned cars on the road.

They camped that night in Little Sycamore Canyon at Solromar, north of the county line. There were other people camped there and people exchanged news and rumors. One man said that he'd heard the Navy had landed in Long Beach with freighters full of food. Somebody else said that the pandemic had been a germ warfare attack by Arab terrorists. Somehow it was the fault of the Liberals. A woman wearing jeans and a tee shirt said that the Administration had secret refuges where they'd taken all the rich people and given them vaccinations and that they had started the pandemic as a way to stay in power. Why else had they canceled the election? Tony didn't say very much.

The next day they passed hillsides covered with Spanish bayonet and prickly pear. Cecilia showed the girls how to gather the cactus fruits. That night they camped above Pt. Mugu on Calleguas Creek. The girls hiked up the creek until they found a pool of green water and they filled their bottles. Tony came back to camp with a dozen avocados wrapped in his shirt.

They reached Oxnard before noon the next day. The countryside was agricultural and there were pumpkins and sugar beets in the fields and they gathered two large sugar beets, which was all they could carry. They didn't see very many people as they walked through Oxnard and they didn't talk with those they passed. There were bodies rotting in the streets and ruins of smoldering houses on every block. They didn't want to stop so they ate Tony's avocados while they walked. New housing developments built on farmland extended the limits of the city for two miles. There was no break between Oxnard and El Rio.

Tony was headed for a camp he knew on the outskirts of El Rio, near the gravel pits. There were about forty people there. A lot of them knew Tony. They had lots of food and they took water from the duck ponds. One of the people knew Inez's father but didn't know where he was. Maybe he was at the Indian Rancheria, the man said, but he hadn't seen him or heard any news of him. The Rancheria was sixty miles away, at Santa Ynez.

Tony's friends said that there was hardly anybody left in the city, that there were whole blocks with no survivors. The SeaBees at Port Hueneme had tried to set up camps until they ran out of food. People stole hundreds of boats at the harbor to try to reach the Islands. Others had moved to camps along the river or out in the fields.

ൡ ൡ ൡ

After a week there was a new outbreak of the disease along the river. People called it "white measles." Panic began to spread in the camps. Tony Romero got sick. The girls decided to go to Santa Ynez. They didn't hug anybody goodbye.

They walked north on 101. The sky was full of smoke and the sunlight had a reddish color. After they crossed the Santa Clara River they could see individual fires from the scores of developments spreading up the valley. There were huge cookie cutter tracts where the fire had spread to whole blocks. In the distance fires had spread to the mountains and the chaparral was in flames.

After six miles they came to Highway 126 and had to backtrack to avoid walking into town on Ventura Boulevard. They walked another three miles until they were near the ocean and rested in the shade of an overpass to eat lunch. They heard motorcycles approaching but they didn't have anywhere to go. Two bikers on choppers came up to them and stopped. They wore guns in shoulder holsters and no helmets and were covered with tattoos.

They looked at the girls for a while and asked them where they were going. The girls didn't answer and one of the bikers asked again. Inez said that they were going to Santa Ynez to look for her father. The two bikers looked at each other. The thin one shrugged and Amanda heard him say something to the other one about going the back way through Cuyama. The big one seemed to agree and they told the girls to hop on. Amanda asked if they were taking them to Santa Ynez and the big man answered yes. There seemed nothing else to say.

Inez climbed on behind the thin one with the black hair and the headband. Amanda climbed on behind the man with the long beard who had a sawed-off shotgun strapped behind his seat. The big man pulled Amanda's arms around him and ordered her to hang on and they roared off. Amanda thought he looked a little like one of the presidents that she had seen in her history book, except he had parts of his beard braided. She thought the other rider looked like an Indian.

In Montecito they pulled off and cruised the exclusive homes in the hills. The bikers seemed to know where to find the three and four car garages that had vehicles from which they could siphon gas. Ashes were falling all around them from the brush fires in the mountains. It was like it was snowing. Some of the flakes were whole leaves that Amanda could recognize.

Somewhere near Goleta they passed a caravan of three Hummers bristling with weapons going the other direction. Someone in the middle Hummer took a pot shot at them just for the hell of it. The bullet wasn't even close and they roared on.

Near Gaviota they stopped and camped on the beach. One of the men had a pot and built a fire and they all ate hot chili beans with spoons. The bikers mostly ignored the girls. They drank warm beer and laughed at how it foamed and speculated on what their friends were doing in Bakersfield. After a while they asked Ynez about her father and where she thought he might be and listened carefully to her descriptions of the Indian Rancheria and the Casino. One of them said that it was probably better that they got there in the day-time. The bearded one was called "Moog" and he called the black-haired man "Fly." Moog gave the girls a sleeping bag, though it was so warm they didn't need it. Moog and Fly just slept in their clothes on the sand.

In the morning they started early and were in Santa Ynez before nine o'clock. A man in a cowboy hat was guarding the Casino with a rifle. Moog and Fly circled the parking lot once slowly. Fly told Inez to stay behind him and not to get off the bike unless he said. Moog told Amanda to unhook the shotgun and hide it on the right side of the bike. They rode up to the entrance and stopped about thirty feet from the man with the rifle, who aimed it at Fly. Fly had parked about fifteen feet past Moog, directly facing the man, so that they formed a narrow triangle, and had left his engine running.

17

"We're looking for Rudy Vallejo," Fly said to the man with the rifle. Moog had his arms folded. Amanda hung on behind him.

"Not here," the man said.

"Is he alive?"

"Don't know. Why are you asking?"

"This is his daughter," Fly answered.

The man looked Inez over. "Okay, I'll take her to him."

"You don't look like Rudy Vallejo," Fly answered back.

"Where Rudy Vallejo is is our business," the man with the rifle said, "and that makes his daughter our business."

Moog had quietly taken his shotgun from Amanda and had it pointed at the man before he had finished speaking. "I think we'll be on our way," Moog said, "as long as you don't move."

The man with the rifle didn't move or say anything. Fly wheeled away in a big circle and came back farther away with his gun out. Moog started his engine and roared off, aiming the shotgun as long as he could. Fly roared after him, zigzagging. A shot passed over their heads. The girls hung on tightly.

"Your dad's not here," Fly yelled to Inez. "He's probably dead. We're going to Bakersfield."

∾ ∾ ∾

They passed through Santa Maria without leaving the freeway. They couldn't see the city but they could smell it. Fog mixed with smoke and in the eerie darkness the heavy stench had become an aerosol that saturated their clothes and their lungs. Across the river they turned east on Highway 166. Hundreds of people were camped around the reservoir. Some of them were on the highway and waved to them to stop but they didn't. Five miles farther inland the road made a sharp bend and they stopped for lunch where there was a pool of algae covered water, which they all drank.

Past Cuyama they turned north and entered the valley at Maricopa, on Bitterwater Creek, and then went over to 99. Bakersfield was shrouded in smoke and they could see fires burning north of town. There was no one at the clubhouse but there was a note on the table from Nan-Girl that said, "We're at the House."

It was already evening so they decided to spend the night. Moog and Fly were leaning against the wall of the clubhouse quietly smoking marijuana. They could hear the girls talking about them inside.

"Who do you like better," Amanda whispered, "Moog or Fly?"

"Fly," Inez answered. "Moog's really nice but Fly's cuter."

"Yeah, me too," Amanda agreed. "Moog's really nice though."

Moog looked at Fly and gave him the finger. Fly passed him the joint.

In the morning they scoured the city for supplies. A few cars were moving and there were people on the streets but nobody bothered them and they crossed north over the bridge into Oildale and cruised east along the river. For five miles the oil fields were a burning wasteland. Scores of fires filled the air with billowing columns of black smoke. Some men at a crossroads told them that people had broken into the refinery looking for gasoline and that the security guards had fired on them and killed several, and that hundreds of people had come back in the night and set fires, breaking pipelines and blowing wells and storage tanks.

Linda had a house on the river on a ritzy cul-de-sac, her inheritance as the only daughter of old oil money. The neighbors hadn't been happy but private property had triumphed. Five of their club members were at Linda's house: Nan-Girl and Bobby, Yellow Dog, Marcy, and Linda. Jerry had died in the first week of the pandemic; he'd been the club president. There were two other women there with their two young children. Yellow Dog said the women's names were Margo and Suzy.

"New prospects," he laughed.

By October the members of the Roadkill M.C. had collected all manner of supplies and equipment. They had a truck with gas and used it to get more. They took over the two houses on the adjoining properties, convincing the remnants of the staff and the other squatters that they were better off with the Roadkills, and brought everything of value up from the clubhouse. Their arsenal was awesome. They were ready for a siege.

Linda decided she liked being a schoolteacher and took in Inez and Amanda to soothe her widowhood. Margo and Suzy, who had never been close to a motorcycle in their lives, were having trouble with the culture and bickered with the men. They were considering moving out when Linda told a Mexican couple with a baby that they could stay there also. Somehow that changed the dynamics and the women stayed on. Luis and Rosa had been camping at the Mexican village that was forming about a mile down the road. It was never clear why they had left the village to join the Roadkills. In mid-October an eccentric Japanese artist and engineer named Akira joined them. Then an elderly Basque sheepherder named Agosti joined the camp and they were eighteen, counting the baby.

They were an odd group and the club rules had to be changed so that everyone could be a member. That was Linda's idea. Moog and Yellow Dog and Fly, as the three bonafide members, had to council to talk about it. Bobby was still a prospect but they included him and they all spent a day fishing and decided it was a good idea. Everyone there could be a member. Yellow Dog thought that Margo and Suzy should only be given half-memberships because they were so bitchy. Fly had a quiet grin and told him that if he had the balls to bring it up at the meeting he'd vote with him.

The question came up about the initiation, and whether or not the new women would have to "pull the train." Moog thought the women would do kinda like they damn well felt like. Yellow Dog asked about the girls. Fly was particularly insistent that they couldn't join until they were sixteen, and that they were off-limits until then. Moog said that maybe everyone could make up initiations and write them on a piece of paper and everyone would have to pull one out of a hat. Yellow Dog said that he was going to write "Give Yellow Dog a blow job." Moog said that was fine but that he had to remember that Bobby might get it, and that Bobby bit, that he knew from experience. This brought general guffaws. Bobby was sorry that the club as he knew it was ending before he had his name and his colors.

Yellow Dog said that they should at least have to get naked and do *something* in front of everyone. Moog said that they had to recognize the new nature of the state of the world, that they had to find some balance between being one percenters and some kind of family values.

Fly thought maybe the answer was that the initiations, whatever they were, had to be in front of the group, members and non-members. Yellow Dog wanted to know how they could have sex or have people go down in front of the children.

Fly shrugged and said that anyone was free to go if they didn't want to be part of the club.

"What if they want to stay but don't want to be part of the club?" Moog asked.

Fly thought for a while and said that had to be okay, that if the club wasn't something so good that the others really *wanted* to be members then maybe they weren't doing it right. Or maybe the non-joiners were just "free riders" by nature.

"'Free Riders' might not be a bad name," Yellow Dog mused.

Bobby said he liked the old name.

"What about 'Rangers'?" Fly offered. "That's the umbrella organization. We can be 'Rangers, Roadkill Chapter.'"

By the end of the day they thought they had resolved things. They had also caught two fish. When they went back they found out that Linda, Nan-Girl, and Marcy had had their own meeting. They weren't so far apart. Everyone agreed that they should have a party. They chose Halloween. Linda seemed to know what day that would be.

They held the party outdoors and everyone came, even Agosti. They put a motorcycle in the center and surrounded it with several pumpkins. The girls added a dried sunflower and long streamers they made from an orange bed sheet. Fly added a human skull he'd found. He said it was only fitting. No one disagreed. Somehow Agosti found a sheep. They slaughtered it and roasted the meat on spits over a fire. There was lots of wine and beer.

They formed a circle at dusk and Moog got up to speak first. He shook up a beer and opened it and sprayed the altar with foam. Then he talked about the history of the Roadkills and how what they wanted was a free life in a world too full of bullshit and that they had that now and so they were closing the club. That they were opening a new club to be called the Rangers and that they were going to be the Roadkill Chapter. That there weren't any other chapters, not even this one yet, but that there would be. That there had to be an initiation to be a Roadkill Ranger, but that they weren't sure what that was yet. That if you were under sixteen you could only be a prospect, but that anyone else could join if they wanted to, if they could come up with an initiation that everyone accepted.

There were hoots when he finished and a jug of wine was passed around the circle. Amanda and Inez were allowed to drink a little and they both took swallows. Linda got up next and welcomed everyone and said that she knew that Jerry would have liked what was happening here now and that she welcomed the new women as her sisters and the new men as her brothers.

Yellow Dog got up next and said that he thought that Margo and Suzy should only be half-members because they were bitchy.

"So which one of us is the bitchiest?" Margo asked.

"You are!" Yellow Dog said.

Everyone got up and spoke. Fly talked a lot about the need to stick together and that by sticking together they might make it.

"The world we lived in before is not going to come back," he said. "I put that skull in the center to remind us of that. We were a band of brothers and now we're a band of brothers and sisters. We've all lost a lot of friends and family. But we have a good place here and we're offering it to all of you to be a part of, to be part of the family."

Amanda and Inez were both shy but they both spoke. Inez was blushing and just said that she was glad to be there and that she liked it there. Amanda said that she didn't know if she wanted to be a Roadkill Ranger or not. That she might like to go look for her father sometime if things got better, but that she was thankful to Moog and Fly and that she wanted to be useful and to help the circle.

Everyone applauded. Some people started getting up to speak a second time. Nan-Girl said it was time to start the party. Bobby put a CD on a boom box.

All agreed it was a great party, especially when it started getting silly. Rosa wanted to know what the initiations were about, that she wanted to join but that these Roadkill hombres should show them what it was all about. Moog and Fly and Yellow Dog and Bobby answered the challenge and took their pants off and did a conga dance around the fire, kicking their bare asses around in time. Linda and Nan-Girl and Marcy got up and danced facing out in a circle around them with their shirts off. Rosa gave a clue as to what had attracted her to the Roadkills and got up and did a strip tease. Pretty soon everybody was up.

Agosti and Akira brought out guitars and sang strange Japanese-Basque ballads. People feasted on the mutton with relish and ate cooked pumpkin. Late in the evening, after much wine, a repressed side of Margo came out and Yellow Dog got his blow job.

They had a club.

∾ ∾ ∾

Interview: Jason Kilpatrick

Aged ninety; conducted in 2081 by Janet Conway
Archives of the Scholar's Guild, Berkeley

Jason Kilpatrick: I was thirty years old at the time of the Collapse. Now I'm ninety. I may be the oldest living person in the Confederation. I was the youngest hedge fund manager in Silicon Valley. We leveraged a hundred to one on our assets and had government bailouts and subsidies built right into our algorithms. It took two million to buy in and even then we were picky. When the Saudis defaulted we got a congressman to add a rider to a national security bill that guaranteed our bonds for fifty billion dollars. When Congress censured him we hired him as a lobbyist at five million a year. It was a great deal.

We specialized in privatizing public assets. I earned over two hundred million a year. I had a hunting lodge in Alaska, a resort in the Bahamas, and my own jet. I was never one of the super-rich but I was a contender. About a million of us owned half the wealth of the whole country. Now I see what a mess we made of the planet.

Imagine one of those old subdivisions, say with ten blocks and around thirty houses per block. That was the way people lived. Now imagine that one of those households owned four whole blocks, and that another four households owned another four blocks. That's the way it was.

The Collapse was a good thing for me. I found love. I found Mary, God rest her soul, a real woman who knew how to work and how to have fun. I organized the Whale Tribe schools in the South Bay and set up our ethanol distillery. Mary and I helped set up the farms on the big golf course and I worked there. And I liked the work I did. I had more fun working than I ever had before the Collapse, and I had more free time and I had real friends. So the Collapse was a good thing for me personally. I was a lonely man before the Collapse. I tried to fill my emptiness with wealth and making money, but now I know I was a lost soul.

A lot of people are bitter about the Collapse. They think the government should have done something. The death of so many people was a tragedy, of course. I lost my whole family. But we were wrecking the earth. Now the ocean is coming up because the ice is melting. We all knew, but none of us wanted to change. So the change came to us. I like the way people help each other. That's what people are supposed to do. No one should wish for the old world to come back. I was there and I was at the top and I know better.

Even before the epidemic became widespread, I had stored up as much food and other supplies as I could. As soon as the first person got sick at work I closed the office and told everybody to stay home. The telephones went on working for a week after the blackout came, but then they went dead. Cell phones didn't work. The emergency broadcasting network made occasional announcements, mostly just telling people to stay calm and to stay home.

The government, what was left of it, had no idea what to do. They had a few army and guard units, but what was there to do? They'd get one power plant back in operation but so what—what could they do but turn on their own lights for a week.

My business partner took the jet to Alaska. The disease was already there when he landed in Fairbanks, probably brought there by someone like him. So he tried to fly to the Bahamas. I don't know if he ever made it—the satellite phones stopped working. Most of what was left of the jet fuel was used up that way, by private jets flying around the world looking for someplace to land.

I had friends who had a large reserve in upstate New York, near the Canadian border. They had their own guards, police, and doctors. They were fine for four or five weeks—I talked to them by satellite, and they went on having parties and playing tennis. Then everyone seemed to get sick at the same time.

At Westport, they put up barbed wire and concrete barricades and shot intruders, but it didn't save them either.

I stayed in California at my place above Portola Valley. I could have gone anyplace in the world. My girlfriend was staying with me. When the telephones stopped working my girlfriend took the Miata to go check on her family. I never saw her again. I basically hid out for three months. I didn't light candles at night and I tried not to make any noise. I had a telescope, so from the top of the hill I could check out what was happening in Palo Alto, Sunnyvale, Cupertino, and all the way to San Jose. I looked for signs of order but didn't see any. Fires were common.

There was a break in the weather around Christmas. I took the Humvee and a small arsenal and went on a foraging expedition. People were still dying everywhere. Corpses were piled along the streets and the smell is something I'll never forget—you couldn't get away from it. Dogs pulled the sheets off the bodies and nobody rewrapped them. Supermarkets were either emptied or under armed guards— but I was headed for a pet food distributor.

When I got to the warehouse there was already a woman there loading a pickup truck. That was how I met Mary. She started joking—asking me if I had any good recipes to swap. Actually, she asked a lot of questions—all very friendly and flirtatious. I realized later that she'd learned the whole story of my survival before I even knew her name. Then she made some decision and invited me to the Silicon Shores Christmas Party—that was what they called themselves— the "Silicon Shores Club." They were a collective—there were about eighty of them, mostly pulled in by Mary. They lived near the golf course in East Palo Alto.

We filled my Hummer and her truck and I followed her to East Palo Alto. I gave them all the food and ended up staying for a week, and then for another week. Mary was friendly but stand-offish at first. After two weeks I decided to move in permanently with the collective. We drove two trucks to my place and loaded up with everything that looked useful and I grabbed some personal items that I still wanted. Other stuff we cached. It turned out to be useful the next fall for acorn gathering. Mary was a woman who liked her freedom, but eventually we started living together.

In those days there was a lot of violence. Everyone wanted to be a survivor and some thought that killing other survivors increased their odds. There were bandit gangs that killed everyone they saw, except for the young girls, and later them also. After the Hunger Years people were different. After the Hunger Years people tried to survive out of a sense of duty—not because they were afraid of dying or had any particular fondness for life.

The collective went on absorbing loners. We scavenged, gathered, fished, defended ourselves from the bandits and the armies, and made friends with other collectives. That was in the second year I think it was. More people died of thirst than from starving that summer. People drank salt water and went crazy, or died from dysentery. We took water from San Francisquito Creek and treated it with iodine. That probably saved a lot of us. The third year was the worst. I think we ate every rat left alive in Silicon Valley. Fishing was poor. Many in the collective got too weak to work.

Mary had friends in Santa Cruz and we drove the Humvee over on a mix of oil and ethanol—I'd been distilling wine and liquor. In Santa Cruz they fed us and gave us two six-foot rolls of nylon netting that you could make fishnets with. The Humvee died in Santa Cruz. An old Chevy took us partway over the mountains on ethanol but then it died so we had to walk the rest of the way, lugging the rolls of netting.

We didn't have much luck with the fishnets—we were all too weak.

We lost two thirds of the collective. We would all have starved, but in February two whales beached themselves in the mud flats. The blubber gave us enough energy to send whale meat out to the other collectives that we knew. We sailed whale meat all around the Bay and made deliveries to the big groups living near Stanford and around the reservoirs. After that we were known as the Whale Tribe. We're still called that.

That was the worst year. Nobody starved to death after that, though we were often hungry. We'd work all year to build up some surplus of food, even if it was just acorns and grass seeds. I don't think anybody survived who wasn't in some kind of group. The whole valley was a ghost town.

The next summer Mary's friends from Santa Cruz showed up with a big truck loaded with vegetables. They helped us plant beans and squash in the golf course. It rained that summer, which was lucky for us. The Stanford Collective was better off—they had more water— but they didn't have the Bay. We traded with them and helped each other a lot.

For a long time what I missed most from the old world was coffee. Now I miss my dentist.

∾ ∾ ∾

Amanda

From Janet Conway's Stories of the Collapse
Kern River, 2022–2029

The Kern River turned out to be one of the better places to live in California in 2022, though in relative terms only. For one, there were a lot of swimming pools in Bakersfield and people rigged tarps to catch rainwater to keep them full. There were large stocks of food. Twenty thousand people still lived in the city, scavenging. Fresno was much worse off.

The pox came through again in the summer of 2022 and hit the city hard, but that was true everywhere. Cholera followed, which was worse, especially along the river. Bobby, Suzy, the two boys, and the baby died. Others moved in.

Late that fall a Latino boy ran into the Roadkill Compound to tell them that a gang of police were attacking Mexican Camp. Fly, Moog, Yellow Dog, and two others jumped on the choppers and roared down to help. They should have come in silently. Moog was blown off his chopper by a shotgun blast that almost cut him in half. Yellow Dog killed two of the men in the gun battle that followed. They both wore badges. After that day Yellow Dog hung up his guns. Margo strapped them on.

The Roadkill Rangers expanded, shrank, and expanded again. The groups along the river began to fall into two categories: open and closed. Some, like the Rangers, maintained extensive contacts with other groups. Others chased off strangers at gunpoint. Among the open groups there were occasional exchanges of personnel, as people would relocate for reasons of romance or inclination. Within local areas this was usually easy, though people who were expelled from a group might have to travel a long ways to find another group that would take them in. Camps of drifters and ne'er-do-wells appeared.

By 2023 the population of Bakersfield and the outlying areas was down to ten thousand and in the next two years it shrank further. There were more incidents of fighting and stealing. Gradually people learned how to grow food and to gather. In Amanda's words, "We ate a lot of things that we don't usually eat." Some groups raised dogs.

In 2029 both Amanda and Inez gave birth to children by Fly. Or, in Amanda's case, she *thought* it was Fly. She wasn't completely sure. They were both boys.

The Second Decade
2031–2040

By 2031, ten years after the Collapse, the population of the United States had stabilized at four million. There were another million in Canada, four million in Central America, and some six million in South America. World population was about eighty million, about the same as the early Iron Age. Infant mortality was high everywhere, but people were learning how to stay alive.

There were widespread heat waves. Carbon dioxide levels approached those of the early Eocene. Industrial outputs of CO_2 had stopped, but a long chain-reaction was in progress, and CO_2 in the atmosphere is long-lived. Permafrost thawing was releasing large amounts of methane. The manmade aerosols and other particulate matter that had been masking the heating from greenhouse gases were gone. There were no cloud-forming contrails. Skies were clearer than they had been in three hundred years and the earth cooked beneath a naked sun. In the West, summer temperatures of 110 degrees Fahrenheit were more and more common, the heat spells lasting for a month at a time. High pressure systems in the interior kept out the cooler air of the jet stream. New records would have been set everywhere, if anyone had been keeping records. It never seemed to cool off at night.

Refugees from the cities lived in the ruins of small towns. Sometimes those who were isolated in the mountains moved down to join them. Nobody wanted to be alone. There were too few people in the world to want to be alone. There was too much death. People knew they needed each other. Established rural communities pulled in closer. People would gather weekly or more often at some central location to trade news or to socialize, and all the empty houses or cabins near the meeting areas were soon occupied. Bicycles were widely used, tubes being patched and repatched.

Sometimes there were tensions between refugees and "natives," those who were already established on the land before the Collapse, especially if the natives had distinctive persuasions. The refugees were almost always a mishmash, racially and culturally, so they settled on being Californians.

A group of farmers near Fresno were able to pool enough diesel to bulldoze gravity fed irrigation canals. People hoarded canning jars. Gold experienced a brief resurgence as a medium of exchange until nobody wanted it any more. "Gold? No thanks, already got some." A rumor that gangsters in Tennessee had broken into Fort Knox didn't help. Goods continued to move as barter or credit. A person's credit was the same thing as their reputation.

Hoarding and depredations were local. There was some killing. A group of mercenaries in San Diego, led by the son of the "last elected governor of California," claimed to be the legitimate government. They called themselves the "Black Watch." They took over Fallbrook with armored personnel carriers and slaughtered several hundred Mexicans and Mexican-Americans who had formed a community there. A band of avenging Mexican insurgents, led by a man who called himself "Joaquin Murrieta," blew up their fuel depot and over the next six months picked off most of the mercenaries one by one.

Mostly, though, everything was too bad, too near to starvation for anyone to be able to organize any large-scale actions. Mostly people helped each other, as people have always done in hard times.

People were full of ideas. Aging electricians and line workers were still concocting schemes to bring back power, though at a local level. Large generators would run for a while, then sputter out. In 2032, Christmas lights were on for an hour on a large redwood tree in downtown Santa Cruz, and again on New Year's Eve.

A group in Martinez managed to fabricate a twenty-foot still, and were able to produce small amounts of fuel oil out of crude salvaged from the hold of a tanker. It was never very much, but it proved the concept. A few barrels of diesel were traded upriver to Sacramento for grain. Machinists in Sacramento were able to use generators to operate enough machinery to fabricate another still, which they floated down to Richmond. Skilled machinists were in high demand.

In East Los Angeles a group of ex-CEOs banded together to organize a large-scale food-for-work program, intending to distribute goods still stored in warehouses. It might have worked, too, had the entrepreneurs not insisted on private ownership of the company. Labor hadn't had so much power since the fourteenth century.

In a way it was a hopeful time. There were still roads,

machines, and large quantities of viable manufactured materials. The Pandemic seemed to have spent itself. Of course, it was hot.

Many believed that the current situation was temporary—that with hard work and ingenuity the world as they had known it could be rebuilt—that oil would flow—that cars and trucks would again move on the highways—that supermarkets would somehow begin receiving deliveries.

Most had a pioneer spirit, eager to apply ideas to build new water systems and new engines of power. But these were not frontier emigrants, the sons and daughters of emigrants, nor the grandchildren of wagon trains: they weren't born to self-reliance and hard labor, and they lacked the unquestioning optimism of Manifest Destiny. Besides, it was easier to scavenge.

In 2034 there was a large earthquake in Oakland, breaking all five bridges. Most of the damage to the bridges was minor—one or two missing sections—but there was no way to repair them. Many of the skyscrapers toppled. Somehow the Pyramid Building in San Francisco survived. Scattered sections of freeways collapsed all around the Bay.

The Sacramento Valley seemed to flood every other year. Tulare Lake filled with water. Flocks of birds appeared. A trickle of water in the broad delta of the Colorado River was once again flowing into the Gulf of California. Farmers opened Haiwee Dam. After a hundred-year hiatus, the lakes in the Owens Valley filled with water.

It was getting harder and harder to find working batteries. Any solar panel that could be found was in use. Some people were using electric golf carts and recharging them from the panels. There was still a lot of legacy wine and liquor around. In fact, distillers used vodka as the starting material for making ethanolic fuel.

Corn was failing all over, threatening a new famine. Seed corn over a decade old was less and less viable, and because of the "death genes" that had been inserted into the genome by global corporations new seed produced stunted crops, or never germinated at all. People began collecting grasses, and planted barley. A Johnny Appleseed type traveled to the Hopi in Arizona to beg for viable seed. Other corn came up from Mexico. After that everyone grew "Indian Corn." People improvised mills or ground it the old way with stones.

The use of solar electricity, storage batteries, and inverters led to a network of octogenarian amateur radio operators—an enthusiasm quickly adopted by the youth. People built windmills. Electricity was too good to lose. Radio gave the young a reason to learn the mysteries of letters and numbers—it stretched their horizons. They learned geography. Isolated communities in other parts of the country sent greetings, and tales of woe. Some groups wished to remain isolated, and their location secret, and forbade radio.

Other than those few with solar power, there was no illumination after dark. Flashlights were saved for emergencies, as were candles. Storytelling flourished. Children wanted to know why the world was the way it was, and adults tried to make it all make sense. "Pioneering" was a common theme, along with "castaways." Those who knew it told the story of Robinson Crusoe, or Swiss Family Robinson.

Occasional vehicles puttered or whirred along the highways,

which were still passable for long stretches. A small medical college in Davis was teaching basics. A biochemist and her husband, a beer maker, were trying to produce penicillin.

In the Holy Land a new prophet walked out of the desert. He preached the Word beyond the Book and called on all the monotheists to give up idolatry in all its forms, that even to refer to God by a name or phrase was blasphemous. He called on Jews, Christians, Sunnis, and Shias to end their petty bickering and unite in the compassion of the Unseen. He performed miracles and thousands joined the new creed from all three religions. Services took on a plethora of forms in mosques, temples, and churches.

In 2039 a Noah character from Africa with a coal-fired steamboat introduced antelope and other large African mammals to the steppes opening up over Northern Europe. That was good, since their savannahs in Africa were drying out. In Inner Asia horses returned to the Ferghana Valley.

∽∽∽

The White Death

from Janet Conway's Doomsday Book,
compiled between 2081 and 2093
Archives of the Scholar's Guild, Berkeley

According to Michelle Marks, whose father was a government scientist, there were three different diseases involved in the Pandemic. Two of them were engineered, created as weapons. The Americans developed the smallpox. They didn't realize that the vaccinated troops, though asymptomatic, were infectious carriers. The influenza was probably Chinese. No one was sure how they ever thought they could contain such a mutable virus. According to Michelle's father, "Both sides were desperate." The cholera was wild, and opportunistic.

Michelle Marks said that while the genomic sequence of the small-pox was certainly a military creation, her father never believed it was the army that actually released the virus. According to Marks's father, bio-hackers in the United States had stolen the code and sequenced their own virus, which they were planning to use to blackmail the army to stop using nuclear weapons in the war. The government was ready to negotiate with them, too, but the hackers had been careless and the bug was already out. The first cases, according to Mr. Marks, had actually been in the United States, in Georgia, but they had been kept so secret that when the disease broke out at the front and crossed over to the Chinese, the Chinese had assumed it was an attack and had retaliated, even though they knew their own influenza weapon wasn't safe.

It is difficult for us to imagine what life was like before the Collapse, though the ruins of that culture surround us. Though our world today seems brimming full of people, the population before the White Death, by my estimations, was fifty to a hundred times what it is today.

One might wonder where there was room for so many people, and how there was enough food for them to eat. Indeed. We might call it the Hydrocarbon Culture, or the Oil Culture. Unimaginable quantities of coal and oil and gas were mined and burned. It was as if they were burning all of the forests in the entire country every four or five years, and doing this decade after decade. The hydrocarbon fires fueled giant machines, and these had to be tended by armies of workers. The Oil People created huge farms, covering whole counties and states, and forced food out of the ground by mixing explosives into the soil.

In effect, the whole earth exploded. In just three or four generations they brought the earth's savings of three hundred million years up out of the ground and into the air where it oxidized. The great conflagration affected every part of the globe, and everything that lived on it.

∞ ∞ ∞

Corporatism

from Janet Conway's Doomsday Book

Almost everything in Pre-Collapse society was owned or controlled by corporations, entities created with the sole purpose of amassing wealth and power. They used the governments to protect and enrich themselves.

Corporation Culture was like a slave society, where everything was owned. Ownership, in fact, was encouraged: machines were owned; the land itself was owned. Everything was based on money. This money was not at all like our own scrip. Money in the Corporation Culture was a huge oligarchic industry. The industry printed it and controlled it. They sold money and they rented money, and money inevitably collected and concentrated, like leaves in an eddy in a stream.

We might wonder why everyone agreed to value money, why they continued to sell themselves for it, and even to steal, fight, and die for it. This is perhaps what is most difficult for us to understand. Evidently it was just "impossible" to get along without it. By inflicting hardship and starvation on those without money, those who had it were able to maintain its value. Physical torture was used when fear alone was insufficient. Groups who tried to opt out of the system were suppressed by armies. The system developed a life of its own, a whirlpool that consumed more and more of the resources around it. Money was a fire itself.

All food, production, machines, and services were controlled by corporations. The whole purpose of a corporation was to accumulate more. We could say that they worshipped a God of Hoarding, and that therefore hoarding was considered a virtue, and a behavior to be emulated. As to why those who hoarded were esteemed beyond those who worked to provide for their communities, there is much to be said. If one of our children were to act out in this way, trying to grab all the food and toys for himself, he would be chastised. With a society based on such behavior, I believe the Collapse was inevitable, even without the Pandemic.

∾ ∾ ∾

Jake

Sierra Ridge, 2032
from Janet Conway's Stories of the Collapse
Archives of the Scholar's Guild, Berkeley

The Old Poet died at ninety. The community he had done so much to found and nurture came out for one of the largest circles in the history of Sierra Ridge. They had a small battery-powered amplifier and people read favorite poems, or their own poems, or told stories.

The Ridge had sent out the news by radio, both citizens band and short wave. When the telephones and the cell phones had stopped working, the Ridge had quickly reverted to its twice-daily CB breaks. Except for a few Pelton wheels, almost everything was solar: they'd never been on the grid. There was probably more electric light on the Sierra Ridge than anywhere else in the state. They ran electric chainsaws.

They also had an international network of contacts in the literary and intellectual communities, and probably knew more about what was going on in the rest of the world than the CIA. If there still were any CIA.

Short wave broadcasts were relayed from station to station. They were called the "News Relays." Mostly it was done in code. Morse code transmissions could carry great distances if the D layer was behaving. Voice contacts were common, but less reliable.

Brief eulogies arrived from all over the world. It had seemed impossible that an American could win the Nobel Prize, so hated had the country become in the international community, but a book of devastating political poems and critiques in his late seventies had won the Old Poet the prize one year before the Collapse. The book had virtually been prophecy, the causes and progression of the Collapse uncannily sequestered in metaphors and images scattered through the poems.

Greetings came from China and Japan and Korea, from Sweden and Estonia, from Germany, France and Central Europe, from Russia, the Middle East, and from Africa. The radio was manned twenty-four hours transcribing code.

The Old Poet had been preparing himself and his community for the collapse for fifty years. He even had a glass dump on his land, in case it might be needed for flaking arrowheads or tools. People had electric pumps for their wells, but there were always hand pumps in the barn that could be reattached. Spring boxes with gravity feeds were common. In the few flats and sinks that had any soil there were organic gardens. Apple trees had been planted up and down the Ridge for a hundred and fifty years. Still, the Ridge community had turned out to be far more dependent on the fossil fuel economy than they had thought. The mills and woodshops ran on generators. People were used to driving the five and ten mile distances from Maidu Hill to the North Diggins, not to mention the twenty miles to town, or the fifty miles to Sacramento or Yuba City.

For the most part, their forest cabins were clustered in certain neighborhoods or watersheds. Ten families lived in the drainage of icy French Creek. Fifty lived on a tiny spur above the river. There were over a hundred scattered across Maidu Hill, and several hundred more in a score of other tiny watersheds and benches.

When the Collapse hit they already had their own schools, wineries, mills, gardens, power, and two generations of experience. They had a machine shop, a small illegal distillery, and some of the state's more extensive private libraries. Impressive arrays of 12 volt appliances were in operation. People knew how to use outhouses and how to conserve water. There were deer, wild turkeys, and wild pig, in addition to domestic animals. There were horses, people who knew how to use them, and a sizable herd of free ranging cattle. Nonetheless the Collapse was traumatic, if not on the scale of the urban disasters.

ᘉ ᘉ ᘉ

Jake made a political speech. He talked about the difference between personal property and the ownership of resources. He talked about different forms of political organization and the opportunity for the Ridge to encourage and support the other collectives emerging around the state. He said that they should trade their surpluses, which were substantial, with other collectives like their own.

He warned about the possible emergence of a new feudalism. Some people were still claiming ownership of large tracts of land and trying to collect rents in labor. He warned about mercenaries and gangs of bandits. He talked about the possible forms of large scale confederations and non-coercive action and regional gatherings.

He said they should try to form a network of communities, each within a day's journey of another, all in contact by radio, and proposed a series of year-long cultural exchanges with like-minded communities in the valley, on the coast, and around the San Francisco Bay. He said that they should form a confederation without a capital, linked by personal friendships and general meetings that would rotate from community to community.

He said that if they could promulgate the principles of voluntary cooperation through example, they might be able to isolate any groups trying to form large militias or armies and contain them.

He said that the Collapse had given them a chance to explain the intrinsic pathology of military oligarchic states, with their insatiable material acquisitiveness, to everyone. And that they could avoid making the same mistake. He said they needed stories to explain this, and that they had to be taught to the children.

It was a good speech. People hooted. None of Jake's ideas were followed up on, in any specific way, but it didn't matter. Events followed their own momentum and things worked out much as Jake had outlined.

The Old Poet was given a Buddhist funeral, somewhere between that befitting a monk and a fox. They burned his body in Big Meadow on a huge pyre of manzanita branches. The *Shingyo* was chanted by the circle in Sino-Japanese and in English.

The Collapse had occurred fifty-four years after the Human Be-In in Golden Gate Park. On Sierra Ridge, the pecan and almond trees, the small groves of black and English walnut trees that had been planted in the early seventies were mature and still bearing.

ལྦ ལྦ ལྦ

The first General Rendezvous and Jubilee of the Shasta-Tehachapi California Confederation was held on the spring equinox of 2034 in Davis. Hundreds attended but it was hardly representative of the state.

Petrolia and Humboldt Bay sent representatives on bicycles. Santa Cruz sent a contingent on an all-electric flatbed with twenty solar panels as a roof. Amanda and Ynez left their children with Fly and joined Margo and Yellow Dog to make the long trip north to represent the Roadkill Rangers. They sputtered in on ethanol-converted choppers. Some walked. Some rode horses. Two wood-fired steam wagons arrived from Concord.

There were representatives from Chico and Paradise and Red Bluff. A lone man arrived on foot from Helena, on the North Fork of the Trinity. Dozens of communities in Humboldt, Mendocino, and Lake counties sent contingents. There were groups from Napa and Sonoma and from coastal communities north of Marin. Groups arrived from Berkeley and San Francisco and Modesto. Groups arrived from places no one had heard of. Religious communes sent groups. A Black Muslim group from the South Bay attended "as observers," as did the Karok nation from the Klamath. The Chinatown tongs sent a group. In many meetings there was simultaneous translation in English and Spanish.

A festival atmosphere prevailed but there were many workshops on topics ranging from political matters, such as a possible charter, to issues related to technology, to discussions on earth-based spirituality. One group discussed founding regional moots as a kind of appeals court to solve problems that could not be resolved at the local level.

Many had little experience with consensus decision making and progress was slow. There were issues of collective defense and discussions on what to do about the bandit gangs. Jake Matson, as part of the Sierra Ridge Collective, again tried to encourage his idea of year-long cultural exchange residencies.

Very little was decided in the meetings, but the parties were great. Even if no agreements had been reached on the particulars of the Confederation, its essential existence was already a reality. No decision was even reached about where or when to hold the next General Rendezvous and Jubilee, and four years passed until another gathering was convened, again at Davis. The Second General was poorly attended. Regional get-togethers, however, became common, and that was how it worked.

∞∞∞

As the First General drew to a close, Jake decided that he should take his own advice and left the Jubilee with the Santa Cruzans. Two of the Santa Cruzans wanted to go to the Ridge, so there was plenty of room on their truck. With the panels on top the flatbed looked like a safari tram. Everyone cleaned up the grounds for a day, though there was very little loose trash, and they pulled out on the 30th of March.

Jake talked a lot to an auburn-haired woman with green eyes named Debbie, who had been a graduate student in mathematics before the Collapse. She liked science fiction and politics and Jake was in love before they reached the Carquinez Bridge at Benicia.

Jake did everything he could not to be obvious: he talked to the other people, or he'd keep quiet, hanging off the back of the truck. Then he'd catch her smile or their eyes would meet and Jake would beam.

They pulled off in Martinez and drove to the reservoir to let their batteries recharge for the rest of the afternoon. They were welcomed by a group calling themselves the Steamfitters Union. They'd built the steam wagons and Jake had met some of them at the Rendezvous. Most of the older men had worked at the refinery. Jake wanted to know if there was still any oil in the hundreds of giant tanks covering the hills. One of the men replied that there wasn't much, but that "there might be some jet fuel at Concord." Debbie wanted to know if the refinery were still operable.

"Might be," the man named Sam laughed, "if we'd stop taking parts out of it. But what then, you see any oil tankers?"

"A little gasoline could go a long ways," Jake put in.

"A little gasoline is not what this place is about," Sam said. "Trust me."

"What about a little kerosene?"

Sam laughed. "Well, that could be useful. We're thinking about that one. But we had to give the steam engine higher priority. We have to run tools and we have to move this stuff around. And this stuff is heavy. Like I say, we're working on it. But in the meantime we have to eat. It's pretty much the fishermen keeping us going now, and the gardens."

No one could think of anything else to say. Sam farted.

"We eat a lot of beans," he added.

The Steamfitters all lived within walking distance of the reservoir and said goodnight and went home. The Santa Cruzans laid bags or blankets down where they could find flat ground and went to bed. Jake found a spot on the grass behind a hedge. He was lying on his back with his hands behind his head when Debbie walked over with a rolled blanket under her arm and asked him if he were sleeping alone. Jake wasn't sure whether to answer from past tense or future tense, so he just sat up and said "Hey."

"What is it about me and shy men?" Debbie asked no one in particular. Then she laughed, put down her blanket roll, and sat on it, facing Jake. "Maybe we should talk about it?"

Miraculously, Jake managed to say that he didn't think that was a good idea. They did much better not talking.

∽ ∽ ∽

In the morning Jake and Debbie hung together and found they had lots to talk about. The batteries on the truck were charged and the truck pulled back onto 680. As they drove from Martinez, Debbie said that if Sam and his friends didn't get diesel in production before they died it wasn't going to happen. Jake agreed.

They stopped again in Los Gatos to let the batteries come to full charge before heading over Highway 17. They were ready by late afternoon. They'd just gotten started up the hill when they saw a man lying face down on the pavement a little down the last exit before Lexington Reservoir. There was another man crouched over him and he waved at them to stop. They parked and went over to see how to help. The man lying down rolled over and they both pulled guns and told everyone not to move. Three other men and a woman crossed the highway from the other side of the truck. They all brandished guns and ordered Albert out of the cab.

The man who had been lying down smacked Jake in the head with his gun and knocked him down. Blood poured into his eyes. The short-haired man who had been crouching put his arm around Debbie's neck and pulled her against him and put his pistol to her temple. He told everyone to start walking. Jake was still sitting on the asphalt.

"You too!" the short-haired man said.

"I'm waiting for her," Jake said without getting up.

The man looked at him awhile, deciding what to do. Jake had his arms on his knees and looked back. The man pushed Debbie to the ground and walked over to Jake and brought the pistol to the middle of Jake's forehead. Jake could see the bullets in the chambers of the cylinder. The man told Jake to open his mouth. Jake did. The man pushed the gun against the roof of Jake's mouth and forced his head back.

"If I ever see you again I'll kill you. You got it?"

Jake stared back into the man's eyes. After a while he nodded. The man pulled his gun back and kicked Jake in the ribs.

"Now get going."

They did. They had a sixteen mile walk to Santa Cruz.

The bandits all hopped onto the truck and turned it around and headed back down toward Los Gatos. They fired four or five parting shots that ricocheted off the pavement.

49

"That's what we get for not carrying guns," Jake said.

Debbie said she wasn't sure about that. They were all alive.

∾ ∾ ∾

Jake went around armed for two months after that. From time to time they would get news of the electric truck. It showed up in Gilroy and Jake wanted to mount an expedition to get it back. He found men who were willing but Debbie talked him out of it. Later he heard that the short-haired man had been shot in the head and that the truck had changed hands. Someone said that the truck was being used by farmers in Hollister. Jake stopped wearing his gun.

Debbie lived on the San Lorenzo River in a house near the cemetery with two friends. The cemetery turned out to be excellent gardening land that Debbie helped work with a hundred other people. They pumped water from the river with solar. Jake settled in and was as happy as he'd ever been in his life.

Debbie was a programmer and had a computer that would still boot but she never turned it on anymore. What was there to do with it? For a while she and Jake watched movies but more and more they found them boring and slightly depressing, especially movies set in cities. Comedies weren't funny. Westerns were better but a little silly. Reading was more satisfying or they would just go to bed and snuggle and enjoy each other.

When the earthquake hit Oakland in late fall it had been raining for two weeks and slides covered Highway 17 at several places near the summit, as well as most of the other roads in the mountains. Buildings downtown collapsed, along with most of the houses in the flatlands. Highway One north was washed out in numerous places.

Debbie's collective lost a water tank. A mudslide took out half of the house of two friends up the canyon, along with the two friends. Jake and Debbie adopted Sasha, their seven-year-old daughter, who had been sleeping in the other room.

∽ ∽ ∽

Interview: Jackie Simpson

Aged sixty-three; conducted in 2076 by Janet Conway
Archives of the Scholar's Guild, Berkeley

Jackie Simpson: I was eight years old at the time of the Collapse. Both of my parents died in the Pandemic the same week. We lived in Santa Rosa. My best girlfriend lived in the mountains east of the city, about ten miles away, on the road to St. Helena, so that's where I went. Her father got sick but lived; her mother died a few weeks after I got there.

In November when our supplies were running out we all moved down to the vineyard. Almost everybody who was still alive on the road had already gathered there. More survivors moved in from town.

There were almost no families left, and we didn't really have anything in common except that we had all lived in the area. People act different ways in crises—some share, some steal. Some do worse. During the Hunger Years the group changed a lot. Some of the malefactors were murdered—those who stole or hoarded. I think everyone knew who had killed them but it was never spoken of. We ate a lot of raisins and walnuts.

Other places it was much worse. There was a lot of cannibalism. Some groups, that's all they did—killed people and ate them.

I married Jim, a young man in the community, when I was sixteen. We made up a ceremony and it was a good party. Our group had gotten pretty big—a couple of hundred. We had the vineyard, good water, and some orchards, but my husband and I moved to another cooperative a few miles away, where the people were more like-minded, spiritually. A lot of the communities took on quirky beliefs.

Sonoma was a good place to be. I went to the General Rendezvous at Davis, and most of the communities supported the idea of the Confederation. Not all. There were still groups that wanted a regular government that had authority, with police and jails and stuff. Some of them banded together and had elections and called themselves the County Government but nobody paid much attention to them and pretty soon they just had the name. So we called them "the County" and they were just a part of the Confederation like all the other groups.

Two of my children survived, two sons, and they built a mill to press walnut oil, run by a waterwheel, which is still in operation.

∽∽∽

Jake

Santa Cruz, Sierra Ridge, 2039
from Janet Conway's Stories of the Collapse
Archives of the Scholar's Guild, Berkeley

Jake and Debbie and Sasha made a trip to the Ridge in 2039. They rode bicycles, though they spent a lot of time patching the inner tubes. They carried dried fish, raisins, walnuts, dried millet cakes, and a Smith & Wesson .38. They went through Pacheco Pass to avoid the ruins around the Bay. Near the summit they passed the electric truck. It had been stripped. Jake figured that they had ruined the batteries by letting them discharge too much, or that the panels had stopped working.

In the valley there were water towers, windmills, ditches, pipes, and fields of soy beans and wheat. Crude thrashing devices were run by hand or by improvised engines. Some of the farms had animals. As they climbed the foothills they saw some sheep.

The trip took a week. The Ridge was still prosperous, if darker. More and more generators had to be run, where they could be, from water power. A machinist on Deer Creek had teamed up with a blacksmith and was making Pelton wheels. Ram pumps, which could push water uphill from a stream, were also in demand.

At a Christmas party a man from Maidu Hill hooked up a digital projector and showed "A Christmas Carol." Everyone was glad when the movie was over and they could go back to the party.

Jake and Debbie stayed for a year. Then they wanted to go back to where it was cooler. A young man and a young woman from the Ridge went back with them. It was a cultural exchange.

The Third
Through the Fifth Decades
2041–2070

Great parts of the arid West were almost completely depopulated from drought. Streams dried and wells failed. It was dry in the South as far north as Tennessee. Texas and Oklahoma became one vast desert, stretching through New Mexico to Arizona. Eastern Colorado was dry and the drought extended north into the Dakotas. The Missouri River reached new lows.

In desperation, some communities began dynamiting dams, a practice that spread to California and the Pacific Northwest, where people were thinking that salmon were more important than lakes. For several years, blowing up dams acquired a religious-like character—that by blowing up dams the earth could be returned to a state of mythical purity and a vaguely remembered abundance. Unfortunately, the dam demolition generally did more harm than good—especially to the downriver people. Liberating a captive river is actually a tricky operation, requiring time and many intermediate steps.

A small team who knew what they were doing used thousands of pounds of air force TNT to blow neat holes in a dozen of the largest dams on the Columbia, creating some spectacular waterfalls. Nobody cared about being neat with the dams on the Colorado.

In 2038 a series of earthquakes in Greenland loosened great masses of melting ice and some of the largest glaciers in the world slid into the sea, flooding coastal Florida and maritime lowlands all along the east coast. Sea level had already risen five feet, and rose five feet more. Salt water poured into the Sacramento Valley. Tidal currents flowed through the streets of the state capital. Half of Stockton was under the new bay. The Great Bay stretched from Sacramento to Tracy. Vallejo was underwater and a finger of the Bay reached into Petaluma. The sand lots that had made a fortune for James Lick on Montgomery Street returned to sand. In Berkeley, San Pablo Avenue marked the shoreline.

The weight of the encroaching water in the Los Angeles basin broke open a fault near Long Beach, collapsing most of the freeways and all but the most overbuilt of the skyscrapers in downtown L.A. Nobody cleaned up the rubble.

In Old Europe there was no reason for anyone to stay in the cities and no one did. In Prague, the towers and arches that had defied gravity for half a millennium waited in patience, perhaps wondering how many more centuries would pass before men would once again pass among them. As much as stones can wonder.

As legacy technology and manufactures wore out or were broken, only those communities closest to natural sources of food, water, and firewood were able to survive. The others migrated, died out, or shrank to tiny subsistence bands. The Oklahoma dust bowl spread to Kansas and Nebraska.

By contrast, the Ohio Valley experienced a regrowth of wilderness. Rain was plentiful, temperatures were mild, and broad-leafed plants flourished. The deer population had been hunted almost to extinction, but small mammals were abundant. In Vermont it seemed to rain all summer. It rained in Nevada.

Higher levels of carbon dioxide should have encouraged tree growth in the mountains, a balancing mechanism that could in time sequester large quantities of carbon, but there was a bug in the program—in this case a bark beetle that ravaged lodgepole pines throughout the Rockies.

In California there were more mosquitoes than anyone could remember. Houses around the state were collapsing from termites and it was becoming more difficult to salvage usable lumber. Windows were salvaged where they could be found. Sometimes houses were burned for the nails. Chinook runs experienced extreme vacillations, virtually disappearing on some rivers only to spring back in record numbers five years later.

South of the Tehachapis, in Southern California, flash flooding became common in the summertime. Four feet of intensely salty water covered Lake Badwater in Death Valley. Long extinct lakes in the Antelope Valley and the High Desert began to fill. There was a large die off of oak trees, though the very oldest and largest trees seemed more resistant.

Shepherds drove in flocks of sheep from Nevada. A few ranches had milk cows, or cattle. Cheese was common, but was usually goat. Wheat and barley were both grown in the Central Valley, if playing back-up to the growing bay. Corn, beans, peas, and soy beans were other popular crops.

There were few solar panels that still functioned at all. One by one, solid state devices stopped working. Plastics had become brittle and splintered or shattered. Rubber grew hard and cracked. Some people tried wrapping their bicycle rims with cotton pads held on with wire. People walked a lot. Occasional handcarts and jerry-rigged electrical flatcars operated on flat stretches of railroad tracks.

With a few exceptions, "closed" communities had a harder time than the others, but often there were religious sub-groups within larger communities. There were a few Jewish communes. Keeping a kosher house was almost impossible, but many Jews found simple ways to keep the Shabbat.

Justice was mostly a local affair. Most communities convened juries as they were needed; others tried to solve disputes in general meetings. Thieves and those who were intractable to peer pressure were usually "hated out": verbally abused and left out of community events until they moved on and tried to find some other place to live. In many areas a system of quarterly regional meetings evolved to coordinate efforts of local communities. These meetings also offered a chance for appeals or resolution of cases that deadlocked on the community level.

The first generation to mature after the Collapse had a difficult time. For one, they were not many. Their parents' stories seemed fantastic, and the skills of the older generation were mostly irrelevant. Mostly Generation One were excellent scavengers. They knew where everything was and they seemed to lack the hoarding instinct of their parents. They had grown up in a culture where people helped each other by necessity, and it seemed natural. They also knew all the adults in their community, and who among them to go to for help with their projects. They were tinkerers and curious about the piles of junk around them, if impatient with descriptions of theory. If a fuse burned out they shorted it with a piece of wire and the next time the equipment malfunctioned something probably burned out that they couldn't see. Or replace.

A group in Santa Rosa figured out how to make storage batteries that worked. Or mostly worked. Until they ran out of sulfuric acid. One of the adults they knew had been on a submarine.

Small news broadsides occasionally appeared, and were read in their entirety by those who could—usually out loud for those who could not. Public readings became popular. If many could not read, interest in the written word was high.

Groups of young people often lived together, taking over a house or several adjacent houses. They always came to community meetings and circles. In rural communities that were growing food, some of the youngsters took pleasure in improving on their elders' techniques. They were good at organizing community-wide work projects, such as digging long water ditches. Plastic pipe was salvaged any place it could be found, but was less and less reliable.

A devastating fire swept through the Sierra foothills.

The Strike Against the Newport Bay Company

Record of Father Garibaldi
written circa 2046, the year 35 N.C. (New Calendar)
collection of California College, Pomona

Terrible things happened in Newport and Irvine, and all through Orange County. Many say that we need a government to enforce laws. But I was alive before the Collapse, and there were already terrible things happening in Orange County when we had a government, but they were kept out of sight or hidden in other countries. And the very government that some are now trying to reinstitute perpetrated crimes just as brutal as any committed by the Newport Bay Company or the rebels, and on a much larger scale. Whole countries were impoverished, with the people reduced to penury or wage slavery in a global economy stacked against them. Union leaders and community organizers were tortured and killed by the thousands—in a dozen countries—the torturers financed by the companies in the comfortable portfolios of those enjoying the pleasures of quiet Newport Bay.

They cut up Lupe alive. Sue Sampson was tortured. They killed Ramon with torches. We tell hero stories: how Lupe resisted the torture—how she died without telling the Company what they wanted to know—but that is not what really happened.

Some of the story was recorded by Bishop Sagrillo, who kept a diary of those years, before the Security men murdered him. It is true that Bishop Sagrillo colluded with the Company for a while—this I can never quite forgive, though that is my sin. But we must admire a man who changed when confronted with injustice, knowing that to do so would mark him for death. Some of the story comes from Lupe's mother, who escaped, and some from those who assisted us while working for the Company, who must not be named.

Still, none of the story is as bad, or as evil, at least in scale, as what transpired daily around the world before the Collapse. That makes writing any of this difficult—that so many have tried to recreate the same system of dominance and injustice when we at last had a chance to live in accord with the Savior's teachings. But perhaps we will still. The story takes place in what was Orange County, around Newport Bay.

∾ ∾ ∾

In the year 25 N.C. the Upper Newport Bay was a favored place of the oligarchs of the One Hundred Families. Lido Island was underwater of course, as was Balboa Island, but the bluffs and the highlands were quite beautiful, as they are still. At high tide one could sail right out across the Balboa Peninsula, if one took care to miss the ruins of the churches and the Newport Beach Grammar School. Mussels and starfish grew over the remains of the houses—those still standing—waves and storms battered everything. The Lovell House lasted longer than some of the others, but even its concrete frame collapsed as the sand was washed away from beneath it.

All of the coastal land was owned by the Newport Bay Company. The Newport Bay Company had over two thousand employees, and paid many thousands more as day workers with their own scrip. They had subjugated the independent fishermen and controlled all the boats, and the Company owned all the nets and manufactured tackle. The poor had to use canoes to fish at night with torches and cormorants.

The Company had developed a water system in the San Joaquin Hills, repairing old reservoirs on San Diego Creek. The old Big Canyon Country Club was irrigated. Half of the regular employees of the Company patrolled the streams, reservoirs, and ditches, to keep the poor from stealing water. Only Company scrip, the blue "Newport Notes," were accepted in payment for water. Those who refused to work for the Company had to get by with water from Bonito Creek, which was so polluted that people got sick and children died from dysentery and cholera.

Fashion Island was a fortress warehouse and barracks. The Company staged many entertainments for its workers, usually what they called "high culture." Classically trained musicians were in high demand. To be fair to Harold Wilkerson Lee III, the CEO and principal stockholder of the Newport Bay Company, we should say that he saw his enterprise as the last refuge of civilization, the last bulwark against a slide into a new Dark Ages.

Harold Wilkerson Lee III liked Mozart and Plato. He read and reread *The Republic*. I can only guess that he skipped the part where the owners could earn only five times as much as the workers, but otherwise he liked it. Harold Wilkerson Lee III believed that all the great accomplishments of civilization had been performed by the elite of the population, by people like himself and his family, and the others of his class.

In addition to selling water, the Newport Bay Company operated schools, clinics, and courts. Company farms and orchards and fleets provided food. In addition, the Company had treaties and trading agreements with other companies, like the San Onofre Corporation south of San Clemente, and some of the inland fiefdoms. Sometimes there were squabbles and border disputes, even little wars, but nothing that threatened the stability of the system. Little border wars even opened a new market for the Company: they could sell protection. And it wasn't only on the frontiers that people needed protection—gangs of young men often raided homes and dwellings that didn't display the blue sea lion that was the Company's logo. Most of these depredations were carried out by the Company's own soldiers, and Harold Wilkerson Lee must have known that. Harold Wilkerson Lee surely would have said that these tactics were regrettable, but that in times of crisis, "things must be done."

There were already, at this time, the anarchists to the north: the "Confederation," but, for the present at least, they posed no threat to Harold Wilkerson Lee or the Company. The Confederation was disorganized and they didn't have an army. No, the real threat was from the workers themselves, from union organizers like Ramon Olivera, and even more so from the masses of peons, the *desperdicios* who refused to work for the Company. That was why it was so important to the Families to band together, and that was why the Company gave stockholders and other propertied families special rates and special deals.

∾ ∾ ∾

Like many young people in Orange County, Harold's son Rawlins had grown up bilingual. Harold had a Mexican mistress himself, and his son had been raised by a Mexican nanny. Harold had thought that being bilingual would be to his son's advantage—that it would help his son in expanding the Company and their estate—but he began to have doubts. He wasn't even sure how bright his son was. Rawlins read a lot, but that didn't always mean that one was bright.

Harold even inquired of doctors if perhaps the disease that had partially crippled his son had also damaged some of his brain cells. That would explain a lot.

Harold Wilkerson Lee was worried about his son, whose full name was Harold Wilkerson Rawlins Lee—his mother had insisted that her son share her name. According to his friends, Harold sometimes wondered if his son's mother, in thus insisting on the break with a family tradition, had contributed to the problem.

Harold thought his son was spending too much time in "Brown Town," with the Mexicans. Not that there was anything wrong with young men of good family going to Brown Town for a little action and good times. Not at all. But Rawlins wasn't going there with any of his friends from the Compound; he was going there by himself, and he was mixing. Harold knew he was sweet on a Mexican girl. He'd found out. She was a cantina singer who played the guitar and sang ballads. Harold knew her name and where she lived and who her parents were. He wanted his son to be happy, of course, and there was nothing wrong with having sex with Mexican girls—he was no racist—but you weren't supposed to fall in love with them.

∾ ∾ ∾

On Saturday night, September 15, 2046, Harold Wilkerson Rawlins Lee was feeling particularly happy. He'd spent the afternoon in bed with Lupe, and Lupe had agreed to marry him. Lupe called him "Rawleens," and even that made the young man smile. And he loved how she laughed. And he was amazed and grateful that such a gifted and beautiful woman as Lupe would love him.

They recognized that the marriage could be a problem, on both sides, but Lupe thought that Bishop Sagrillo would marry them. She had already sounded him out, actually, the week before. Lupe was carrying Rawlins's child, but Rawlins knew that Lupe's decision had nothing to do with that. Lupe had made that clear. So when that night his father asked him to share a bottle of wine with him Rawlins gladly agreed. He had to tell his father about his engagement, sometime.

Rawlins's father seemed to be in a particularly good mood also. He wasn't criticizing him and he didn't give his usual lecture about the importance of defending Civilization. Nonetheless, Rawlins was wary. After the third glass of wine, when his father started to rhapsodize about the glories of Culture, Rawlins was careful not to interrupt. When his father casually mentioned that he had had lunch with the Bishop, and that the Bishop was in full agreement with him on the importance of protecting the heritage of civilization, Rawlins was careful to question him about that casually. His father seemed almost gleeful, stating that the Bishop was indeed a very cultured man.

Actually, the Bishop had come as a beggar. The Newport Bay Company controlled the water for the whole basin, and, therefore, its very life. The water systems may not have been on the scale of the Roman aqueducts, and were far more ephemeral, but still, the water system was a spectacular feat of engineering, and it seemed only right to Harold Wilkerson Lee III that he and the Newport Bay Company should profit from their investment.

Rawlins was surprised at the implications of what his father was telling him. It was well known that Ramon Olivera was going to call for a strike after Sagrillo's Mass at the Irvine Downs. He had thought that the Bishop was supporting the workers, and he said as much. His father laughed and said that the Bishop was a realist, and that he had offered to build the Bishop a cathedral, so it was a win-win situation.

Rawlins had said nothing after this. Then, as an afterthought, his father had smiled and added, "After tomorrow the workers will show a little more gratitude to those who provide for them—that Ramon Olivera is going to get a big surprise."

After that Rawlins's father changed the subject, and Rawlins let him droll on about what it had been like to listen to a real symphony orchestra, and how, if he had his way, an orchestra would be his legacy to civilization, along with the Company. When the wine was finished they were both ready to excuse themselves and retire. They hugged and parted.

Rawlins waited an hour in his room. Then he left through the door in the kitchen quarters. He had his own set of keys. He needed to tell Lupe, and to get a warning to Ramon. Maxwell Hamilton, chief of Security for the Newport Bay Company, followed him, of course. He was in touch with Company Barracks through walkie-talkie.

ⵣ ⵣ ⵣ

They beat Rawlins but they didn't kill him. Maxwell Hamilton, for some reason, demurred on that point. The Boss had never actually said that the traitor was his son. He'd just said that the traitor would leave the mansion and lead them to Ramon and to be thorough. Still. One of the guards pulverized Rawlins's right hand with a singlejack. Maxwell didn't berate him but just said that that was enough.

The girl had been more difficult. Difficult, but not that difficult.

They put Ramon Olivera's battered head on a pole, and implanted the pole on the Irvine Downs. They dumped his entrails at the base of the pole.

~ ~ ~

Harold Wilkerson Lee III had slept for several hours after finishing the wine with his son. Then he had dressed, and was drinking scotch in his office when Maxwell Hamilton knocked on his door in the hours before dawn to make his report. His uniform was spattered with blood and there was blood on his face.

Maxwell Hamilton saluted. "It is accomplished."

Harold Wilkerson Lee said "Very good" and waited, perhaps enjoying his subordinate's uncomfortable awkwardness.

"What else?"

"Your son was there, sir."

Lee said nothing.

"He's alive," Hamilton added.

Harold Wilkerson Lee III then turned his back on Maxwell Hamilton and gazed out the window without speaking. After a few more moments Lee dismissed Maxwell Hamilton and told him to wash up and to put on some clean clothes.

~ ~ ~

Bishop Sagrillo recorded the events of the next three weeks in his diary. He also issued a proclamation, which, though believed by many to be self-serving, was not inaccurate. Harold Wilkerson Lee just thought it showed that the Bishop was soft, that he let emotion get the better of him, instead of reason—that he wasn't strong enough to make the tough decisions necessary to save civilization.

According to the diary the Bishop himself spoke out after the mass, announcing the strike. His diary also tells how, two weeks later, Harold Rawlins Lee murdered his father, using a knife in his left hand, and how Maxwell Hamilton assumed control of the Company, and how Rawlins Lee had been publicly tortured and executed, and the beginning of the Long Terror. Then the diary ends.

ᐱᐱᐱ

Interview: Inez Vallejo

Age sixty-eight; conducted by Janet Conway, 2077
Archives of the Scholar's Guild, Berkeley

Inez Vallejo: I was twelve at the Collapse. I came to live here with the Roadkills on the Kern. We changed a lot after the Hunger Years, and we grew a lot. We took in a lot of new members. We did a lot of traveling and trading. Amanda's son, Moog, became a cartwright.

After they opened the dam at Lake Isabella, some of us moved up to the hot springs at Miracle. We were some of the first to start raising horses. Moog and my son Rudy and some of the girls had driven a small herd of mustangs down through Walker Pass. They had traded for them with a big load of corn flour and soy beans that they hauled over in goat carts.

We set up trading posts at Walker Pass and at Tehachapi. Rudy went down to Tejon and they built a lot of defenses along with the trading post. That's what became the fort. A lot of emigrants and refugees would come over and we'd get a lot of news about what was going on in the south. The refugees usually arrived hungry and with nothing, so it wasn't much of a trading post. Rudy would always feed them and help them and ask them to give something back when they could. Years later wagons would come up from the valley full of grain and olive oil and dried fruit and dried meat. Those people never forgot and they always supported the Confederation. Sometimes groups of them would go up and stay for a month to work on the fort or help with the corrals.

Amanda and I were friends until she died. I raised her second baby.

ཞ ཞ ཞ

Looking Death in the Eye

Story collected by Father Garibaldi
papers of California College, Pomona

Chavez and thirty of the rebels were trapped in a blockhouse in Santa Ana by Morris Samuelson's army. Samuelson promised them safe passage out of the city if they would surrender and take an oath not to take up arms thereafter.

Chavez made a speech and said he believed Morris Samuelson, that he had grown up with him and had fought with him in the militia after Riverside burned, that there was no more honorable corporatist than Morris Samuelson. But that he himself was not afraid to look death in the eye, and would not surrender.

Twenty-one accepted the surrender. Chavez and eight others stayed.

The Nine. Looking death in the eye.

Each man came out firing.

Looking death in the eye.

Morris Samuelson was good to his word, or so he thought. The Company had all the rebels murdered by the San Onofre Corporation on their way south, without his knowledge.

Looking death in the eye.

The Second Half-Century

2071–2120

In the North Atlantic, the Gulf Stream wavered and faltered, and the waters of the Caribbean warmed to new highs. The entire Gulf Coast was wracked by hurricanes of unprecedented force. Northern Europe and the east coast of North America experienced alternating extremes of weather: two and three year winters, the snow never melting, followed by three years of heat and drought. In western Africa the narrow agricultural belt thinned and almost disappeared. Western Australia became drier than ever.

The hottest places in North America continued to be Texas, Oklahoma, and the northern deserts of Mexico. The Dakotas were warm, but only by their previous standards. In Saskatchewan, the wheat belt kept moving north, and people migrated with it.

The melting of ice and permafrost had a multiplicative effect: exposed land warmed and exposed more land. Melting permafrost released large quantities of methane, with twenty times the atmospheric warming power of CO_2. Greenland's icebergs drifted northward and collected in the Arctic Ocean. The Southern Hemisphere took more than its share of the heat.

By 2100 sea levels had risen twenty feet and continued

rising, sometimes half a foot in a year, for the next three centuries. A new bay appeared in California, submerging the delta
country and stretching from Knights Landing to below Stockton. Salt water lapped against the ruins of the state capital in
Sacramento, and at high tide reached two feet up the walls of
Sutter's Fort.

As the last of the Old People—those who had grown up
before the Collapse—died in the 2060s and 2070s, the population of the United States began inching above four million,
almost entirely along the coasts and rivers. In California, the
population was about what it had been at the beginning of the
Gold Rush. There were very few people alive who had ever
seen an airplane in the air. There were many who didn't believe
the stories. Children played a game called "Collapse" where
they would set up long rows of wooden blocks and short sticks
on the ground and then run through them, kicking over as many
as possible without stopping or slowing down.

Groups near ruins would specialize in collecting and trading scavenged materials. Certain items became increasingly
scarce and precious: matches, shoes, lumber, fishing line, rope,
storage batteries. People looked for the old-fashioned refillable
cigarette lighters, refilled them with alcohol, and husbanded
their flints. Clothes were patched and repatched—treadle sewing
machines got a lot of use. It was hard to find any resin that still
worked—fiberglass boats became impossible to repair. Sail
material was scarce, and tore easily.

Ammunition began to run short, as did smokeless powder.
Primers were very scarce. Groups who hoarded large powder
and ammunition supplies and wouldn't share or trade some-

times had their depots blown up. A group north of Berkeley tried making their own nitrocellulose, but after several large explosions they gave up. Farming groups in the valley began to leach nitrate salts out of their compost piles for saltpeter.

Electrical systems were patched together however they could be. Alternators and bearings could still be salvaged from cars. People built windmills and waterwheels. Still, electricity was a luxury. There were very few light bulbs anywhere. Sometimes fluorescent bulbs could be coaxed into working. Mostly people went to bed when it got dark, though there were a lot of regional differences.

Several communities managed to connect to each other with telephones, using batteries and splicing together downed power lines. A few CB radios were still transmitting. Communities tightened up. Loners were looked upon with suspicion, unless they were Rangers.

In Los Angeles, at the La Brea Tar Pits, a group who called themselves the Wildcats built a still and were producing small amounts of fuel oil for illumination and other purposes, but they found few customers who had enough to barter to make the venture worthwhile. Warlords from the San Bernardino Valley tried to take the operation over with forced labor, but the workers revolted. Slavery seemed to be an idea whose time had passed, at least in California.

A more vigorous attempt to reinstitute slavery occurred on the plantations in Mississippi and Alabama. The slavery was not racially based—whites were imprisoned as often as blacks, by plantation lords of both races. However, without a central government to enforce the Peculiar Institution, these attempts were rarely successful. Escapes and revolts were frequent, and the plantation lords were never able to create the large scale forces needed to protect their "property" on a regional basis. Also, there were roving bands of escaped slaves who would raid and burn any plantation holding others in bondage.

In San Diego malaria and yellow fever appeared, and quickly moved north.

The Church of Jesus Christ of Latter-day Saints in Utah, with no central authority, split into factions. The "Free Mormons" embraced polygamy, community sharing, and a bewildering array of theological tenets.

In San Francisco a hundred Buddhist monks arrived on a three-masted junk from China. Only a few San Franciscans had any idea where China really was. The Buddhists, however, knew where San Francisco was and had sailed right through the Golden Gate, where they were greeted by their astonished kin. They brought tea, live tea plants, and rice, as gifts. The Scholar's Collective, in Berkeley, sailed across the Bay to meet them.

The Buddhists stayed for two years. A Jewish trading collective, several members of which were themselves Buddhists, circulated a subscription for a company to build one of the junks. Their plan was to sail to Mexico, or to Costa Rica, for coffee beans. Few had ever tasted coffee, but all had heard the stories. The Chinese supervised the construction, along with a second junk for a Chinatown group.

By 2080 the greatest threat to the human species was global warming. Smoke hung over the western half of North America turning the light to an eerie red. Across twenty degrees of latitude changing rainfall and temperature patterns had left vast belts of dead trees, standing brown forests that eventually burned in fires that lasted for months. The smoke had a slight temporary cooling effect, but within a decade the temperatures rebounded with doubled fury. Tumbleweed and other Eurasian species spread over the hills but did little to control the erosion. New deserts appeared covering thousands of square miles. The Sand Hills in Nebraska began moving for the first time in a thousand years. Great sand dunes, rivaling the Sahara, advanced where there had never been sand before. It seemed like it was always windy. It was a hard place to live.

It was a traumatic interglacial—a time of contraction rather than expansion. Fishermen in the Northeast still passed on their great-grandfathers' stories about cod.

On the plains, buffalo began to out-compete the feral cattle, but the herds still grew slowly—the climate was changing too quickly for the range plants to keep up. People occasionally saw more exotic animals: antelope with tall spiral horns, and gazelles—descendants of escapees from private reserves.

In California it seemed like it rained all winter, or it never rained at all. The summers were scorchers. There was a pall upon the world. Something bad had happened—it was too clear. There were still bones and skulls and collapsing buildings and rusting hulks of steel everywhere. No one was sure whether or not it was their fault, or their parents' fault, and therefore their fault, or if they were victims and God was unfair and they should be angry.

At a shallow lake at Folsom, on the American River, a group built a sawmill. A waterwheel ran a generator. When the generator broke they moved the mill and ran the saw directly off the waterwheel. They had a legacy circular blade and didn't even need a Pitman arm. All the logs were skinny.

Flower gardens became wildly popular. Seeds and bulbs were exchanged over great distances and communities competed for their floral reputations. Something about the expenditure of soil, water, and labor on flowers gave people back a sense of pride and confidence.

In 2095 herds of pronghorn spread around both ends of the Sierras and reentered the Central Valley. Domestic animals also proliferated, for a while. Ten doublings could increase the size of a herd a thousand-fold, and there was a spike in the numbers of sheep and cattle. Deer returned in abundance to the burned over forests. Mountain lions were common, and hungry enough to be a menace to people. Bear seemed to be doing well. Many communities had milk cows. Most people ate a lot of meat.

All the cattle were free ranging—longhorns did better than other breeds—and there were problems keeping them out of gardens and farms. Barbed wire was salvaged, and fences were repaired, often to be cut again by those who found them an obstruction.

The "free tribes" generally held land in common, and thought others should do the same. More and more of the communities became religiously based, and sometimes little inclined to mix. Ranchos became common in "free range" country. Some of them tried branding cattle as ownership, but there were so many wild cattle and so many disputes that the practice was gradually abandoned. Nonetheless, disputes arose over rangeland

and springs, between cattlemen and shepherds, and between both of them and farmers.

There were lots of festivals. People always seemed ready for another holiday. Every full moon was an excuse for a party. Solstice and equinox were added to more traditional holidays, and in some communities, the "cross-quarter" days. Of the cross-quarter days, May Day and Halloween were the most important, generally the occasion of large, community-wide celebrations, and a time when the young and other wandering travelers tried to be home. "First Harvest" was celebrated on August 1.

Thanksgiving, Christmas, and Easter survived, as did, somehow, Flag Day, which was celebrated like another Fat Tuesday, scores of groups and collectives staging performances and flying their banners. Square dancing made a comeback, along with the more exotic and individualistic erotic and trance dancing. There were circle dances and conga chains. People made drums on African designs with wood, rawhide, and goatskin. There was reaction—some communities abhorred the general sexuality and licentiousness of the parties and forbade all dancing—but merriment was against them.

Alcohol was widely produced, distilled, and consumed— enough that many considered it a serious problem. The two most common drug plants grown in private gardens were tobacco and marijuana, followed by opium poppies.

In 2105 the earth tried to adjust for the thirty feet of water pressing down upon the Central Valley, and the San Andreas Fault broke loose in what was probably the largest earthquake in the geological history of California. The earth rocked for half an hour. Anything standing fell. Huge waves washed away tidal communities. The last standing skyscraper in San Francisco, the Pyramid Building, toppled and disappeared beneath the waters of the Bay. Reverberations and associated earthquakes in the Sierras broke whatever dams were still intact. Perhaps the tallest manmade structures north of the Tehachapis were the two cooling towers at the Rancho Seco nuclear power plant—the hyperbolas had rolled with the punches.

Railroad tracks were bent and twisted at so many places that even handcars couldn't go very far. Two groups who had been trying to build steam engine locomotives gave up. Even oxen-pulled flatcars had few stretches on which to operate.

During the second half of the first century, Humboldt Bay was one of the more prosperous areas in the whole state, as much of Humboldt Bay as still existed. By 2100, Ropers Slough was a large cove that came in three miles, nearly to Fortuna, and stretched from Table Bluff seven miles to the outskirts of Ferndale. Southern Humboldt Bay was open ocean. The South Spit was completely submerged and waves crashed against the bluffs from Beatrice to above Fields Landing. The Elk River emptied into a narrow two mile inlet behind Spruce Point. Eureka was surrounded by water on three sides, connected to the mainland by only a mile of dry land at Cutten. East of the city a beautiful protected cove reached nearly to Freshwater. On the west side, waves broke over most of the North Spit at high tide. Fairhaven and Samoa were both underwater. Only the northern half of the Samoa Peninsula protected Arcata Bay, which covered half of the town of Arcata itself. There were no roads connecting Arcata to Eureka.

Second-growth redwood forests spread throughout the fog

belt, growing tall and thick. On the north side of Eureka at Cooper Slough a sawmill had an operating steam donkey. About three thousand people lived around Humboldt Bay and the surrounding hills, half the population of the whole county. Old redwood houses resisted termites, and a number of them were kept in repair and people lived in them as nuclear families. Many others lived in collectives and tiny autonomous communities. There were two big Christian communes and other, more esoteric intentional communities. Ad hoc collectives formed whenever such organizations were necessary and there were lots of meetings.

The bay was rich, and the hills were rich. Tomatoes never seemed to ripen, and corn didn't do well, but it was good country for peas and potatoes. There was good bottom land along the rivers. Deer were abundant, and the elk were on the rebound. Smokehouses dotted the coves and inlets. The rising waters seemed to favor the crab population, which proliferated, and crabs were a staple of the local diet. At Trinidad the locals managed to harpoon occasional whales from skiffs and a wooden yacht and they rendered enough whale oil to burn in lamps all around the bay. Fish offal and sharks were rendered into oil in a cove south of Eureka. Fishermen brought in sole, rockfish, salmon, smelt, flounder, and lingcod around the bar. Sheep and turkeys were raised in the valleys and hills and Humboldt became well known for its woolen goods.

Around the Great Bay there was widespread alarm among the elders over the precipitous decline of literacy and the possible loss of all written knowledge, or that it would become the sole preserve of isolated religious orders. All too often books were used as items of personal hygiene. Someone said that the children needed new books—about radio or ethanol or steam engines or hunting—that the old books were all about another world for which the young had little interest. Someone found a small printing press and learned how to use it. The poets, and the historically minded, thought that they had words worth printing and got in line. One of them wrote a story about the Collapse.

A group of Washo from the Carson River made a successful expedition to Texas to collect peyote.

∾ ∾ ∾

Esther

Humboldt Bay, 2090 (the year 69 New Calendar)
General Histories of the Shasta-Tehachapi
Confederation of Free Communities
Archives of the Scholar's Guild, Berkeley

When Esther told her mother that the deacon's son had molested her, her mother told her that the deacon's son was a fine Christian gentleman, and that she should be more careful about how she dressed. That had happened when she was twelve. Four years later, when it was the deacon, she didn't say anything to her mother.

She tried to stop going to Bible class, but her father wouldn't let her not attend. They wouldn't hear of it. "Of course you have to go. The deacon himself teaches it."

Instead she began to ask questions, questions of doctrine and paradox. "If God knows everything, and how everything will turn out,

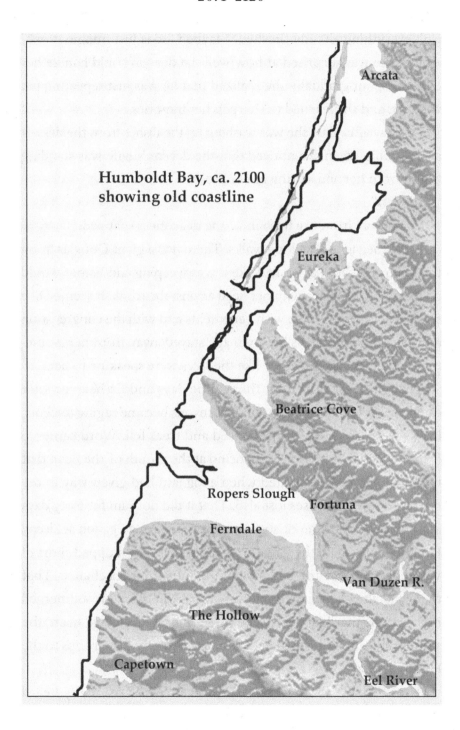

Humboldt Bay, ca. 2100
showing old coastline

Arcata

Eureka

Beatrice Cove

Ropers Slough

Fortuna

Ferndale

Van Duzen R.

The Hollow

Capetown

Eel River

isn't everything already finished? Maybe God is just imagination?"
At first she was surprised at how well the deacon could handle her
questions, but gradually she realized that he was just repeating pat
answers, and she learned to sharpen her inquiries.

One day after class she was washing up the dishes from the dessert
at the spring when she noticed that the deacon's wife was standing
across from her and staring at her breasts.

"What?"

"Stay away from my husband," the deaconess snapped.

Esther began to take long walks. There was a giant Douglas fir on
the Mattole Road that looked like it was weeping and Esther would
go there and take naps with her head against the trunk. It seemed like
she was always in trouble with her parents and with the congregation
and even the other girls her own age stayed away from her. Sometimes on her walks it seemed like the trees were speaking to her.

That winter it rained for thirty-nine days and Esther's mother
caught the fever. The streams in the canyons became raging torrents;
banks were undercut and collapsed and trees fell. Word came up
from Capetown, on Cape Mendocino at the mouth of the Bear, that
two men had been drowned when a log jam had given way in the
river, and several houses lost also. That it did not rain for forty days
and nights was a matter of some import to the congregation at Sleepy
Hollow. Once again the Creator, in His mercy, had stopped short of
world destruction and had given humanity another chance. That
there had already been a flood was clear from the ruins submerged
in the sea. Esther had never seen these ruins, but she had heard the
stories, and some of the men had seen the ruins on their trips to the
Humboldt Fair.

After Esther's mother died, the voices she occasionally heard became louder and spoke more often, and she began to talk back to them. Not all the time, but sometimes. She found that there were certain places she could go where the voices were particularly clear.

When she sat at her loom, weaving, she heard a man's voice, but he spoke in a language that she couldn't understand. When she followed the sheep down to water them on Oil Creek she heard a woman's voice. The woman told her that her name was Ruth. Ruth told her stories about the world outside the Hollow and about things that had happened in distant lands and in the far past, and sometimes in the future. She told her about palaces and court intrigues and about famous lovers who had been her ancestors.

When spring came her father told her that he was going down to Capetown, on the Bear River, to stay for a while with the congregation there and that he would come back with a new wife. That afternoon, when she was watching the sheep, she heard Ruth's voice and Ruth told her that she was going to go to Humboldt Bay, and that Esther could follow her if she liked. Then the voice disappeared and Esther followed the way she thought that Ruth had gone, north and east through the forest.

The forest was dark and thick, with huge fir, cedar, and spruce trees. There was lots of poison oak and Esther did her best to avoid it at first, but then she just walked through it. It was dark when she got to Buzzards Peak, and she cut some fir branches with her sheath knife and made a bed for herself with her blanket, which she had just happened to take with her that day. She had also brought along a nice soft cheese, and some corn pone. She found a spring a little ways down the mountain and then returned to the summit to sleep. She heard some shots fired to the west, and maybe some voices shouting her name.

That night she dreamt of a desert place. She thought it must be the Land of Moab. She saw Ruth standing by a well, with her gleanings tied in a bundle. Esther approached her to say hello but when she got close the woman she thought was Ruth suddenly turned and pointed at her with a witch's hand and started shrieking and laughing. That woke Esther up. She could hear animals walking and snorting nearby in the forest. Deer, she hoped. Esther didn't sleep anymore that night until the false dawn began to lighten the east. Then she slept until the sun was up.

Esther followed the ridge above Barber Creek until she reached a promontory. She could hear the long lines of breakers to the north hidden in the fog. She continued east until she was on the flatlands by the river. There was a farmhouse near the creek with layers of bark and moss-covered planks laid over the roof. The occupants were evidently out tending to their animals so Esther helped herself to some breakfast—real wheat bread and butter—and left a note of thanks. She waded and swam across the Eel just below its confluence with the Van Duzen, holding her blanket and her clothes over her head. The sun was beginning to burn through the fog and she sat on the far bank until she was dry.

Esther followed 101 north for three miles until she reached the outskirts of Fortuna. She tried to move down to the trees by the river, so that no one would see her, but the marshes soon forced her to return to the highway. She followed the highway another six miles until she was descending from Table Bluff and the highway dipped beneath the rolling white breakers of the Pacific Ocean. It was late afternoon and Esther was hungry and she saw some structures built on pilings and some docks in a cove to her right.

There was a path leading down to the docks and as Esther

descended she could see more structures and an old two-story house with a shingled roof. Esther climbed the steps of the porch and stood in front of the door, not sure what to do. She was just reaching for the door when it opened and a young woman who might have been Esther's older sister if Esther had had an older sister said "Oh," and "Hello."

"I think I'm supposed to be here," Esther said.

The woman looked at her for a few seconds and shrugged and smiled and said, "Okay, come in."

Esther walked down a hallway and turned through another doorway into a dining room, where a dozen young men and women, all somewhat older than herself except for one red-haired boy, stopped eating and all looked at her. The woman who had opened the door for her followed her into the dining room and said, "Everyone, this is ..."

Esther was staring at the food on the table as much as at the faces that were turned toward her.

"My name is Ruth," she said.

Esther had never introduced herself before. Everyone she had ever known had already known her name. The Shipwrights found her a chair and gave her a plate of food and waited while she clasped her hands together and prayed before they resumed eating. They did their best to eat normally, making small talk with each other while their guest wolfed down her dinner. When her plate was empty, which happened rather quickly, everyone could see her longingly eyeing the food pots, which were out of her reach in the middle of the table. Marilyn, the woman who had answered the door, finally broke the ice by asking Billy if he would please pass around the peas. And Ruth's face brightened, and she found her voice again.

Ruth stayed on at Beatrice Cove. Sailmaking suited her for a while—she could lose herself in the work for hours—but she remained an eccentric, even by Shipwright standards. She organized séances, and once she was over her shyness, turned out to have quite a bossy side. But her true gifts emerged when she discovered brewing. She seemed to have a secret connection with plants, for finding them, tasting them, and knowing what they would do. She brewed yarrow beer and wormwood beer. She concocted a poppy beer for those afflicted with insomnia. She brewed chamomile beer, elk clover beer, spruce beer, and a dozen others. The Shipwrights traded her beers up and down the bay and beer making soon supported their longer term projects.

After two years passed Ruth wrote a letter to her father telling him that she was well and happy and that she was asking the spirit in the great fir tree at the top of the Hollow to send him peace and blessings. She signed the letter "Ruth," but added "Esther" in parentheses. She gave the letter to a trader who was going all the way to Cape Mendocino and who promised to drop it off on the way, but she never received any answer.

A year later she tried again and received a letter from the deacon telling her that her father was well but that her missives were unwelcome. Nonetheless when her daughter was a year old she and Billy borrowed a donkey and made the long trip around the bay and the Slough and over the pass to the Hollow. Ruth arrived on the donkey's back carrying her child and even the frosty deaconess was hospitable, though neither the deacon's wife nor the deacon stopped by to visit. In fact, only a few of the young people, the teenagers, seemed interested in Ruth and Billy at all, and even the teenagers would come by surreptitiously, meeting them outside when they were on a walk to the big fir tree, or when Billy was out restacking the collapsed wood pile. Martha, her father's new wife from Capetown, treated Ruth respectfully, if with reserve. They were about the same age.

Ruth noticed that Martha hadn't taken care of any of her mother's things. Not that her mother had had a lot of things. The quilt was torn and soiled and thrown in a corner. None of her mother's clothes had been saved. Ruth had hoped to use some of her mother's clothes to make something for the baby. Ruth also noticed that Martha spent a lot of time at the deacon's. Martha said she was his secretary. Secretary of his you-know-what is what Ruth thought.

Ruth's father seemed confused and oblivious to everything—he called Ruth by her mother's name and referred to the baby as "Esther." There was no point in staying, and after two days Ruth and Billy returned to the Cove. Two weeks later a young man from the Hollow named Caleb knocked at their door and told Ruth and Billy and the other Shipwrights that he had run away and could he stay there? Just for a while.

∽ ∽ ∽

Interview: Leland Royce

Aged seventy-five; conducted by Janet Conway, 2089
Archives of the Scholar's Guild, Berkeley

Leland Royce: I published *The Reporter* for almost twenty years. At first *The Reporter* was a broadsheet, printed on both sides. As paper became scarce we printed on whatever we could find, so the format varied a lot. I wrote editorials to support the Confederation, which at that time was still mostly an idea. Still is, actually.

The Reporter

*** December 12, 51 N.C. ***

Mechanics Club hosts talk on Cement, Plaster, Wattle

"Dried cattle dung is excellent to mix in with the mud and lime," Mr. Justine said.

***

Cattle stampede wrecks farms near Modesto.

Formally, the Confederation hardly existed—there were no articles and no signatories—but I wrote about it as if it were a functioning entity. In a way it was, but in a way it wasn't. My subtitle was "News of the Confederation," and just that got people to thinking about the Confederation and talking about it.

The *Bay News,* from San Francisco, was more interested in commerce and technology. They weren't anti-Confederation—they just thought more in local terms.

There hadn't been a General Rendezvous for over ten years when I started publishing. Now we have them every year and they actually do things, like coordinating support for Tejon and the other posts on the frontier. We set up a committee on standards. The Emergency Response Team, which, again, is mostly a coordinating body, has been effective in helping communities with shortages. Most of the real work is done by the Regionals.

The Reporter

*** September 12, 55 N.C. ***

Stewart London, Founder of Scholar's Guild, Killed in Explosion

Mr. London was born in Berkeley in 2008. When the Berkeley Riots erupted in 2022, Mr. London's father, a professor at the university, attempted to protect his family by hiding them out in the chemistry building along with a few colleagues. The thirteen-year-old Stewart was the sole survivor, managing to escape by hiding in the hills near Lake Temescal. London eventually found his way to Yosemite, where he lived for some years.

After attending the first General Rendezvous of the Confederation in 2034, Mr. London returned to Berkeley, where he remained. London organized cleanup and salvage operations at the university and built up a group of friends and like-minded colleagues. He is perhaps best remembered by his chairing of the meetings of the Scholar's Guild with a miner's hammer.

***

Too Many Dogs in Berkeley.

Bay News

*** November 1, 2077 ***

New Calendar Year 56

Salvagers from the Whale Tribe discovered a large quantity of sulfuric acid this week in the ruins of a factory south of the Bay. Twelve drums were found. Excavations are continuing and there is every hope that more useful materials will be uncovered.

***

Bay News

*** April 21, 2079 ***

New Calendar Year 58

The Mechanics Club of San Francisco has placed a large waterwheel into the Golden Gate channel off Fort Point. The wheel is submerged horizontally, attached to floats, girders, and cables, and uses tidal currents to pump salt water into a tower. The water is used to run the mechanics' generators and belt-driven lathes in their shop on the bluffs.

***

The Reporter
*** April 7, 59 N.C. ***

Trouble in Tulare

In an attempt to avoid another range war in the San Joaquin Valley, Buddhist and Catholic leaders from this city traveled south to Visalia to help facilitate a day of negotiation. The host community provided brined olives in abundance. Other communities of our Confederation also sent gifts, hoping that further bloodshed can be avoided. Redding sent a cart of new rope. Clear Lake sent some of the year's best bud, along with necklaces of dried flowers made by the community's children, wishing peace and goodwill.

When asked about the success of her mission, Sensei Sandra of the Two Bays Zendo said that she wasn't sure—but that the flower necklaces were a big hit—and that everyone stayed for a second day of talking and enjoying the delicacies. The gifts impressed all sides that the Confederation favored a spirit of giving. "This dispute wasn't really based on need," Sensei Sandra said.

***

I'd report on the regional courts, the moots. Everyone liked to read about that. And we reported on militia musters, and did a lot to get a regular rotation system accepted. I think we were the first to call for the annual "month" that each person should give to work for the Confederation.

Publishing *The Reporter* was my own project at first, in Sacramento. I was part of a mechanics' collective. Eventually the whole collective got involved and we called ourselves the Printer's Guild, Local 1. That included everybody in the whole cooperative, whether they did typesetting, reporting, delivery, or cooking. We traded and bartered and depended on goodwill. Then I started including a "Reporter Coupon" as part of each issue. Four of them would get you a paper, so there were more and more of them in circulation and they got a lot of use as general currency.

When we decided to stop publishing the Guild threw a big party to redeem any scrip that people didn't want to keep. We charged out-

The Reporter
*** August 20, 58 N.C. ***

**CHLOROFORM PRODUCTION IN
CONCORD HAS BEEN ABANDONED
FOR THE HARVEST.**

***

**Cyclone cuts through East Bay, two
tornados in Fresno area.**

Bay News

*** January 13, 2092 ***

71 N.C.

Janet Conway, historian and author of the *Doomsday Book*, died this week in Berkeley after a short illness.

***

rageous prices for drinks and food. Most people kept their coupons— they were worth more around the Bay than what we were giving for them. Still, there were no hard feelings.

After that most printing came out of Berkeley.

∽∽∽

Interview: Billy Samuels

Conducted by Francine Conway
2100, Humboldt Bay

My escape was a lot like Ruth's, and we both ended up with the Shipwrights. I was only twelve when I ran away from the Temple, and I'd been with the Shipwrights for three years when Ruthie showed up. I was raised at the Temple of Planetary Gnosis, out near Petrolia. The hierophant was called Master George, and I found out later that he was an opium addict. We were taught that everyone outside the Temple were persecutors, who wanted to destroy us, and only the men at the highest levels were allowed out of the compound. I joked with Ruthie that the New Baptism Saints, where she had grown up, was an open community compared to the Temple. At the Temple compound, the Guards patrolled the perimeter fence with crossbows.

I left at night, when they thought I was asleep in the dormitory, and hid in the woods. I was as afraid of the outsiders as I was of being caught by the guards, so I mostly moved at night. I eventually got down to Salmon Creek and had a little camp. I'd come down here to the cabins at night to steal food from the Shipwrights. After a while they just started leaving food out on the porch, like I were a feral cat or something, and one night Jimmy and Marilyn stayed up and called to me and I came in.

The Temple guards found out where I was and tried to make me come back. At first they tried persuasion, but when I said I wasn't going back they used threats. The Shipwrights told them to fuck off and things got ugly. We had to ring the fire bell and send up a flare to call the neighbors. Folks around here aren't partial to Master George and the Temple.

The ironic part is that a year later we saved Master George's life. Master George was out in a skiff with two other men in Ropers Cove. Even Master George took a hand when the smelt were running. They were seining, which isn't a good idea in a small boat because the net gets too heavy. A fog came in and they got turned around and capsized on the shoals. I was out with Jimmy and Marilyn—we were after smelt also but we were using dip nets. We could hear the cries for help coming through the fog from out by the breakers. We never found the other two men but we saved Master George. Jimmy and Marilyn wanted to throw him back in when they found out who he was because of what he'd done to me, but we brought him in. He nearly died from the hypothermia. Maybe the opium saved him. We tied him up in the barn and he went through withdrawal right there. He got better after five days but we kept him another week. After that we let him go and I think he went to Clear Lake, and then on south somewhere. He couldn't go back to the Temple. Word had gotten out that they had held a big funeral at the compound for Master George and the other two men, and that the chief of security had married Master George's wife, with whom he'd been having an affair, and had taken over the leadership.

I've seen Pre-Collapse maps of the bay and I think the water is still coming up. All of Ropers Cove between Table Bluff and Ferndale used to be dry land. Now the ocean comes all the way to Fortuna. In a hundred years the only harbors around here will be in the canyons.

Folks here are sympathetic to the Confederation, but we don't have that much to do with them. We feel more a part of the Columbia River League. We're going to float lumber down to San Francisco on log rafts, if we can ever finish our steamboat.

The Second Century
2121–2220

In 2121 there were no parades for the centennial of the Collapse. Anyone who remembered it was dead. In California it began to rain in the summertime, and sometimes fog covered the foothills of the Sierras. Sturgeon were coming back to the rivers.

Higher temperatures in the Amazon reduced transpiration from the forest, resulting in less rain. A drought moved westward through the whole northern Amazon, trees dying and falling like dominoes.

In 2150 Greenland was bare. Much of the Arctic ice was gone and it was still getting warmer. Sea levels had risen forty feet. Three oceans jammed currents of warm water against Antarctica. Monsoon-like rains fell for months at a time and the sinking water drove huge conveyor belts of thermal energy from the tropics to the poles. Mountains of ice were on the move across the continent. It was as if the earth, sensing her fever, sought to cool herself with icepacks. Ferns, heather, and scrubby beech trees began greening the exposed gravelly soils, gobbling up carbon and setting into motion a new food chain.

In the United States there was an explosion in the alligator population—the reptiles expanding into lagoons and marshes all the way up the flooded Mississippi. Malaria followed.

With increased rainfall in northern Nevada, along with the destruction of the dams on the Truckee River, the water level in Pyramid Lake rose 120 feet. Trout were again reaching their spawning streams. Walker Lake rose two hundred feet, surpassing 1930 levels and submerging the huge ammunition depot at Hawthorne. In Utah, the Great Salt Lake alternated between record highs and record lows, as drought and flood traded decades.

Twenty feet of water lay over Sacramento. More and more of California's best bottom land was being submerged every year. The Sacramento Valley had become a great bay, already stretching 125 miles from the Sutter Buttes to Modesto. Inlets of the Bay covered most of Napa, Petaluma, Fairfield, and Concord. Nobody had built any dikes. Each storm the water seemed to move higher.

In San Francisco water covered Market Street past the old Civic Center to Divisadero, and reached Valencia Street in the Mission. Water over the Marina District was forty feet deep. Waves smashed anything still standing on 46th Avenue in the Sunset. Alameda was underwater. In Berkeley boats were moored along San Pablo.

On the east coast, half of Manhattan Island was under the Atlantic, and most of the boroughs. Not that it mattered. It was the same with Boston and Cambridge—only the hills and the heights were dry. Delaware Bay covered most of Philidelphia. Much of Washington DC was underwater. The Potomac Inlet washed against the burned wreckage of the White House and the deserted Capitol. At the base of the Washington Monument the water was twenty feet deep.

In China, most of Tianjin and Jiangsu provinces were covered by the Yellow Sea. All of Vietnam from Ho Chi Minh City south was underwater. Most of Cairo was under the Mediterranean. The Suez Canal was unnecessary. The North Sea reached Hamburg.

On the east coast of England the Humber Inlet formed a huge bay stretching from north of York to Doncaster, Lincoln, and connecting with the Trent. The Wolds were an island. The Wash came far enough south to cover Cambridge. The Thames Inlet surrounded Buckingham Palace. Canterbury was a port, the long inlets washing up against the ancient cathedral. The town was much as it had been seventeen centuries before, when the Saxons had built their low hovels amid the ruins of Roman buildings.

In 2170, the Gulf of California breached a low pass south of Mexicali and spilled into the Imperial Valley, flooding Calexico, El Centro, and liberating the Salton Sea for the first time in eight million years. Oysters grew there and left their shells, separated from their relatives by ten thousand feet of sediment. Salt water covered Indio.

As the waters of the Great Bay lapped against Marysville and Yuba City in 2180, the Chinese community built houseboats. With judicious forethought, they also built shallow junks, with bamboo lathe sails. The farmers saw a good thing coming and planted forests of bamboo along the rivers. The climate was favorable. As the Bay covered Marysville in 2200, the Chinese floated up and down the valley to other ports. A few electrical pylons still reached above the waters of the Bay and provided convenient moorings.

Bayside communities in the valley began living by fishing. Along the Sierra foothills people raised goats, but lost more and more to mountain lions. Acorns were still collected each fall as emergency food, and often needed. Most people found it easier to hunt feral pigs with dogs than to raise them penned. Catamarans were the way to cross the valley. San Francisco, in a small way, was becoming a maritime trading center, though many boats sailed all the way in through the Carquinez Strait to the new ports at Concord and Tracy.

A tallow industry developed at Chico, producing candles. Tanbark and hides were floated to Santa Cruz, where locals operated a tannery. The Sierra Valley filled with mustangs and was becoming a choice place to live. Grapes, wheat, beans, and a large assortment of green and red vegetables were traded up and down the Great Bay from Shasta to Tehachapi.

In 2152 a ship entered the Great Bay with a Semitic crew who called themselves "Phoenicians." The ship was festooned with legacy armaments that gave every indication of being operable. They had sailed halfway around the world and offered for sale coffee beans, opium, and Chinese women, and demanded a trade of hashish, hempen rope, grain, and dried meat. When the port of Concord refused them entry because of the slaves, the Phoenicians threatened to level the city, and fired an exploding round into a warehouse, which caught fire and burned. The intent of the Phoenicians was to show that they weren't kidding, but they greatly misjudged the tenor of the citizenry.

The city of Concord sponsored a collection to buy the women from the Phoenicians, and the trade was concluded on the night of the new moon, after which the young men's militia staged a feint, attacking from the shore with rockets, while two volunteers, who approached from the dark side, mined the ship with kegs of powder. The explosion was spectacular and the ship sank.

In 2171 a man named Joshua Royce gave a sesquicentennial address to the Scholar's Guild in Berkeley on "Pre-Col Society." The lecture was open to the public. When he described the compulsory education, and that while most could read, few actually did, the laughter was deep and general. Other descriptions of Pre-Col life—the wage slavery and the hoarding—brought incredulity and shaking heads. The over-population. How stupid could they have been?

In a more somber tone he described the huge deadly armies that defended the elites, the wars that were fought—whole cities bombed and destroyed. He talked about the massive corruption of the government, the propaganda and the prisons and the sham elections controlled by "corporations."

"It was called democracy but it wasn't at all what we mean by that: it was really an oligarchy. Representatives weren't even required to do what the people wanted them to do," he said. "The whole society was based on accumulating money, but the money wasn't really money, it was more like a scorecard in a big game run by the corporations, but an utterly ruthless game, impoverishing the majority of the population, and most of the world."

In conclusion Royce told the audience that in an even older civilization, Rome, the whole city would go crazy over a chariot race.

Rosa Inez Vallejo gave a talk called "The Perils of Getting By." She described the legacy technologies they were using, and the varied and innovative ways that they had been adapted. However, she warned that their own cleverness in improvising and repairing Pre-Col equipment and machines was backfiring,

101

that by "getting by" they were neglecting any basic manufacturing for themselves.

"Even our storage batteries are one-of-a-kind, hand made articles," she said. "The Electricians Guild spends all of their time teaching the basics of lead-acid battery construction—at least the plates could be manufactured by machines."

She described Pre-Col chemical plants that manufactured sulfuric acid, and compared them to their own sulfur stills, which, she said, produced weak and impure acid and never enough to keep up even with the demand for batteries. "Where would we come up with vanadium?" she asked.

"Because we are able to 'get by' with black powder from our composting, we abandoned our efforts to make smokeless powder and nitrate explosives. For which, again, we would need sulfuric acid."

When she warned that even supplies of zinc, which seemed plentiful, could be used up in another generation, someone from the audience quipped, "Oh, we'll get by." There was general laughter.

Zhou Win-lip, the club elder, gave the philosophical address—the main attraction for the general public—about modes of discourse for natural comportment. Win-lip compared decision-making processes in collectives and in the Confederation with river meanders and island and habitat formation. "Efficiency is not always what it seems," he concluded. This remark, to everyone's delight, drew whistles, applause, cat-calls, interruptions—everything but a melee. The guild's own wine was served for the party. Two musicians, a pianist and a trumpet player, presented an excellent rendition of a Bach allegro.

The next summer a band of Mormon traders came through Donner Pass with a mule train of ores, minerals, and rare metals to trade for explosives—they were mining and building and had heard that some of the Californians still had Pre-Col ordnance. They were working on a self-pumping well. Rosa Vallejo thought they'd probably pull it off—that their ideas were sound. "It's basically a hydrostatic centrifuge coupled to Archimedean mechanical advantage," she said. "If trees can do it, we can too."

There were fewer and fewer trees. The forests hadn't adjusted. Few trees or shrubs could survive such radical swings of temperature and rainfall. The Ericaceae did well. Artemisias and other mayweeds were able to roll with the punches, and even flourished. Nothing seemed able to kill pampas grass, or Scotch broom, or gorse.

In the spring of 2178 a new flying insect appeared that seemed to hatch out of the ground. They were smaller than the common fly, larger than gnats, and swarmed around people in great numbers. They didn't bite but they loved to fly into eyes. A bug expert who was queried shrugged and said "diptera." So everyone called them "dips." The insects had such a great base of diversity that one species picked up when another died back. They'd had a lot of practice. Mammals were having more trouble. Infant mortality was so high that people rarely named their children until they were one or two years old. Still, if a child managed to reach adolescence, he or she had an even chance of dying with gray hair.

In 2180 a chess craze spread across the Bay, with championship matches held at the Mechanics Club in San Francisco.

A group of scavengers planned a trip to Arizona, where they hoped things would be better preserved. They found a whole palette of tiny Dremel burrs, much in demand by those practicing dentistry with treadle-driven drills.

In 2199 atavistic cattle wandered into the valleys of southern France. Monks in the Dordogne celebrated the new century by painting pictures of the aurochs-like beasts on the walls of their monastery.

∾ ∾ ∾

Ranger Fly

141–156 New Calendar
General Histories of the Shasta-Tehachapi
Confederation of Free Communities
Archives of the Scholar's Guild, Berkeley

Young Fly of the Kern Roadkills Collective had grown up with meetings and he didn't like them. The hypocrisy was the worst—when people would make up all kinds of arguments to support what was obviously selfish aggrandizement. The greedy ones, the grabbers who seemed to have no shame at all in trying to take from the collective. That was the worst, but that would be endurable if the group could ever act effectively to censure and stop the grabbers.

But few in the collective seemed even to have the ability to reason well, or they argued from some sense of law or custom and not from first principles. Even when the answer to a question seemed, to Fly anyway, obvious, hours could be spent hearing everyone's stupid opinions.

Fly didn't like the work that much either. And more and more he didn't like the company. They even called him "the misfit"—jokingly, and in a comradely way, but it was truer than they knew. Hadn't Ocean and her gang of girls made him the butt of their jokes?

Fly began spending a lot of time by himself in the mountains above the Kern. He'd stay away for a week at a time, or a month at a time. He always felt better after these sojourns. Then he was glad to see people and carouse with his friends. At least for a night or two.

So Fly decided to become a Ranger—one of the trackers and watchers—the loners who acted as the frontier sentinels of the Confederation. Rangers were well respected, and always welcome at camps and homes. For one, they were always full of news.

Confederation militias had built forts at Shasta and Donner Pass. The Rangers manned these posts as well as the old Roadkill trading posts at Walker Pass and Tehachapi. But Fort Tejon was Ranger headquarters. That's where the Chief lived and that's where, in the spring of 141 N.C., the seventeen-year-old Fly found his way.

The Chief had interviewed him, walked with him, and told him he could stay for the summer training, and to get himself set up in the bunkhouse. That had been a happy time. There had been outdoor classes, in groups of two or three, with senior Rangers, learning woodcraft and trailcraft. But there had also been classes in history, technical classes on explosives and firearms and signaling, and remedial classes in reading, writing, and numbers for those who needed them.

A guest lecturer from the Scholar's Guild had given a talk on history and political theory—this last, according to the lecturer, mostly about all the ways that men can enslave each other. The Chief himself had sat in on that talk, and had added his own remarks about the important part that their guild fulfilled—and the importance of protecting what he called their "great experiment in freedom."

But at the end of the term Fly had the biggest disappointment of his life. He remembered the Chief's words exactly.

"I like you, Fly, but you're not right for the Rangers. Rangers depend on knowing how to be invisible, but we do that by turning sideways. You, you're invisible all the time. It's like you don't have a shadow, you don't have a soul. And you have to find it. That is the most important thing that you have to do—maybe the only important thing. But I can't afford to have you doing it on Ranger time. It's been a pleasure having you here. Stop by if you are in the area."

The Chief had held out his hand, but Fly hadn't shaken it.

After that Fly spent more time than ever in the mountains and on the deserts—any place there weren't a lot of people. He was, truly, homeless. He honed his skills until he could track even Rangers, and stay hidden from them. He learned how to join a camp of traders, or a camp of Indians, easily, with a good story. And he learned how to get people to talk. He traded news, and told people what was going on in other parts. When people began to call him "Ranger Fly," he didn't correct them.

Two years later Fly was shadowing a Ranger that he'd spotted on Bubbs Creek, west of Kearsarge Pass. Fly knew he was a Ranger by the way he moved, and by the way he hid his camps. He was an older, Hispanic-looking man. Fly followed him down the Kings River for two days and then southwest on Indian Creek toward Cherry Gap. Fly figured he was headed to Squaw Valley. Fly was about to slip away when the man suddenly stood up from where he was making camp and threw a hefty rock at the boulders in which Fly was hiding.

"C'mon in and have some tea, for God's sake. You've been following me for two days."

Fly did so.

The man made a very small fire and heated water. He threw in some roasted chicory root and a few crushed holly leaves and passed the cup to Fly. After Fly had taken a sip of the tea the Ranger asked him his name.

"Fly."

"Ah. Of course. Ranger Fly," the man had answered. "I've heard of you. People talk about you. Ranger Fly. Pleased to meet you, Ranger Fly. I am Juan Carlos."

The man smiled and held out his hand. "Juan Carlos the Ranger, in my case, not Ranger Juan Carlos. I don't know why."

Fly made his decision right away. After all, the man had known his every move for two days—what was the point in lying to him?

"I'm not really a Ranger."

Juan Carlos looked at him. "I reckon I know a Ranger when I see one."

"No, you don't understand. I was rejected by the Chief."

If Juan Carlos had been sitting on a stool he would have fallen off from laughing. Suddenly he stopped and adopted a serious expression. "Rejected, you say. The Chief didn't hire you on?"

"No. He told me I had to find my soul."

Juan Carlos laughed again and shook his head. "We were all rejected by the Chief, Ranger Fly. That's what a Ranger is. Anybody he passed works at Tejon. Didn't the Chief tell you to report?"

Fly thought for a moment and nodded. "He told me to say hello if I was in the area."

"How long ago was that?" Juan Carlos asked.

"Two years."

Juan Carlos started laughing again. "Well, Ranger, maybe it's time for you to report."

Fly headed for Fort Tejon the next day. When he got there, a week later, he burst into the Chief's office without knocking. The Chief looked at him intently a few moments, nodded slightly, and then said the same thing to Fly that he said to every Ranger, whether they had been out for years or for a week.

"Where you been?"

So Fly told him.

❧ ❧ ❧

To Rosa Vallejo, great-great-great-granddaughter of Inez Vallejo, it was a boot-strap problem. They needed transport. For boats they needed lumber and sails. For lumber and sails they needed manufacturing. For manufacturing they needed transport.

They needed sawmills. For that they needed lumber, and they needed energy. For that they needed a steam engine. For that they needed metal fabrication. For that they needed metallurgy. For that they needed coal and for coal they needed transport.

"We need some surplus so that we can specialize," she often said. "We need irrigation ditches and flumes so that we can produce surplus."

Rosa knew they needed more rope and they needed sails. For sails they needed canvas. For canvas they needed cotton and looms. Wasn't cotton how it all got started, with cotton mills in England?

They desperately needed pipe. They needed plastic. To make plastic pipe they needed chemical plants. For chemical plants they needed equipment. How can you boot-strap metallurgy? How do you boot-strap a factory? Each step assumes that you have something that you have to make. No wonder mankind spent a hundred thousand years in the Stone Age. No one around the Bay was even making glass.

"How did the Egyptians build pyramids?" Rosa wondered. "How did the Phoenicians build ships?"

ᕲ ᕲ ᕲ

In the year 149 New Calendar, the laboratories of Charley Wu in the old university buildings at Davis fronted the Great Bay. From the roof of the building, gazing southeast, the blue waters of the Bay stretched to the horizon. The laboratories were the headquarters of the Drugger's Guild, and their most important product was penicillin. The headquarters of the Doctor's Guild were nearby, and the two guilds argued about who had been the first to organize themselves. There were many guilds operating in the Confederation of the Great Bay, but the Drugger's Guild and the Doctor's Guild were the strongest and the best organized.

Guilds were much more than professional organizations: to join a guild was to join a community and a way of life, with a lifetime of communal responsibilities. Guilds tried to be as self-sufficient as they could, and had their own houses, schools, and farms. Each guild had its own system of organization, some, like the Mechanic's Guild, loose, and others, like the Doctor's and the Drugger's, tight. The tightness or looseness of a guild followed naturally from the time necessary to complete an apprenticeship.

The Doctor's Guild, which had also formed in Davis, evolved from the master-apprentice relationship by steps so natural and necessary that it was already functioning as a guild years before it was named and formally organized. While doctors lacked hospitals and the machines and instruments of Pre-Collapse technology, they preserved basic medical knowledge. Apprentices still learned anatomy and the microbial theory of disease. They used microscopes. They knew what x-rays were even if they could rarely produce one. They knew about infection, and they depended upon the druggists for their meager supply of antibiotics.

The druggists grew penicillin by fermentation. It was pretty basic stuff—whatever they could find—but it worked. A hundred and fifty years of an antibiotic-free environment had weakened the resistant strains. They were out-competed.

The Drugger's Guild included apothecaries and chemists, herbalists and farmers, their families, and, through marriage, links with other guilds. Specialization within the Guild was common, but the Drugger's encouraged everyone to take a hand in the fields and in the kitchen, and mostly everyone did. While penicillin was probably their premier product, the Guild also supplied the Great Bay with a hundred other medicines, vegetable and mineral.

Some of the guilds were simply loose associations of local collectives—there were a dozen ropemaker's guilds, each specified by its location: "Redding Rope" or "Chico Rope." But even these would have annual conventions and assist each other in time of need, and would usually accommodate members who wished to relocate. The Tanner's Guild of Santa Cruz was vertically integrated to include numerous local collectives engaged in everything from soap making to lumbering and cheese making.

There were three electrician's guilds: Bay Electric, an association of the numerous locals around the Confederation; San Francisco

Electricians, which catered to free-lancers; and the Franklin Guild. The Franklin Guild was the smallest and was almost a secret society, with esoteric initiations and secret handshakes, and was devoted to research. Many of its members were also members of one of the other guilds. The Franklins maintained laboratories and pooled their discoveries. In 2190 they embedded thousands of stainless steel needles in metal cones that they mounted on poles or dead trees, charging batteries and running small motors from the earth's electric field.

∾ ∾ ∾

The use of gold as a medium of exchange made a small comeback in the Second Century. A minting collective in San Francisco cast small gold coins fashioned to look like miniature sand dollars. Appropriately enough, they were called "bay dollars," which was quickly shortened to "baydles." "Baydums," or "bay dimes," were flat and a tenth the weight of a baydle, though generally worth more than a tenth of a bay dollar. No one would take a baydle when they could get seven baydums, just because of the extra weight and that baydums were a more immediately useful piece of currency. Besides, baydums were worn in necklaces, pierced and linked together. A ten baydum necklace might be traded for two baydles. The bigger the pile of baydles, the less each one seemed to be worth. This seems contrary to reason, but was just the result of a free market: no one wanted a heavy pile of gold. Hoarding was actively discouraged both through social pressure and through boycotts or other direct action.

Scrip, as IOUs, might be written by anyone. Certain guilds would issue scrip as commerce demanded, but it never became a general currency. For one thing, the value of scrip generally decreased over time as the scrip became harder and harder to redeem. Scrip that was five years old was only worth a fraction of its face value. Who wanted to redeem old scrip? Some guilds were better at this than others. Still, in effect, scrip carried negative interest, further reinforcing the anti-social nature of hoarding. A person's status and prestige were based on his generosity.

∾ ∾ ∾

In the fall of 156 N.C., Ranger Fly was headed back for Fort Tejon as fast as he could go without using the main roads. Fly had gone south with another Ranger to see the new salt marshes in the Imperial Valley. Then he had gone over to the Colorado River at Old Blythe. That's where he'd heard the news about the bandit army. He headed west right through Joshua Tree to Desert Hot Springs, then had turned north. The route through San Gorgonio Pass and the San Bernardino Valley would have been easier, but dealing with the lords and barons of the fiefdoms was always touchy, even for Rangers. "Major" Stedman, the Lord Mayor of Colton, had threatened to hang any Ranger as a spy. So Fly skirted north along the dry foothills of the San Bernardinos and the San Gabriels, and then across the southern edge of Antelope Valley. He climbed up through Oso Canyon and Peace Valley and Gorman, and approached the familiar fort from the south.

It was the Vice sitting behind the desk. The Vice varied the usual greeting.

"Fly, how you been?"

"Where's the Chief?"

The Vice paused a few moments. "You haven't heard. Assassin got him."

Fly didn't say anything.

"Just a guy," the Vice said. "He's in the hoosegow if you want to talk to him. Been there a month now. We don't know what to do with him. Stedman's got his wife and daughters, his son too, told him he'd spare them if he killed the Chief. Guy believed him. How you been?"

"There's a bandit army in Arizona. They took Flagstaff—killed the men, raped the women, sold the children. Stedman probably bought some of them. The communities ransomed as many as they could."

The Vice let this sink in. "How big is this army?"

"At least two thousand," said Fly. He wondered if the Vice would believe him. No one had ever heard of an army that large. "They've been picking up gangs all the way from Texas. They're on horses, with a camel train. Word is they're headed for California."

"Weapons?"

Fly shrugged. "Sabers and muskets. A few blunderguns. They count on speed and numbers."

The Vice blew some air between his lips and thought for a moment.

"You'd better alert the Confederation. Not much we can do here. Or anywhere, really. The radio's down so take a fresh mount and leave tonight."

೧೪೧೪೧೪

The Invasion
156 New Calendar

The call for a general muster spread quickly around the Bay. Everyone seemed to know that the leader of the Texan army was named Darvo, and suddenly there were lots of stories about him. How he planned to build castles at both ends of the Bay, that there were two hundred women in his harem; that he would spare the inhabitants of the Bay and let them keep their lands if they made offering to him of earth and water, but otherwise would be merciless. Many claimed to know a friend of a friend who had actually seen the pyramids of severed heads at Flagstaff. Many opposed the muster, for reasons ranging from pacifism to a pragmatic futility, that in this case resistance promised certain death. After all, had not Darvo spared Taos?

Mostly, though, around the Bay bullet molds were busy. Saltpeter pots boiled day and night. Swords were sharpened. Pikes were mounted on new poles.

There were rumors that the fiefdom king, Major Stedman, had formed an alliance with Darvo's bandit army and was going to lead a second army north to attack Tejon, then march down the Grapevine and trap the Confederation militias in a pincer.

The Rangers sent out all of their available scouts.

∾∾∾

Fly rose very early, but when he reached the meditation hall at Two Bays Zendo, zazen was already in progress. He removed his moccasins and his hat, bowed at the door, and found a straw cushion along one of the walls. He bowed to the cushion, turned, bowed to the hall, turned back around and settled down, facing the wall. No one turned around to see who had come in.

When the four meditation periods were finished and everyone had made their prostrations, the servers brought in tea. It was ephedra tea—the Zen sect had been enjoying stimulants for a thousand years.

Everyone faced in and drank the tea in silence. Only when the cups had been put away and the timekeeper struck a last bell did Roshi Sanj acknowledge Fly's presence.

"When a Ranger comes to zazen there is usually trouble in the world," she said.

Fly tried to choose his words carefully. "There is a big gang from the Staked Plains and the Dust Bowl," he said. "They have horses and ride with guns and sabers. They've been raiding the Mormons and the Indians and others on the east side. They kill the men and make slaves of the women and children. They hit Flagstaff and they seem to be moving west."

For some time nobody spoke. Then Roshi Sanj asked what was the mood among the Rangers and traders.

"Many wish to fight," Fly answered, "either in the passes or by striking them by surprise in the desert."

"What would you do," Sanj asked, "kill them?"

"Not all of us are agreed," Fly answered.

 av av av

The Confederation councils met in Tracy, most of them arriving by boat.

Rosa Vallejo was elected Commander, but no one had any overall plan. Local militias were usually twenty to thirty men and women. They'd need to coordinate a hundred of them if they hoped to defeat the bandits. South of the Bay, in the San Joaquin Valley, fear verged on panic.

There was a lot of talk about Pre-Col weapons. The Suisun Bay Collective said that they would build a couple of gunboats, as a navy, mounted with Pre-Col cannons. This was an unpopular idea. Someone wanted to know who would protect them from the navy. Suisun Bay said that they were going to build the gunboats anyway, regardless of what anyone said, and that they would all thank them for it later.

Rosa Vallejo complained about the state of communications.

"How can we proceed with any coordinated plan of defense when it takes a week to get communiqués to my commanders in the field?"

A committee of volunteers was created to set up relay stations. Nobody who had a working radio wanted to give it up, but many of them agreed to join the "Defense" and be part of the network. Someone said they should use heliographs. Where there were wires of any kind people set up telegraph.

∾ ∾ ∾

Roshi Sanj began her march with twenty-five people. They followed the Great Bay south. By the time they reached Modesto their ranks had swelled to several hundred. No one carried any weapons. Rosa Vallejo herself took a catamaran across the Bay from Tracy to try to dissuade them from going any farther, telling them that such a march was suicidal. She told them that they would be of greater service to the inhabitants of the Confederation by joining the militia, but did not call them traitors. Sanj thanked her for her concern, but said that they were intent on meeting with the invaders and when they did so they would share with them whatever provisions they had with them, including their lives. Vallejo stayed for tea.

Between Merced and Fresno more and more companies of militia on horseback passed the marchers, heading for Bakersfield and Tehachapi. There was dust in the air.

ᘛᘛᘛ

Ranger Fly was in a large circular hogan, not far from Paradise on the edge of the Great Bay. He had brought the harmel seeds from Nevada and they had ground the seeds and cooked the bark from the acacia roots. The participants gathered at dusk and placed themselves around the edges of the hogan. The floor was meticulously swept and there were fresh cedar twigs piled to form a mat under each person's seat. The pot, with a wooden ladle, was in the center. After the invocations, each member came forward to drink from the bowl. Fly took his turn and returned to his seat, to await the onset of the journeying.

Tentative drumming and rattling built for twenty minutes until the purging began, when the tempo and intensity of the drumming increased to support the vomiters. Sometimes the server or anyone able would shake the rattle directly over the head of whoever was purging. And they journeyed.

Fly had crawled out of the hogan. The intensity had caught him by surprise. What had he expected? The manzanita shrubs around him had acquired a portentous attitude. Each one had individuated and seemed to be waiting with expectation, silent but very alive. He sat with that, offered tobacco, and felt the condor spirit approaching him from behind and to his left side. This time he had not called her. She had come unbidden. She was very old. She was from the world before.

Once we were slaves in Egypt.

She still had the iron ring and a few links of broken chain around her neck.

They have murdered my children.
They have enslaved my sisters.
They burned me. They mocked me.
They stripped me and bound me in chains.

Fly bent over and touched his forehead to the ground and she spoke more clearly. She whispered of freedom and of great soaring wings and she sang of devastation. Once she had been young and beautiful but even the gods age, given enough millennia. Fly thought maybe her name was Rachel. Or maybe it was Lilith.

They cut my groves and burned my forests.
They trampled my gardens.
They poisoned my water.
They bred monsters from my corn.
They would not listen to my waterfalls.
They could not hear the speech of my bees.
They stole my black oils and set fire to my earth.
They built nations of death and they died
    and I am no better than they.

Fly felt a beak chewing at his neck and he knew that he would not take part in the ambush. He also knew that the invasion would fail. The spirits, the invisible beings, were returning to the earth. The ghosts were coming alive. And they would bring other messages and other secrets. He could already hear the shouts and the songs coming from inside the hogan.

൚ ൚ ൚

The invaders had to pass through the country of a large group of allied tribes who were called "the Havas" by people around the Bay. These were a racially mixed group of nomads, including many Mojave Indians, who since the Collapse had grown greatly in numbers and lived along the Colorado River. The Havas had acquired a reputation for ferocity, and almost all of them were members of one of their warrior societies, including the women.

The Havas waited until the bandit army had constructed a bridge and crossed the Colorado near Topock and were approaching one of their villages at Needles. The leader of the bandit army was named Darvo, and the Havas had left a scarecrow in their village with the bandit's name on it with a noose around its neck. Darvo was infuriated and burned the village to the ground. Just as the bandit army was preparing to move on, groups of mounted Havas appeared harassing the flanks of the army and taunting them. Darvo chased after them for two days until the Havas had drawn them southwest into the waterless Chemehuevi Valley.

At this juncture Darvo began to have second thoughts, shouting out to his adversaries that they were cowards who were afraid to fight, and made ready to reverse his course. But before he could do so one of the women's war lodges, the Badger Society, began to make feints, again taunting the bandits. One of the leading women of the Badger Society, named Calxi, had had a dream in which a fox was annoying a bear by barking at it. In exasperation and anger, the bear had charged after the fox into a thicket of thorny bushes, whereupon it had become a naked man and she had woken up. She shared the dream with her sisters and that was how they had devised the plan. The women rode naked, wearing only broad stripes of white, black, and ocher war paint. They insulted Darvo personally with jokes and lewd gestures, and provoked him into pursuing them for two more days. All of the Havas were expert slingers, and did great damage with their rocks and leaden balls. They drew the bandits south for another forty miles, through the Ward Valley and into the driest part of the desert.

The bandits were camped on the edge of a large alkali sink and the Havas then sent word to their camp that they would fight them in the morning. That night, while the bandits were in a large war council, the Havas drove off all of their stock, including their horses, camels, and mules, in a daring if costly raid. Without water or mounts, the great army broke up into small groups, and the Havas picked off the stragglers. Only a fraction of them got back to the Colorado.

Darvo had left a rear guard at the river to protect his bridge, but the Havas had convinced a company of them, who were from Arizona and had many relations among the Hava, to destroy the bridge. In this, however, they were not successful. Darvo's captain, who was named Elias, surprised them as they were cutting loose the bridge, and a standoff ensued. The captain convinced the officers of the rebel company to parley under a flag of truce, to which the rebels assented, but the captain murdered all of them as soon as they arrived at the council. The remaining rebels fled down the river, and Elias was able to salvage and repair the bridge. Even so, few of the bandits got back to Texas.

But the war fever itself left wounds all over the Confederation. Small bands of irregulars roamed the frontiers and plundered small farms and communities, helping themselves to whatever provisions they could find, all in the name of "defense." "Official" Confederation militias even made up flags and marched under them, pursuing the bands that were considered "outlaws." It was a bad time. News got out that several large haciendas near Delano had sent emissaries to Darvo offering intelligence and support in exchange for favorable treatment. There were repercussions, including tar and feather.

At Fort Tejon the Rangers were hoping that Major Stedman would indeed show up and attack them: vengeance was in the air and the Rangers were more than ready. Wisely, Stedman stayed in Colton.

သာသာသာ

Mechanics Club
Chess Championships

San Francisco
Bay News, *December 14, 158 New Calendar*

Richard Polglase, twenty-one, of the Grass Valley region was declared the champion after being undefeated in the tournament, with twelve wins and four draws. Martina Freemore, of this city, placed second after losing to Polglase in the last round. Martina, also undefeated entering her last round with Polglase, managed a draw with white against Polglase's French Defence, but then lost with the black pieces.

All of the contestants crowded around the board as the two contenders squared off for the final game and Polglase pushed forward his King Pawn. Martina responded in kind, and then murmurs and exclamations filled the room as Polglase offered up a gambit on the Bishop file. When Polglase offered up a second Pawn two moves later, the referee had to ask for quiet.

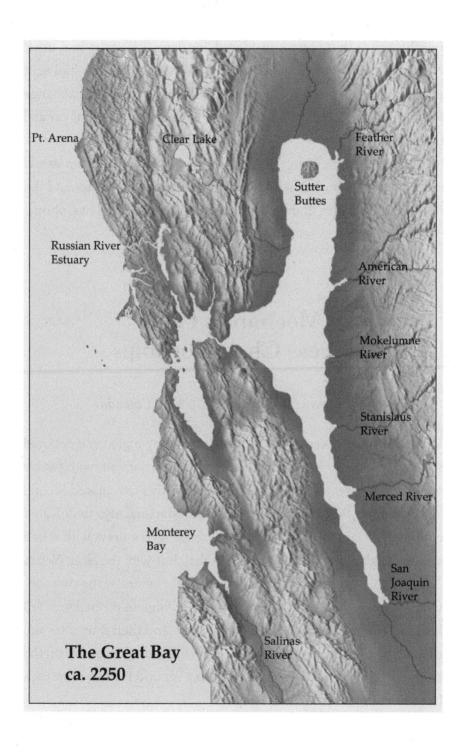

Pt. Arena

Clear Lake

Feather
River

Sutter
Buttes

Russian River
Estuary

American
River

Mokelumne
River

Stanislaus
River

Merced River

Monterey
Bay

San
Joaquin
River

The Great Bay
ca. 2250

Salinas
River

erds of African lions from somewhere had made them-
ome on the warm plains of Kansas and Colorado.
d cattle and other domesticated animals easy pick-
es worked their way down south through the Rocky
and decimated sheep populations. Men and women
ept with the bow and often found it preferable to a
most of which were now loaded from the muzzle.
bears were seen north of Mt. Shasta.

ornia's Central Valley, Marysville was under twenty
er and the Great Bay washed through the streets of
urlock was a port. The Bay covered the Napa Valley
le. The Russian River Inlet extended to Healdsburg
ort Park. Marin was becoming an island, only con-
he mainland by a narrow isthmus near Cotati.

rancisco the Mission District was underwater to
ghts. Potrero Hill was an island and most of China-
nderwater. Telegraph Hill was an island at high tide.
le, Watsonville, and Salinas were underwater. Mon-
ent inlets up the Salinas and Pajaro river valleys.
unedale, and Aromas were Pacific Ocean ports with
ishing fleets.

xnard and most of Ventura were below water. Tony
amp above El Rio was on a small point with some
e edge of a little harbor.

ngeles the ocean came in ten miles. Hawthorne,
nd Bellflower were under two fathoms of Pacific
arrow peninsula of hills connected Inglewood to
s. There was an excellent sheltered harbor on the
of Torrance, and another one southeast of Santa Ana.

The Third Century
2221–2320

None of the climate models for global warming had accurately
predicted what occurred, but all of them were partially correct. None of them had been able to predict the feedback loops
that accelerated the great melting of the western ice cap of
Antarctica.

By 2250, sea level had risen eighty feet. If Antarctica continued to melt, sea levels could rise another two hundred feet.
Typhoons moved to high latitudes in the Atlantic, mixing the
waters. The Gulf Stream gradually found a stable course, and
heat began moving again to the British Isles and Northern
Europe, ending their short little ice age, but not the global flooding of the ocean.

Nobody could actually see the sea level rising: the water
advanced by storms and floods. After a high water subsided,
people would simply not move back to their old homes, or they
would, until the next big storm pushed them out again.

All of the lowlands of Northern Europe were underwater: the
Netherlands, coastal Germany, Bremen, Hamburg, much of
Denmark, and half of Belgium. The Oder formed a large bay as
far south as Berlin. The Elbe was an estuary at Wittenberg, covering the farmlands all the way to Osterburg. The Rhine was
sea level ten miles from Düsseldorf. Bordeaux was underwater.

The Po was a broad inlet all the way to Parma. Bologna was just a few miles from the coast.

In Central Europe three kings ruled the Free State of Bohemia, elected by citizens' councils and recallable at any time. From the mountains, men and women who knew country ways moved down to the rivers and plains and grew food and raised animals. It had been a good place to live for forty thousand years and continued such, the warmer winters expanding the choices of crops and orchards. Rafts of logs again floated down the Vltava.

In Egypt, the Nile Estuary began at Beni Suef. In Iraq, the Persian Gulf came to within fifty miles of Baghdad.

In England the Thames opened into a broad estuary at Windsor. One could moor a boat to the Castle and float with tidal currents to Buckingham Palace, which was below forty feet of water. In London, only the high ground was dry. Brackish water covered Eton and would flood Maidenhead at high tide. Liverpool and Lancaster were submerged. Carlisle was underwater. The Trent was sea level at Nottingham. Most of Edinburgh and Glasgow were flooded. Northern Scotland was almost an island. Gloucester was submerged.

The Sea of Azov found its way around a dam and began pouring brackish water into the Caspian Sea, which snaked north to Uralsk and Volgograd.

The Amazon delta broadened, parts of Manaus were flooded year-round. The Rio Negro basin had dried to a veldt, but a veldt filled with rivers, and waited patiently to see who would live there.

Virtually the entire country of Bangladesh was submerged, and all of the coastal cities of India. Calcutta was submerged for miles

around. Rangoon and Bangkok Ho Chi Minh City were underw

China was flooded along t the rivers. The Yellow Sea rea feng and Zhangzhou were sub land near the mouth of the Yar Shanghai, and Nanjing.

Except for a few hills, all fiv below water, as was Boston. I of its suburbs. Baton Rouge w nearest dry land. New Orlea with most of Florida. The Oh wood forest. Monkeys would

In the Great Basin high amounts of water north from In the winter it snowed. In 2 Lake Lahontan began fillin year drought had ended. Ta River. Honey Lake overflow Lahontan was fifty feet deep

Life zones had moved up hundred years of heat had sq zones—but the summer rai woods had reclaimed large expanding in the Sierras fr They liked the new fogs. Al to the increased moisture an temperatures. Deer were a them—there were always y

A few selves at They fou ings. Wo Mountain became a heavy rifl Grizzly In Cali feet of wa Modesto. to Yountv and Rohn nected to In San Bernal He town was Castrov terey Bay Chualar, P makeshift All of C Romero's docks on In Los Compton, Ocean. A Palos Verd inland side

Large estates grew date palms and fruit orchards in the San Bernardino Valley. In Orange County there was surf in Buena Park and Garden Grove. People talked of a herd of elephants in the lagoons near San Diego. No one knew how they got there.

The problem in California was finding good farmland. If it wasn't underwater, it was probably desert. The farmers in the San Joaquin Valley south of the Great Bay managed to keep some ancient irrigation ditches in repair by hand.

The Confederation continued to be a popular idea, though social and religious differences between regions and communities made general agreements almost impossible, except for defense and trading disputes. A "live and let live" philosophy was the general ethos. If one community practiced polygamy and married their girls at twelve or thirteen, and other communities didn't like it, well, what could they do but say they didn't like it and welcome runaways?

The word "America" was rarely heard. The ruins and everything about it were called "Precle," and fantastic stories were told about the people who had vanished. The stories were rarely romantic. It was more as if the Precles had been an occupying army from somewhere else, had destroyed their own civilization, and then had died or gone away—some said in spaceships. Even some historians admitted that the Precles had gone to the moon.

Pottery and basketry took on distinctive local designs. Stainless steel pots were handed down mother to daughter, as were the increasingly scarce pieces of glassware.

Indentured servitude became a common and widely respected practice, especially for felons. Anglo-Saxon legal precedents

127

widely prevailed. Those who had committed grave offenses against another were sentenced in local courts to serve their victims, or their victims' families, for a period of time reckoned commensurate with the offense. This could be several years for a murder, and sometimes evolved into a permanent relationship, the offender being adopted into the victim's family. It was all a family affair: the extended families of both parties generally supported the servitude actively, as a way of avoiding further reprisals or bloodshed.

Literacy rates were still alarmingly low around the Bay. But then, what was there to read, except "Precle." Schools were mostly for adults: trade masters taught others and were invited to give workshops around the Bay. The ropemakers at Red Bluff accepted apprentices, and set them to work in the hemp fields for a year.

An introduced holly called yaupon, a relative of yerba maté, was widely grown for the high caffeine content of its leaves. There was no Chinese tea or coffee.

Toward the end of the second century news filtered into the Bay that the Free City of Boulder was going to hold a Continental Rendezvous to celebrate the bicentennial of the New Calendar, which was actually 2222, year 201 by the reckoning of the Great Bay. Boulder had the highest literacy rate on the continent. While there was no stated political agenda, many believed that Boulder wished to become the new Philadelphia of a Reunited States. The Confederation organized a contingent to make the long journey to attend, as did several of the independent communities around the Bay.

In 2307 Mt. Lassen erupted, joining a string of active volcanoes in the Cascades. There were spectacular sunsets. Teams around the Bay played lacrosse, and met for matches.

In 2310 a huge storm destroyed float houses and docks all along the eastern side of the Great Bay. It was the highest water anyone could remember. The Great Bay was a hundred feet deep in the middle.

∾∾∾

The Great Trek

*from the Great Bay of California
to the Bicentennial Rendezvous in Boulder,
April 1 to July 4, 201 New Calendar*

Journal of Solomon the Monk

Library of Green Rock Temple, Clear Lake

March 31, Johnson's Harbor, Wheatland

The party has been collecting here for a week, and tomorrow we at last set off. There are a great many barges and pirogues tied up all along the harbor, and gifts and supplies have been arriving for days. We have seven small wagons in our party, as well as several single axle carts. Several wagons are to be pulled by oxen, but mostly our party is using mules. One man, a Christian monk, is using donkeys. I have two mules.

We hear that another party, larger than ours, is leaving from the southern trails.

I have decided to keep a diary of our journey.

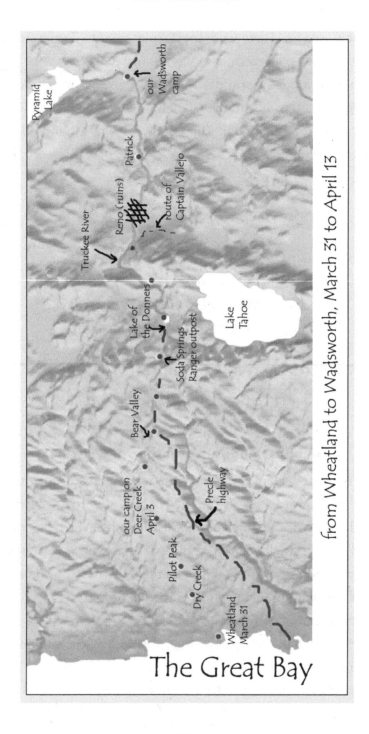

The Great Bay

from Wheatland to Wadsworth, March 31 to April 13

Pyramid Lake

our Wadsworth camp

Patrick

Reno (ruins)

route of Captain Vallejo

Truckee River

Lake of the Donners

Soda Springs Ranger outpost

Lake Tahoe

Bear Valley

our camp on Deer Creek April 3

Precle highway

Pilot Peak

Dry Creek

Wheatland March 31

April 1, Dry Creek

We started very early this morning, but it seems like we were starting and stopping all day. We made for Pilot Peak, which we could
see to the northeast, as directly as we could, but there are a bewildering array of paths and roads in these hills. Making camp was a
great confusion, nobody knowing what to do, and everybody telling
somebody else what was best. We are at the Dry Creek ford, near
the Spenceville Commune, where there are the remains of two
washed out Precle bridges. I don't know why it is called Dry Creek,
as it has ample water and is quite beautiful. We traveled until nearly
dusk, but Mowry Vallejo thinks we only covered twelve or thirteen
miles. I think almost everyone's wagon will have to be repacked in
the morning.

April 2, Pilot Peak

We are camped below Pilot Peak after a short day of only eight or
nine miles. We are at an excellent meadow with artesian springs that
they call Indian Springs. This morning we held a meeting and selected
Mowry Vallejo to be our camp and trail leader, hoping that having
a designated leader will save us from stopping and holding council
at every crossroads. Mowry accepted this position on the condition
that we call him "captain," so we will. We are learning to pack the
things we need for camp on the top of our wagon loads.

There is lots of good grass here for the animals.

April 3, Deer Creek

We made about fourteen miles today and are camped at Deer Creek
in the community of Nevada. We passed a number of farms and

communities, including La Barr, Grass Valley, Town Talk, and Gold Flat, which are well known around the Bay. There is a great deal of excitement here over our expedition and two men of the Willow Valley community joined us with horses. We are now twenty-two: seventeen men and five women.

April 4, Skillman Flats

We proceeded about fifteen miles today up a long ridge and found water here at springs in a forest of large cedars and sugar pine—some of them four and five feet across. We left the wagons on the road and are becoming much more efficient at making camp. Captain Vallejo's style is brusque but humorous, and so far all are pleased with his leadership.

Dogwood along the creek is just beginning to leaf out.

April 5, Bear Valley

We are in the beautiful green meadows of Bear Valley, and our camp routines have become very regular. There is still a lot of snow about, in shaded places, and we can see much more on the mountains ahead, which is a concern to our captain.

April 6, Cisco Grove

We are camped at Cisco Grove on the Yuba River, which is quite swift and very cold. Captain Vallejo has organized a rotation for the grazing and roundup of the animals, and I had the first turn, which caused me some anxiety as I do not know animals well. Redtail, an accomplished muleteer from the Shasta country, sensed my confusion and graciously came to my aid. I will do better next time.

April 7, 8, Soda Springs

It has been a week since we left the Great Bay at Wheatland. Progress has been slow as the road is in very poor condition, with slides and fallen trees that we have had to clear enough to let the wagons pass. I myself have only a two-wheeled mule cart and am quite glad. We reached Cisco Grove two nights ago. For the most part the old Precle highway is our best route, though we have many detours around collapsed bridges and slides.

We are now camped for our second night at Soda Springs, at the old Ranger outpost. There are traders here, who claim to be descendants of the original Rangers. We are making improvements to some of our wagons, resting our mules, making moccasins, &c. This is a beautiful flat valley surrounded by granite peaks just below Donner Pass. We worked at clearing the road ahead. The warm weather is melting the snow quickly wherever it is exposed and we hope to be able to cross over tomorrow.

April 9, Donner Lake

We crossed the pass today following the route of a Precle highway called "40." With some clearing of rocks the road was quite passable. We lunched on Donner Lake and the women stripped and jumped into the water, screaming aloud because the water was quite icy. Some of the men were shamed into an emulation. I myself did not join them. We are camped now at the far end of the lake, and the water flows out to the east.

April 10, near Boca

We passed a Precle highway sign, very large and high, supported by heavy steel girders, which said "weigh station," so we must be near the old border. We traveled through a steep canyon along the Truckee River. The mountainsides here are quite bare of trees, although there are some dead snags that evince it was once forested. There is a new plant here called sagebrush, a low shrub, woody and gnarly, that is quite resinous and with leaves cut into three blunt teeth at the ends.

April 11, Cabela

Today was a long day following the Truckee River through a spectacular canyon that was deep and narrow, with steep peaks on both sides, but we are over the mountains. We are camped in a large meadow, headed east now, where the river flows close to the old highway. The river is very full and loud with its rushing and, though the sagebrush on the mountains is a beautiful pale green, we are clearly in desert country now.

There are very strange Precle ruins here. There is a very large structure here in which six or seven families of Paiutes live, with large openings in the roof that act as smokeholes. There is a large bronze statue of two mountain sheep, twenty feet high, in front of the building. There were once three sheep, but one has been broken away and melted for the bronze. I think the whole building could collapse with a large snow. The people here say they will move along the river into the mountains in a week or two.

We are told that there are three large bandit gangs of slavers operating in the Precle ruins of Reno, to our east. Trading caravans buy protection from whichever gang they first come across, and use them as guards for their passage. We are all quite exhausted and will decide what to do in the morning. The bandits rarely come into the mountains as these people are well known for their marksmanship.

April 12, Patrick

One of the locals woke Captain Vallejo in the middle of last night and warned him that a spy for the bandits had informed on us. After a hurried meeting, Captain Vallejo had us bring in our stock and yoke up the wagons immediately, and we set off in the dark. Captain Vallejo took the four heaviest wagons and the horsemen south along the outskirts of the ruins, hoping to distract the bandits and to meet up with us on the Humboldt, after following the Carson River. The rest of us crossed through the ruins by dark, including the two young women, Angela and Lisa both dressed up as muleteers to look like men. We saw large fires to the south but by good fortune passed unmolested and are camped on the river in the early afternoon, after about twenty-five miles. We would have liked to have proceeded farther, but our animals are too exhausted, and we must rest here. We are about eight miles up the canyon from Sparks, which is at the eastern edge of the ruins.

April 13, Wadsworth

We started early today, just after dawn, and are camped now at a place called Wadsworth, where the Truckee River turns north. Mostly, all day, the only plant was sagebrush. The people here are Paiutes, and tell us that there is a large beautiful lake a few miles to the north. Because of the slavers in the ruins these people have become very fierce, though they have been very friendly to us. Several of our scholars had long discussions with them and, as it has turned quite cold, we had a large bonfire and a most splendid time. Two of the men, with horses, have offered to guide us to the Humboldt Sink, which they say is two difficult days to the east, with little water, so we must carry what we can.

April 14, Boiling Springs

This was a very long day, over twenty miles. There were small lakes of water along the route but all were thoroughly salt, and salt flats extended from both sides of the road.

We are camped at the place called Boiling Springs. There are many geysers of steam and the air is sulphurous. The water coming out of the ground is scalding hot, but people have built a series of small ponds, and in the lower ponds the water is cool enough to drink, though it is very thick tasting. After we watered our stock, and then ourselves, all relaxed in one of the warm pools and I instructed all in the party in the art of Bodhisattva back washing.

April 15, Humboldt Sink

If anything, today was a longer day than yesterday, perhaps twenty-five miles, but we have reached the Humboldt Sink. Fortunately, the sky was overcast today and the temperature cool. There was no water anywhere, and even here we have had to dig to create drinking holes. But there is good grass for the animals, though we have to take care not to let them get bogged in the mud. Our two guides are turning back tomorrow, saying that they do not like the people of Lovelock, which must be our destination tomorrow.

For some miles we passed through a dark green shrub called greasewood, which is thorny and quite sharp and hurtful to the shins, but now we are back in sagebrush.

April 16, Lovelock/river

We are camped on the Humboldt River out past the town of Love-lock. The locals there seemed very sultry and live in shanties of

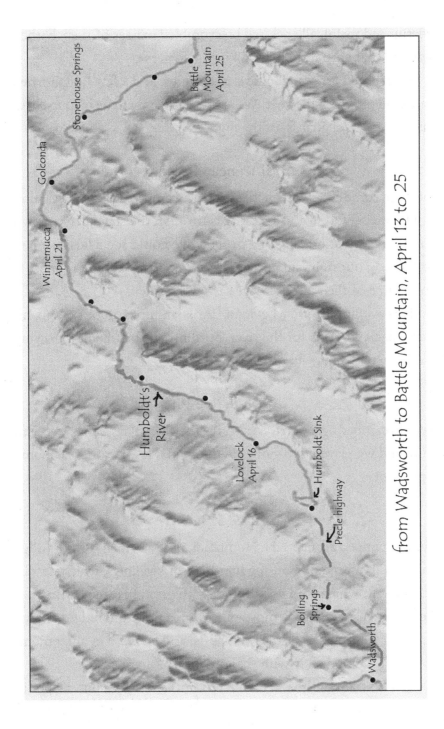

from Wadsworth to Battle Mountain, April 13 to 25

corrugated metal, all enclosed by crumbled masses of rusty barbed wire, so that each dwelling is a kind of fortress.

They breed horses, donkeys, and mules, and a few long-horned cattle, all of which they eat. We are just as happy to be by ourselves, and have posted guards for the night.

April 17, near Oreana

We have come about fifteen miles and are camped again on the Humboldt, having found a vale that cuts through the steep banks down to the river. Just outside of Lovelock we could see a large square fortress on our right, an immense Precle prison, which I suppose is the source of the razor wire we saw in the town.

This evening Brother Levin, a Christian monk in our company, gave special prayers for the river, burning sagebrush and throwing the burning embers into the water.

April 18, Rye-Pitt

We are camped again on the river. Brother Levin has a chess set with him, and we played two games in the sand. He is a rather fearsome opponent.

April 19, Mill City

We are camped again on the Humboldt, near a cement Precle bridge that is still intact, and housing hundreds of swallows, which we disturbed and which told us as much with great insistence. Brother Levin suggested that we move our camp a few hundred feet down the river so as not to disturb the birds, and all were in agreement. We found a good eddy with shallows for the animals.

We all swam in the river, which is not very wide, but deeper in the middle than a man can stand. The water was very mild. I find that young Lisa extraordinarily beautiful, with her dark eyes and dark hair. And all.

The willows along the banks are all leafing out.

April 20, on the Humboldt

Again camped on the Humboldt. There is a tall mountain rising out of the desert to our north. We have seen almost nothing but sage-brush for ten days now. Brother Levin decided that this plant must be the "Queen of the Desert," and rubbed handfuls of the leaves all over his body, so that he now smells like the desert itself.

April 21, Winnemucca

We are camped north of the Precle ruins called Winnemucca. There are many ranches about and an adobe fort above the river. Nobody lives in the ruins, or even ventures into them, the people believing that they are evil and a cause of bad luck. The people elect a mayor once a year by casting ballots: the decision going to the majority, even if only by a single vote. They have a militia but say that they have never had any use for it, which, as they explained, is why they maintain it.

Yesterday a man here was whipped for stealing, being tied to a tree and given fifteen lashes. We did not witness this event, I am glad to say, it having occurred before our arrival, but was the talk of the town. These people also whip their children.

Many of them breed horses. They also raise cattle, though to me the cattle seem completely wild. There are hulks of rusting Precle machinery everywhere. And tanks, cement houses, steel houses that completely seal, and all sorts of other wreckage.

April 22, Golconda

We are camped on the river in a place called Golconda. The people here live in railroad cars and in shanties and raise chickens. They govern themselves by general assembly, as do many of our communities in the Confederation.

April 23, Stonehouse Spring

Today we followed the Precle highway, veering away from the river and climbing over a summit, which, according to my map, saved us several miles. Shortly after the summit we found a water hole, but with many skeletons of horses and cattle in the area. Two of our mules had already drunk of the spring. Our muleteer tried to make the animals cough up the water, which was only partially successful. We also tried to make them swallow charcoal, which they adamantly refused. However, by this evening the animals seemed fine, and even seemed to make the long day's trek better than the animals who did not drink.

We are camped at a very desolate place called Stonehouse Spring. There is a Precle mine here, a huge pit two miles across. Nobody lives here. The place is entirely deserted.

April 24, Mote

A short day. Camped on the river. There is good grass here and the river plain is quite broad. Brother Levin spotted a few locals watching us from the bluffs, but none of them have come into our camp.

I must tell you about Brother Levin. Brother Levin is one of the Fool Monks, followers of the New Prophet whom they call "The Great Fool." He is a jolly man and a little wild, but with a surprisingly good education and, in spite of his rakish attitude, seems to be

filled with loving kindness. He is also an excellent conversational-
ist if called upon, but appreciates silence as much as I do. We get
on well, though he is often a jokester, and we have become friends.
When I offered to instruct him in meditation, he willingly agreed
if I would agree to accept the love of the Great Cosmos into my
heart. When I agreed to this he said, "So now what is there to med-
itate about?" A fool, indeed.

April 25, Battle Mountain

We are camped at a place called Battle Mountain. There is fine grazing for our animals along the river. Perhaps two hundred people live
here. They raise alfalfa for their animals and offer hospitality and
supplies to trading caravans, having numerous joiners and smiths in
the community. They also raise sheep and are fine weavers.

Last night someone evidently stole Jack Sizer's rifle and some of his
powder.

April 26, Argenta

We are camped on the river by a tall mountain. The cliffs are quite
beautiful and full of colors of red and browns. The weather has
turned quite chilly and we made a roaring fire of sagebrush and had
a song contest for songs about the sagebrush. Angela's song was
quite funny and bawdy.

April 27, Dunphy

*This is Brother Levin writing in Solomon's journal. Solomon is a Buddhist
monk of the Zen persuasion, and, if somewhat stiff, is educated and well-
read and we have become fine friends on the trail and I look forward to our
travels together.*

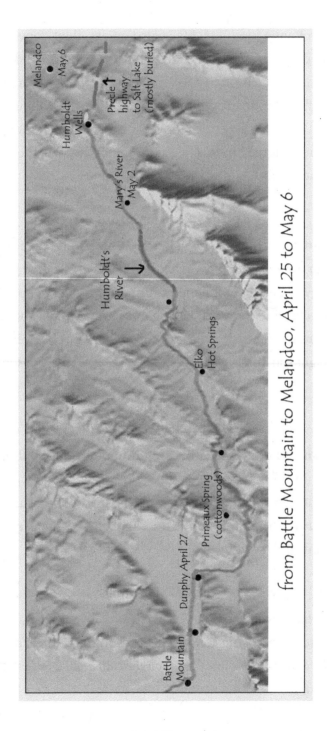

from Battle Mountain to Melandco, April 25 to May 6

I showed Brother Levin my journal and he asked if he could add some comments. You see how he is. We are camped by the river at Dunphy's Trading Post, though the proprietor is not named Dunphy and doesn't seem to do any trading. There are two hills above our camp that Brother Levin claimed were clearly the breasts of a mountain goddess, complete with dark nipples, and he insisted that I accompany him to the top to lay an offering.

Brother Levin was a Christian monk before being converted to the doctrines of the Fool Prophet. I asked him if he were still a Christian and he said "of course." I asked him if that were not a contradiction and he insisted that the teachings of the Fool merely completed the work of Moses, Jesus, and Mohammed; that with true monotheism there could be no difference between one god and another. I asked him if that meant that all gods were false, and he said, "Of course, that's half of it." I told him that I thought he was a Buddhist without knowing it and he just laughed.

They say that the Fool was born in the year of the Collapse, somewhere in the desert in Palestine, and that after his teaching spread into Europe some missionaries came to this continent by boat.

This morning we awoke to a dusting of snow, which makes the sagebrush quite beautiful.

April 28, Primeaux Spring

We are camped at a springs near a pass, in a grove of cottonwoods.

April 29, Carlin Canyon

We are camped outside of Carlin, where a small stream meets the Humboldt.

A number of the locals have come into our camp and have told us many interesting stories about the desert peoples of the area. They say that for many years there was deadly feuding between the communities along the river, but that at present all are at peace, though they had nothing good to say about the people of Elko.

We obtained many excellent supplies from these people, including hides that we can use for moccasins. I traded some of my yaupon tea for cornmeal, my own supply being already very low.

We can see the snow-capped Ruby Mountains in the distance. The land is greener here, and our animals graze easily. We passed yet another Precle prison, the third or fourth on this trip, which always gives me an ominous sensation. It is as if half of the Precle population stood guard over the other half, who were locked in these dungeons.

April 30, Elko Hot Springs

We traveled perhaps twenty miles and are camped at a small hot springs on the outskirts of Elko, which we hear is entirely Precle ruins. We had to bypass a large mountain this morning, through which once passed a long tunnel but is now collapsed, and we had a difficult time following the river.

The mountains really are ruby!

May 1, North Fork

We are camped on the North Fork of the Humboldt. The Ruby Mountains fill the horizon, and surely all of that snow is the source of our faithful river.

This morning we passed through the Elko ruins, which are quite ugly. Hundreds of rusting railroad cars were on the sidings. The desert preserves things well, even wooden fences. We live in a ghost landscape, but it is so pervasive we are blind to it. We are born in it, and can see it no more than a fish can see water.

This open prairie seems endless. Today we saw big horn sheep, all ewes, and several herds of pronghorn.

May 2, Mary's River

We are camped at Mary's River, past a ghost town called Death. There are bogs and marshes to the south of our camp. Our hunters had no luck, so we slaughtered another of our goats. I have given up my vegetarianism, as my supplies of beans and wheat are quite low. I am also letting my hair grow out.

The Precle "energy towers" are all about us, a few still holding copper cables. Brother Levin told me that the copper web extracted energy from the earth and caused time to speed up, which the Precles tried to slow down with massive blood-letting. I asked him if this were a teaching of the Prophet and he laughed and said no, that he had learned this teaching from a wise man.

May 3, Humboldt Wells

We are camped at Wells. There was a Precle town here but it is all in rubble. The Precles seemed to have put steel fences around everything. Shoshones live here now. We will camp here and wait for Captain Vallejo and the rest of our party.

May 4, Wells

We are considering leaving the highway route and following the river because of water. I did not foresee this and copied no maps for this area except for the general map that I drew after the one in the atlas in the Temple library, on which I drew little detail excepting the major rivers. I do have a compass.

We will wait one more day for Captain Vallejo. The two women with their wagon and Jack and Martin Sizer with their wagon are going to try to follow the highway, though the Shoshones say there is no water that way.

These Shoshones live in fine shanties built with tree limbs and corrugated metal and have gardens and horses and sheep. They also eat antelope, which they were happy to share with us. They speak English and are quite knowledgeable about the world and eager for news. The women here cover their breasts at all times, even in hot weather, as they do in some of our mountain towns around the Great Bay.

May 5, Wells

This is Brother Levin writing in Solomon's journal. It is over a month since we set out on All Fools' Day. I hope, however, that my decision today is that of a True Fool (blessed be his spirit), and not merely foolish. Redtail, who had been assisting me as muleteer, is quite adamant about not proceeding further on the Precle highway, stating that there would be no pasturage in the desert for the mules, and no water either. He also spoke of bandits. So we have decided to go north along the river valleys, heading for the Snake. Noah, the trader, agreed with Redtail, so we have decided to travel together. Solomon and I have combined our supplies onto one cart, while Noah and Redtail have agreed to handle our mules as well as their own wagon. Angela and Ynez and the Sizers are going to wait another few days for the rest of the party.

May 6, Melandco

This morning we separated from our companions, who were determined to brave the desert and follow the Precle highway east. Brother

Levin and I, with the two muleteers, followed the track of an older and smaller road north.

The road so far is quite passable, there being much brush growing up through it, but that caused little hindrance to our cart. After about twelve or fifteen miles, as the day was getting late, we pulled off down a small ravine to a good springs with pasturage.

There are some Indians living here at the springs, speaking their own language, who welcomed us and we shared food. I gave them one of the stainless kettles from our cart.

These people grow a strange tobacco, with sticky leaves and scented flowers. Brother Levin enthusiastically shared in one of their pipes, mixing a second pipe himself with tobacco from the Great Bay, which was accepted with nods. I myself do not smoke.

In the evening a man came into the camp who had traveled with some Mormon traders and spoke English. He said that he had seen the Great Bay and had traveled to several of the communities in our Confederation. He helped fill in a number of areas on my map, and warned us that cannibals lived to the north, and that he and his people never went far in that direction. This intelligence frightened our muleteers, but is doubted by myself. Nonetheless, we will turn east tomorrow and follow Thousand Springs Creek.

There are juniper trees along the trail.

May 7, Wine Cup Springs

We are camped at a lovely springs called Wine Cup, on Thousand Springs Creek.

There is a hot spring here and also a very cold spring. A small group of families live here, mostly in caves that they have dug into the hillside. Brother Levin called them "troglodytes," a word I did not know. We were again warned that on the main road north there were cannibals and slavers, so we are glad to be following the river.

The trail was dry all day until we reached the creek. I found the country quite beautiful. Of course, I like deserts. Brother Levin wasn't so happy. Except for this springs, the country seems entirely deserted.

May 8, Thousand Springs

We are camped in Thousand Springs Valley. There are broad boggy meadows here covering several miles, and our mules took their pleasure. The land is flat and level, covered by sagebrush, with some hills to the south of us.

I believe that a kalpa could be defined as the number of steps required to cross through the sagebrush country, which is still inestimable.

May 9, Rock Springs

This morning I awoke to the sound of birds singing. There are meadowlarks, some blackbirds, and some wrens. We have camped at a spring where the water flows out of a large hole in a rocky cliff. We have been crossing ravines. The country has changed, except for the sagebrush. There are junipers on some of the hills, and greasewood and another thorny plant that has caused us all some hardship.

Two families of shepherds are camped here, evidently nomads, who were very suspicious of us until Brother Levin stripped off his breechclout, bathed in the water, and sang silly songs. This seemed to put the shepherds at ease, and they brought us some mutton, though we could not understand their language.

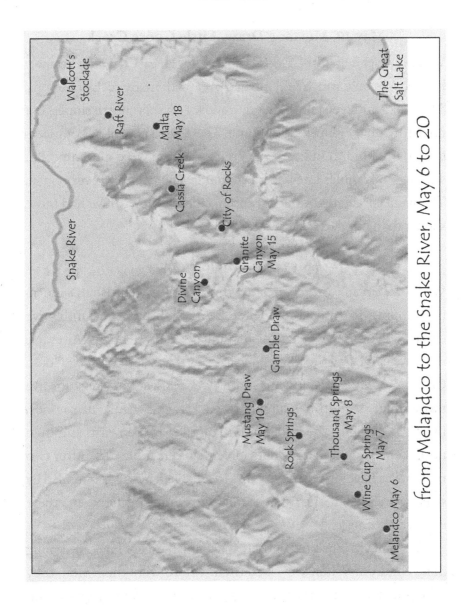

from Melandco to the Snake River, May 6 to 20

May 10, Mustang Draw/Little Goose Creek

We are camped on Little Goose Creek, after an easy day. The country has become hilly, much of it burned over, with many rocky outcrops. The peaks in the distance are quite snowy on their north slopes, but quite bare on the slopes facing south. There were no willows or greenery of any kind to indicate the creek until we were quite upon it, although our mules knew it was coming. The country is very open. The wind sprang up in the afternoon, and we all wish we had more shelter than our carts and our tarps.

May 11, Gamble Draw

We headed in an easterly direction through the sagebrush this morning, hoping to find Goose Creek. After about three miles we descended into a dry vale, which gradually became boggy. After five miles we came to a broad green valley that I was sure must be Goose Creek, though it was flowing south. We followed the creek for five more miles, sometimes having to backtrack because of ravines, mostly keeping to the high bluffs. The river turned east, and then north. The wagon had more trouble than our mule cart. After two more miles heading north we came to an excellent valley bounded by steep ravines where the river meanders in many directions, and there is much greenery.

This valley is inhabited entirely by women, except for some young male children. When we asked them where were their men, they told us that all of the men had gone away on a salvaging expedition the year before, and had never returned.

This is as secluded a place as one could find anywhere, and Goose Creek (so it is called) gives them very ample water, and the women keep cattle and goats, along with a few horses. They are able to grow a great deal of alfalfa, as well as corn and beans and green vegetables.

The women seem desirous for male company, and soon made solicitations of hospitality to each of us, which our two muleteers quickly accepted, but which Brother Levin and I declined. While Brother Levin and I made our excuses as graciously as we were able, the women were somewhat miffed and we both had to endure some rather barbed jibing.

The women live on separate ranches in old patched up shanties, and in wickiups.

May 13, Gamble Draw

We have stayed two whole days here, and as Redtail and Noah seem to have no interest in going farther anytime soon, Brother Levin and myself are going to take two mules and a donkey and continue on our own, leaving as early in the dawn as possible. We have told no one else of our decision.

These women are completely fascinated by spirit rapping, which they seem to practice as a group every night.

May 14, Divine Canyon

Our animals were well rested and we moved quickly today, covering over twenty miles. I am better with the mules than I had thought. Most of the day we followed the river, but several times had to work our way up the bluff because of flooding from beaver dams. The scenery was quite spectacular: great red dirt bluffs and high canyon walls. We passed the ruins of a Precle ranch, thoroughly looted but for pieces of heavy equipment—large earth-moving machines entirely overgrown with vines and trees.

We are camped a mile south of a group of ranches, all in thorough disarray, which the people there call "Divine Canyon." They told us that we were only two days from the Snake River but they refused us passage unless we gave them most of our food and other goods, which we would not.

The men there beat both their wives and their children, and both Brother Levin and myself thought that the dullness apparent in all of them might be the result of continued blows to the head.

There were deadly feuds between several of the families. They drank to excess as often as they could, which was probably every day, distilling various fermented concoctions in a metal kettle built on a brick fireplace. The kettle was covered with an inverted lid, somewhat larger than the kettle, into which they poured water. A smaller pot on some rocks inside the main kettle collected the distillate. A number of the men are missing an eye, the result of their "rough and tumble" fighting in which eye gouging is an accepted infliction.

I told them about the way of the Buddha, and Brother Levin tried to display loving kindness in every way, but they were so surly that we preferred this camp with the scorpions to the lice of their barns. We both lamented our own spiritual shortcomings.

We are both glad to be gone from those women at Gamble Draw. I confess that I never completely believed their story of how all the men left. Several of them told the story quite differently, and they got very annoyed when I pressed them about any details. We are uncertain now how we will proceed.

May 15, Granite Canyon

We are camped in a beautiful grove of cottonwoods just below the pass in Granite Canyon. Late last night, about an hour before dawn, a young man named Jammer whom we had met at the settlements at Divine Canyon came into our camp and woke us, saying that he knew of a way across the mountains and would guide us. We left at first light and after backtracking two miles turned east, crossing many hills and boggy meadows until with some difficulty we came to Granite Canyon and crossed the pass. There is a broad valley to the east of us.

Tall young Jammer is evidently tired of the feuding of his family and has decided to stay with us. He is very handy with snares and caught several ground squirrels within an hour of our making camp here.

May 16, Circle Creek Basin

Today after crossing the broad prairie valley of Birch Creek we passed through the City of Rocks, where there are huge boulders piled up like monuments and buildings. We can still see some of them from our camp, which is near to some Precle ruins. There are pine trees here and we are no longer in the desert.

Brother Levin brought some marijuana out of his "medicine kit," and smoked it with Jammer, who had never experienced that drug, and was quite taken to peals of hilarity. Brother Levin also. Jammer declaimed that it was the most beautiful experience he has ever had, danced, kissed us both, described all sorts of phantasms, and thanked God for his deliverance. I sat up with them in their silliness as long as I could, but after I write this am retiring and will sleep if there is ever an end to their stories and laughter.

May 17, Cassia Creek at Elba

Mountains and rivers are the actual Buddha way, right now. In their expression is complete realization. Because mountains and rivers moved about

153

before the Emptiness, they are alive right now. Because they are the Self before form, they are complete Enlightenment.

That was Master Dogen, as was taught to me.

Today we saw wild horses running across the valley, racing. Brother Levin said that running was what horses really liked to do. I couldn't help asking him how he knew what horses liked to do, as he was not a horse. Brother Levin replied that I was not him, so how did I know that he didn't know what horses liked. I admitted that I was not him, but that he clearly was no horse. Brother Levin told me that of course he was a horse, and jumped twice kicking up his heels, and we both had a laugh with the old sage.

We are camped in lovely green meadows along Cassia Creek at a place called Elba, where there are farmers who are friendly. Beavers in the creek have cut all the large cottonwoods, and only small ones remain. I was able to trade two bundles of yaupon for half a bushel of cracked wheat, for which I was very glad.

May 18, Malta

We are staying tonight at Malta, where the residents have given us a warm welcome. They are farmers here, and quite ingenious in their use of water. They seem to be prosperous but they complain bitterly of the tribute they have to pay to "Patron Walcott," a land baron on the Snake who claims to own all of this land, and demands a rent of one quarter of their grain. This Walcott has a band of hired ruffians who burn the farms of those who are late with their rent.

The people tell us that there are range wars all along the Snake, and they sound much worse than those recorded in our histories in the Confederation. The local barons pay their retainers with gifts of stolen land, granting it to them as tenants in exchange for an oath of service, as well as giving them other gifts and "royal" protections.

The exchanges with the farmers are of course lopsided, the farmers having no organization or power to effect an equal trade, and the barons become rich while the farmers are impoverished. Brother Levin told me that he had talked to some of the young people and that they are planning a revolt, an uprising, and that they are secretly arming themselves.

Jammer has decided to stay here in Malta. There are young women here and other young men and he has made friends quickly. He thanked us both profusely and says that perhaps some day he would like to visit the land of the Great Bay.

May 19, on the Raft

We are camped on the Raft River on some low gentle bluffs. Brother Levin has begun to join me in my evening zazen, but not in the morning, when instead he prepares breakfast.

May 20, at the Snake-Raft confluence

We are staying as guests of "Patron" Walcott, in a special guest room inside of his huge stockade. Patron Walcott is an educated man and seems quite desirous of our news and company.

The stockade is not tall, but is topped by coils of stainless razor wire, of which they seem to have an endless supply, as they also use it to wrap around sticks and clubs, which they use as weapons.

The Patron told us at dinner that his father, who had been the king of all this part of the Snake River, had divided his domain into three parts, one for each of his sons, but that the eldest had taken two of the portions.

He added that he and his brother, Xerfox, whose lands are to the west, had been forced to take up arms to defend even the land remaining to them, that each year their elder brother would appropriate some further portion of their estates. "Each time for a good and worthy cause, of course," our host laughed.

I asked him if it were not a custom among them, as it was with us, for the first-born to provide and ensure for the welfare of the family.

"That sounds like an admirable custom," my host replied. "Such would have saved our people a great deal of woe."

To me, it seemed like another example of the evils of private property. Does not the land belong to those who live on it and improve it? I did not, of course, express these sentiments to my generous host.

May 21, Massacre Rocks

This is a no man's land, with burned and ruined dwellings and farms. We are very worried about being caught by a passing patrol of the combatants, and being attacked before we can explain ourselves.

There are many rocky outcrops about, and high basalt cliffs along the north side of the river, which is quite broad here. There were many rattlesnakes in the camp, which I chased out with my staff.

May 22, American Falls

We are at American Falls tonight, at the great stockade of Kingsnake, the eldest son of the old king. We are obliged to stay a second night, as Kingsnake insists that we stay longer with him than with his younger brother.

This rotund man was a most jolly host, and we received far greater amenities than we had with the "Patron." He said that he had been shocked when his brothers had attacked him, that they had turned their backs on the values and traditions of the family.

He is very interested in sporting events, especially horse racing, and has large stables. Recognizing that we were literate men, however, he wished to take the opportunity to discuss Shakespeare. We had just begun our discussion when his captain came in and delivered a whispered message. Our host excused himself, saying that they had taken a captive and were going to hang him, and asked us if we wished to witness the event. Brother Levin, believing that he might do some good for the poor victim's soul, assented, but I stayed in the manor doing zazen.

When they returned, our host, seeing me in meditation spoke in a whisper to Brother Levin, asking if they should not go elsewhere in order not to disturb me. Brother Levin, who knows me well, shouted at me to get up off my damn ass and assume the duties of a guest.

This king and everyone in his domain by law have to observe the Sabbath. Brother Levin, playing the rascal, asked him which day could be acceptable to everyone as holier than any other? This question confused our host. Brother Levin tried to explain the Fool Prophet's teaching that to favor any one day would be idolatrous, but he seemed to be speaking in a foreign language, for his words seemed incomprehensible to the King, and Brother Levin wisely let the subject drop.

Brother Levin says that Kingsnake is a narcissist, witnessing the many busts of himself mounted on the walls of the premises, and the many banners with his name embroidered thereon, and that he seemed to hear nothing that Brother Levin or myself said to him except for flattery and that which supported his own opinions.

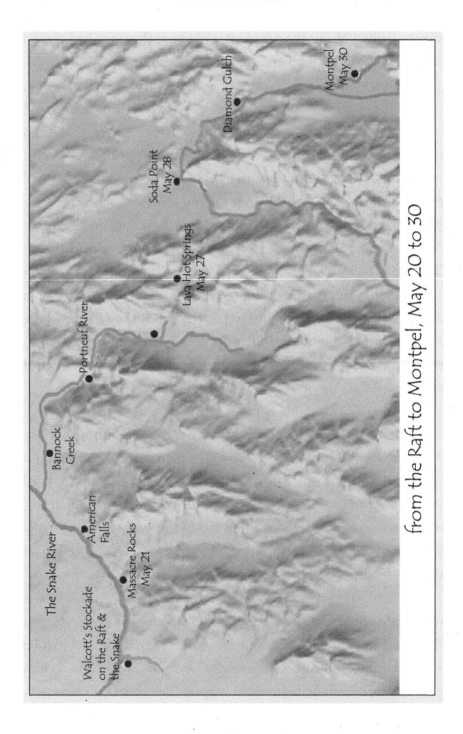

Montpel
May 30

Diamond Gulch

Soda Point
May 28

Lava Hot Springs
May 27

Portneuf River

from the Raft to Montpel, May 20 to 30

Bannock
Creek

American
Falls

Massacre Rocks
May 21

The Snake River

Walcott's Stockade
on the Raft &
the Snake

May 23, American Falls

We are again the guests of Kingsnake. His stockade is built on a bluff above the river, with a small stream that is channeled into the stockade. Kingsnake's wife, the Queen, returned today from a business journey to Fort Hall where she was collecting tribute, accompanied by the palace guard. She seemed interested in myself and Brother Levin not at all—other than that we might be spies, and I confess that an icier woman I have never met. The Queen manages all of the accounts, and seems to direct the war also, Kingsnake's role being merely ceremonial and that not enough to interfere with his sporting. The Queen placed a guard over us "for our protection" and Brother Levin and myself are not allowed to converse with anyone here, other than the captain of the guard. This captain questioned Brother Levin and myself separately and at length about where we were from, and especially what we had seen at the stockade of Patron Walcott. Evidently our answers satisfied him, as he says we will be allowed to leave in the morning and to continue our journey.

To pass the time, Brother Levin and I have been playing chess. I managed to draw a game, which put Brother Levin into a funk.

May 24, Bannock Creek

We are camped on Bannock Creek and are glad to have left the Snake River with its lords and barons. The people here call themselves Bannocks but are clearly a mixed tribe of many races. They have a good spring, and farm and graze the surrounding country, which is quite rich and fertile. These people are numerous and keep themselves well-armed, and say that the kings on the river dare not molest them. The Bannocks have a chief, but he is obeyed only if his counsel is deemed wise, and for that reason they have many long discussions and speeches.

These people have already sent a delegation to the Rendezvous, but they tell us it left a full week ago. They have been very generous in provisioning us with such supplies as we are lacking.

May 25, Portneuf

Today we passed many miles of ruins of the city called Pocatello. The ruins are now almost entirely hidden by a forest of pines, and the country people never go near them, saying that they hold "bad air." We are camped some miles below the city on the Portneuf, where there is excellent grazing.

May 26, Robber's Roost

We passed many ruins in the Portneuf Valley, then turned east, following the river through a defile with steep mountains on both sides. We proceeded along the river, perhaps fifteen miles today, and have a lovely camp by the river at a place called Robber's Roost. There are farms scattered along the valley, and very often we had to pause and share news with the farmers. Few of them had any knowledge of the greater world, or our Great Bay, but all were polite and mannered. None of them appear to be robbers.

May 27, Lava Hot Springs

We passed through beautiful easy country. The valley is broad and open and much like our coastal hills. Farmers here all have milk cows and gave us some yogurt. They know about the Rendezvous but are not at all interested.

Around noon the river turned east and the valley gradually narrowed. The country has changed a great deal. We are in the mountains now, at a hot springs called Lava, which is at the mouth of a narrow canyon with steep sides.

The people here have excellent gardens and grazing areas for stock. Many of the people are craftsmen, working lumber and wood from the mountains and also hunting. They control this very important pass but are famous for their generosity and their festivals, and they charge no tolls to travelers.

We both enjoyed soaking in the springs, as we were sore from so much walking. These people have sex in public, as our Wiccan tribes do in Sonomia, especially at the springs, where carnality seems uppermost in everyone's mind. Brother Levin turned out to be quite a kibitzer, commenting on many details, which surprised me.

May 28, Bear River/Soda Point

This morning we traveled up the canyon and bade goodbye to our beloved Portneuf. Around noon we crossed a narrow pass, blasted out by the Precles, and saw a broad flat valley before us, filled with deer, elk, and pronghorn. On the floor of the valley the road was very poor, overgrown with sagebrush, which slowed our progress. The valley is mostly dry but a group of local people are camped here at Soda Point, on the Bear River, where we are also camped. A great herd of elk bounded out of the river at our approach.

The people here speak a kind of English, but we had great difficulty understanding them, and it is clear that they believe us both to be wandering morons, as they quickly began ignoring anything we tried to say. This pleased Brother Levin no end. They dress entirely in skins, having no woven cloth. It is very windy.

May 29, Diamond Gulch

We are camped on the bluffs above the river, about nine miles to the southeast of a village called Soda, where the people have rebuilt brick houses and practice polygamy. We arrived before noon but stayed and lunched there. They had hanged a young man that morning at the church, and there was still quite a gathering there, right in front of the hanging body. The young man was one of the workers that the propertied men hire for farm work, who had been guilty of illicit sexual relations with one of the elder's young wives. There do not seem to be enough women for the young men, and while the older men often arrange marriages between them and their older wives, whom they have cast off, such severe punishments for adultery are not uncommon. We left them as quickly as we were able.

May 30, Montpel

We are hidden in a large barn on the far side of a community called Montpel. This was a very frightening day. Late last night a young couple from Soda arrived at our camp at Diamond Gulch on a horse, begging sanctuary. They said that they were in love but forbidden to marry, the young woman having already been chosen by one of the elders. Brother Levin and I conferred, and told them that we would accept them but only if they returned the horse. This they both refused, saying that it was due them. Seeing no other options, we set off at once and traveled through the night, arriving here in mid-morning, where the people at once hid us, in case the Sodalites were to arrive in force.

There is great ill feeling between the two communities, and they raid and fight each other often, and the people here have built numerous stockades. These people call themselves "The Rebels," and have

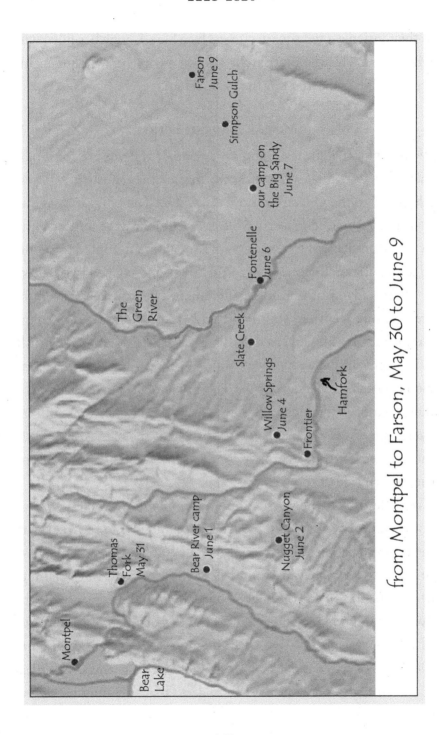

from Montpel to Farson, May 30 to June 9

as their insignia a red square crossed by a blue X, which is filled with white stars. This is a matriarchy and the people obey a queen and are quite adamant that it is the best system.

May 31, Thomas Fork

We left Montpel at first light. Our young fugitives are to remain there, as a trial, for a week, after which time they must either swear allegiance to the Queen or move elsewhere. The polygamists from Soda indeed arrived in force, while we slept, but were refused entry by the Montpelians. In response, the Sodalites attempted to set fire to the prairie on the outskirts of the town, and burned two barns.

On the advice of our hosts, after about twelve miles, we left the creek where it turned south and traveled on a poor trail through completely dry hills and ravines, hardly even supporting sagebrush. After eight difficult miles we came out upon a broad valley completely filled by meanders of the Thomas Fork. The whole sight was quite beautiful, the reds and yellows of the willows mixing with the pale green of the sagebrush and the brown of the hills. After numerous fordings of the stream we found a fine camp near the hills on the eastern side of the valley.

A rude tribe of herders and nomads inhabit the valley with no knowledge of writing. They trade skins and hides for powder with the civilized peoples but otherwise seem quite hostile and mistrustful of outsiders. They are quite adept with the bow. They claim to be descendants of the original "Pioneers," who they say foresaw the "Wrath" and emigrated here from the Eastern Lands at the dawn of history. In spite of their primitive ways they have been quite friendly and shared meat with us tonight and sang songs. The meat was from a large antelope called a "bigant" that they hunt with great stealth. This wondrous animal is a large kind of deer with splendid spiraling horns that Brother Levin believes originally came from Africa. The hunter who had killed the animal ate none of the meat himself, but the sharing of it with others was evidently a matter of high honor.

June 1, Cokeville/Bear River

Another day of twenty miles. The trail along the edge of the valley seems to be often traveled, and the valley is very flat. We are camped on the river.

June 2, Rock Creek, in Nugget Canyon

We have been following the Bear River, which turned sharply east and then north after ten miles of travel. We could see teepees in the valley to the south. The canyons here are quite dry, supporting only sagebrush, though the colors of the earths are quite beautiful. There have been numerous slides covering the road, some of which were quite red. We are camped at a canyon with a stream called the Rocky flowing in from the north.

This place is very isolated, and inhabited by a tribe of hunters who also grow some corn, beans, and potatoes. The women here are very forward, and were very interested in myself, feeling my hair with their hands and even lifting up my robe and chattering and laughing a great deal. I was surprised that they had never seen a black-skinned man before.

They live in wickiup structures, built with willow branches and wattle around a hemispherical frame of long steel reinforcing bars, salvaged from some old Precle site, that were woven and tied with wire with a smoke hole at the top.

June 3, Frontier

This is Brother Levin writing in my friend Solomon's journal. Solomon has come down with a fever and we are staying here until he recovers. We left Thomas Fork three days ago. Our last day of travel was through Nugget Canyon and dry and rugged badlands and high flat-topped plateaus of white sandstone. It has turned very cold and we both suffered some on the trail. We found no water all afternoon and our animals are poorly. Five families live here at Frontier, and the people are quite wonderful and generous. The river here is called Hamfork.

I must add a story about the people at our last camp at Rock Creek. As we left this morning the women were already out with their digging sticks in their fields between the bends of the creek. As we approached the women broke into raucous laughter, the big woman, Lena, falling all the way to the ground on her behind. Evidently one of the women had just come up with a double entendre on digging sticks, with reference, I suspect, to Solomon. That anyone could find a fresh joke about digging sticks after ten thousand years of agriculture I found remarkable. Such were my thoughts.

June 4, Willow Springs

I am recovering well and we came a short five miles today to this place called Willow Springs, where actually there is very little water.

The wife of our host in Frontier insisted on sleeping with Brother Levin last night, claiming that it was their custom, and Brother Levin had to give a number of gifts both to the woman and to her husband, including, I am sorry, a bundle of the fine black yaupon tea that I was saving as a gift for the zendo in Boulder. I asked Brother Levin if sleeping with the woman was not a violation of his vows. He simply laughed and said no.

June 5, Slate Creek/Graham Ditch

One of our mules has died.

Today was very cold and windy. The sagebrush here is stunted and small, and I must say that with the wind and the endless ravines and canyons the feeling of the country was quite sinister. We saw numerous antelope anywhere there was greenery or a seep. In Frontier our host had produced a map from a chest, which he said had been his grandfather's, it turning out to be a Precle road map of Wyoming, and I copied much of it into my journal. This, along with my own map, may be enough to get us through South Pass.

We traveled east most of the day, gradually climbing, until we reached a high open pass, almost indiscernible, where there were snowflakes in the air. After the summit we traveled northeast another twelve miles. We gave all but a little of our water to the mules and the donkey, but our favorite, Jezebel, succumbed, and we left her where she collapsed. We switched the mule and the donkey several times during the afternoon, our cart now being light enough for the donkey to pull on level ground. On hills we must assist.

We are camped at a place called Slate Creek. There is water here but little grass.

June 6, Fontenelle, across river

Today we reached the Green River after a short trek of about nine miles, where there are the remnants of a Precle dam that now create a small falls. The river here is two hundred feet across, but not excessively deep, and the local people, who ride horses, helped us find a passable ford about half a mile to the south where there is a small island in the middle of the river and where the banks were not steep. They call this place Fontenelle. We are camped in some cottonwoods. This crossing consumed the rest of our afternoon. Much of our gear was wetted, but everything dried quickly in this air, including our grains. This journal, and our powder, we carried across safely.

The people here speak a kind of English and were glad to share meat with us, telling us that we must repay them with stories, which we did. Some of Brother Levin's stories stretched the truth. These people wear leggings and shirts made of elk, and Brother Levin and I traded a kettle and some powder for two of them, which are quite comfortable and soft.

The people were very interested in our journey, and even discussed joining us, but they already had plans to move north into the Tetons, as they said it would soon be too hot to stay on the Green. These people are mainly nomadic and carry their possessions in small wheeled carts. They trade sheep to farmers they say live to the south for corn and wheat.

It is still very windy, and I believe that there must be a Windy Hell along with the Hot Hells and the Cold Hells. Brother Levin said, "This country is like an ocean, except that it's prairie."

June 7, Big Sandy

We are camped several miles above the Green River on the Big Sandy, where a ravine cuts through the high bluffs down to the river. We saw some wolves today, and three kinds of horned antelope, including the "bigant" that we first saw on the Thomas Fork. Brother Levin tried to shoot one with our rifle but missed, the powder charge not igniting properly, thoroughly scattering the game. There are large colonies of a kind of ground squirrel here that dig large holes in the ground that seem to lead into a network of tunnels.

June 8, Simpson Gulch

We traveled about twelve miles today, all that our two animals could endure. We are camped again on the Big Sandy where a creek comes in from the north, which I believe is the Simpson. There are snowy mountains to the northeast, which must be the Wind River Range. There is a prominent butte with a flat top many miles to the south southeast.

June 9, Farson

Today is June 10 and I am writing this in the morning while Brother Levin finishes with our packing. We are camped on the Big Sandy, about twelve miles northeast of our last camp. The river here is just a stream that one could jump across in a single leap. There is a fork a short distance downstream from here where the Little Sandy branches to the right. This is a desolate place with many rusting pieces of Precle machinery and equipment.

We arrived at this place quite exhausted, too tired to create proper protection for ourselves from the wind, and were thus huddled at the base of our cart when a troop of nomads arrived on horses. Without speaking to us they made a fire and quickly unpacked their horses, which were well packed with meat. They spoke their own language of which we could understand not a word, but through signs bade us join them in their feast. After dinner, with a rapidity that amazed us, they erected tiny shelters with soft hides for protection from the wind, and one for us as well. I think they were ready to make merry, but sensing our condition, all went to sleep early.

The nomads were up very early, even before me, and had gone through all of our belongings in the wagon, and had laid out a small pile of items that they claimed for themselves, including a package of

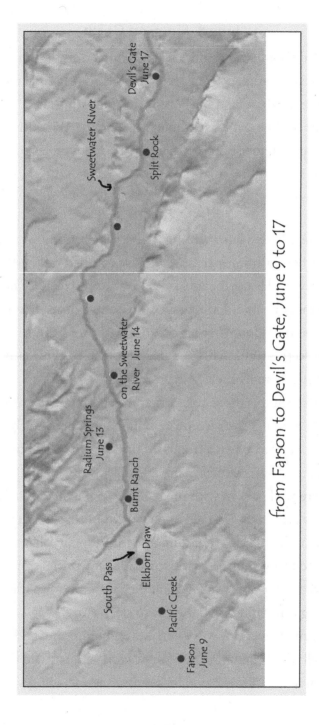

Devil's Gate
June 17

Sweetwater River

Split Rock

on the Sweetwater
River June 14

Radium Springs
June 13

Burnt Ranch

South Pass

Elkhorn Draw

Pacific Creek

Farson
June 9

from Farson to Devil's Gate, June 9 to 17

black yaupon, a small cooking pot, and half of Brother Levin's powder. They seemed to be awaiting our approval of this transaction, and when it became clear that I did not approve, they quickly lost their good humor. Brother Levin sensed the situation immediately and went over to our cart and pulled out the woven smock that he had been saving, and added that to the nomad's pile, at which they all broke into hearty laughter. They then insisted that we take one of their horses, on which was packed several bundles of jerked meat. This was evidently not one of their prime horses, as they made clear by signs that when the horse gave out, we were to slaughter and eat it. Brother Levin believes they were speaking Basque.

June 10, Pacific Creek

We made a good fifteen miles, continuing northeast, and are camped on Pacific Creek where there is a little water, but hardly fodder. I don't know where the mosquitoes are from. The air has warmed considerably and stilled.

We treasure our little bit of grain, as meat alone is not a proper diet.

June 11, Elkhorn Draw/Pacific Springs

A long day through the sagebrush along Pacific Creek. The Wind Rivers seem to be growing taller and more imposing every day. After about sixteen miles we came to a draw, from which we could see South Pass to the east. We followed the draw east another mile, crossing some Precle railroad tracks, and have made a camp on the headwaters of Pacific Creek.

Brother Levin managed to shoot a sheep with great curved horns, and I admit that I am very glad that we have a rifle along with us. We ate the liver and cut the meat into strips for drying.

June 12, Burntford

We have now been traveling through sagebrush for over two months, and today was no different, traveling easterly on a trail overgrown with the ubiquitous shrub, more or less following the railroad bed. Cement posts every half mile marked the trail, and there was a Precle cement marker at South Pass, which we otherwise might not have recognized as the country is so flat and open. A small creek flowing east soon confirmed our crossing. We could see Twin Mounds, a landmark for this crossing, directly to the south. We continued east for about ten more miles, seeing many herds of pronghorn, until we came to a shallow draw filled with orange willow bushes, where the Sweetwater curls back and forth across a meadow, and there was a shanty and a small corral. There were strands of barbed wire across the wagon tracks, but so rusted that I was able to break them with my foot. We proceeded to the river, crossing a patch of snow, but before we could water our animals a young man rode up to us on horseback, accompanied by a pack of dogs, who told us that we were on private land and must turn back. Brother Levin explained our mission, and the young man indeed seemed interested in talking to educated people, but soon his father appeared, a fierce man who had no such interest, and we reluctantly turned back. I repaired the broken fence as best I could, twisting the sad remnants of the barbed wire back into the semblance of a fence. We made a camp a little over a mile to the west, where the river is narrow and there is a beaver dam and some grass.

There were meadowlarks singing today at South Pass.

June 13, Radium Springs

This was a long and difficult day, but the weather is clear and mild. We forded several branches of the Sweetwater, and crossed many ravines and hills to avoid the ranch at Burntford. Several times we had to make detours to get around large patches of wet snow. We passed a bronze plaque today commemorating a Precle named "Willie" who perished at that place, along with most of his party. We are now at a place that I believe is Radium Springs, where there is water and a small meadow. We saw a moose lumbering off as we approached.

A woman came into our camp at dusk, greatly bruised and carrying an infant. We did not hear her approaching, but our mule clearly did, turning both of his ears her direction. After we had fed the woman, when she saw that we were not going to hurt her, she became quite animated. We could not pronounce her full name, which was long, so we have shortened it to "Skopie," at which she laughed and seemed pleased. We can understand her speech very little, but she seems quick at understanding ours. When she saw that neither of us were going to take her to bed she laughed again and curled up with her baby by the fire, singing it to sleep.

June 14, on the Sweetwater

Skopie is traveling with us and has turned out to be an excellent guide. We were about to take the main path, which led north, but Skopie insisted that we follow another path that led due east, until we reached the Sweetwater after five miles. We crossed a ravine to the northern bank and followed the river for ten more miles, where we forded and are camped in a spacious meadow.

Skopie is quite skilled at bareback riding, for which she would strip off her skirt and wear only her girdlebelt. She would frequently scout ahead thus, especially when we approached a ranch, perhaps worried that her tormentor might be there, at such times giving her baby to Brother Levin. She always seemed to know when we needed to climb to the bluffs to avoid the turnings and thickets along the river.

This wonderful woman has quickly and expertly set about making our camp here and has taken complete control over our comestibles. I cannot tell you what a delight she is and Brother Levin and myself are quite taken with her. She laughs a great deal and knows more English than we had thought and talks as much as she can, telling us wild stories with what words she has and signs that she makes with her hands and arms. She was evidently raised in a tribe of nomads that she calls the "Craw" who live to the north, though she says they are not her own people. Of her own people we could discover little, except that they live to the east.

June 15, near Jeffrey

We are camped on the Sweetwater, after a trek of close to twenty miles. We lunched in a boggy-looking meadow, but found little water. Skopie evidently knew the place, took our shovel from the cart, and soon returned with large chunks of ice, which refreshed us more than our stock. However, we were not far from the river, and are camped there now.

We saw more moose today, and some wolves. Skopie made signs that Brother Levin should shoot the moose, but he would not, we still having some jerked meat, whereupon Skopie made a great fuss.

June 16, Split Rock

We are camped on the Sweetwater near a great split rock, after about twenty miles. The land is open and the trail is good. The sagebrush is becoming sparser, and there is a great deal more grass, which suits our animals.

We saw several small herds of bison today, great shaggy beasts with many new calves.

June 17, Devil's Gate

A long day of about twenty miles. We are camped outside the stockade of a community called Momos. The Sweetwater flows through a narrow cleft of rock here and the place is called Devil's Gate. These people believe that they arrived here from another planet, and that there are many planets, and that each man will be given a planet by God at the end of times if he leads a righteous life. They tell us that there is a great rock that we will pass tomorrow onto which their ancestors descended and from which the elect will again ascend. These people are friendly but shrewd traders, very adept in the art of picking and choosing. Brother Levin engaged them in many theological discussions, asking them how God could have only the form of a man, but they insisted that such is the case, and that their prophets have seen him and talked with him.

Brother Levin and Skopie have become lovers.

June 18, Horse Creek

We are camped at a beautiful place called Horse Creek. The prairie has changed, there being less sagebrush and more bunchgrass. Bison and pronghorn are numerous, along with several antelope with curved horns that we had not seen before. We saw a large cat covered with spots, fast enough to catch the pronghorn.

Brother Levin and I quarreled today. There are many killdeer here, who seem to scold us both with their peeping.

June 19, Alcove/North Platte

Today we crossed a range of hills, following an old roadway. This is a country of mountains and dry ravines and cliffs of rusty sandstone. We are camped on the North Platte River, where it makes a sharp bend, at a place they call The Cove.

A hundred people live here and there are trees. These people have fine horses and have many high stockaded corrals, which they say is to protect their stock at night from leopards. They are preparing their fields along the river for corn, beans, and the other vegetables they grow, and they are fine hunters, using short recurved bows that are extremely powerful.

The people here have informed us that this is not a good place to cross the river, but that there is a good ford about seven miles from here and a man and a woman have agreed to guide us, as the woman has relatives living at the ferry.

Skopie is being quite felicitous toward me, as is Brother Levin. We traveled today fifteen miles. The river hosts many wild birds: ducks and geese and swans.

June 20, on Bates Creek

Today we crossed the North Platte where it is joined by Bull Town's Creek. The river there is very wide but placid, and Skopie was able to swim across with the mule, and the horse and the donkey followed. Our cart presented a bigger problem, but our guides and a family living there had several coils of horsehair rope and round boats made of hide, and after ferrying our belongings, we were able to swim and pull our cart through the water.

Leaving our guides, we proceeded several more miles to the northeast and are now following Bates Creek, on which we are camped

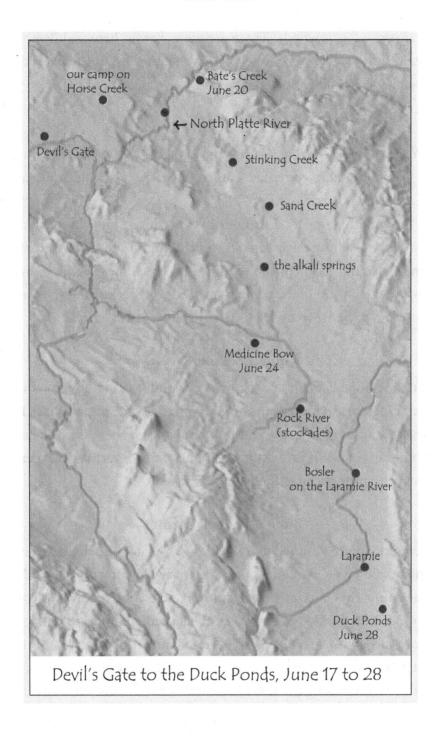

Devil's Gate to the Duck Ponds, June 17 to 28

near some cottonwoods. There are many beaver here and Brother Levin shot a deer. We have erected a shelter with our tarp as it is clouding over and has begun to rain.

June 21, Stinking Creek

We are camped on what is surely the "stinking creek" that we heard of from our guides yesterday. This country is very arid and desolate and we saw no people.

Last night Skopie and Brother Levin seduced me, and we have decided to call ourselves the Splendid Triumvirate. I admit that I am in love but have chosen tonight to sleep alone. Skopie joined Brother Levin and I for zazen but giggled a great deal and soon left and went to bed. We traveled twenty miles today.

June 22, Sand Creek

We are camped at Sand Creek, which is quite small but with good water. There are mountains on the horizon. This place is like the desert prairies of which we are so familiar, and there is no shelter from the wind. We have little to eat but venison, and saw no game today but pronghorn, which kept at a distance.

June 23, Alkali Springs

Tonight we are camped at a small creek that is mostly stagnant and alkaline. We passed a good stream in the afternoon but did not camp there, continuing another five miles to this place. Brother Levin and I are both very concerned about our dwindling store of provisions, but Skopie seems not to be worried in the least, and sang songs as we made camp. In a phonetic compromise, we are calling her baby Raj, and we take turns packing him.

Skopie stuffs his blanket with crushed sagebrush leaves to keep him clean.

June 24, Medicine Bow

This was a long day, but we have come to the Medicine Bow! We crossed some rugged hills through a pass and then through a valley cut by ravines and gulleys even drier than the one before it. There is little sagebrush but some sparse grass and more of the antelope with the curved horns. As we neared the river and the country opened into meadowlands we saw more of the spotted cats at a distance of barely a hundred yards, eyeing us warily. The people here call them cheetahs and do not fear them much.

This is a wonderful community here, much in spirit like those of our Great Bay, and Brother Levin and I feel quite like we have come home, though the manner of speech here is quite odd to us. These people know all about the Rendezvous and have sent a large contingent themselves, which, unfortunately, left several days ago. The people feasted us with a dinner of fish and bulgur, for which we were very thankful, and I gave them half of my remaining yaupon. After dinner there was much dancing, in which we all participated, including Skopie, who seemed to find it all quite delightful.

I danced with a gal with a hole in her stockin',
And her heel kept a-knockin', and her toes kept a-rockin'

June 25, Rock River

We are camped at Rock River, where the people live within stockades as they do at Medicine Bow. They claim that it is because of lions, though we have not seen any. A woman named Jasmin from Medicine Bow has joined us, deciding that she wants to see the Rendezvous after all. Our cart is now so light that it can easily be pulled by our donkey, or by ourselves, and we traded our mule for another horse. The people here make a good powder by boiling urine and straw and an alkaline substance that they have in abundance, and gave us a full horn though we had little to offer in exchange.

There are a number of Buddhists here, of the esoteric practice, and we sat with them.

June 26, Bosler Junction/Laramie River

A long day of travel through a country of alkali, but we have come to the Laramie River. This is a community of Christians who are taught to read in order to study the Bible. A woman here was whipped today for adultery. According to their law, if such a woman confesses and begs forgiveness, her head is shaven, she is stripped, and then publicly whipped. If she does not confess and beg forgiveness she is executed by stoning, as she is thought to be inhabited by the Devil. The man, unless he is powerful, or a deacon, is exiled. Jasmin explained to us that those they believe to be under the power of the Devil are not considered worthy of forgiveness, and that any torture they can inflict upon such wretches is pleasing to their god. Murders also are common here, usually from an ambush, which they call "drygulching."

The deacons here all have good ranches, claiming my namesake as their example, while most of the congregation are quite poor.

I asked Brother Levin if he could not tell them of the ways of the Prophet, but he grimly shook his head, saying that preaching was not the way of his tradition, and that anyway these people believe in the Devil more than in God, and that such hypocrisy was not at all uncommon.

I should add that a young man of the Christians sought out Brother Levin and that they talked together a long time on the banks of the river. Brother Levin called him a Seeker and said that if they did not burn the young man at the stake before he ran away, he would probably find a teacher someplace.

They have several stockades here: the largest, around their church and the homes of the deacons, is of brick and they have mounted on its walls two cannon.

We will leave this place at first light.

June 27, Laramie

We have come to Laramie and are camped by the river in the grounds of a medieval Precle prison. We passed through the ruins of the city, which are quite desolate, and there are no wooden structures that have not been wrecked or burned, though we saw a stone church. Precle wreckage is everywhere, including hundreds of rusting train cars. We saw a few people skulking about, but none of them came out to greet us.

Our scholars have heard that there is a man here named Samuel who is a historian. I had hoped to spend an extra day here to attempt to find this man, or to discover whether or not he is still alive, but Brother Levin and Jasmin are anxious to move on to Boulder, fearing that we will miss the Rendezvous.

June 28, Duck Ponds

We are camped at some stagnant ponds after a short day of ten miles, but Jasmin tells us that it is important to rest our animals here as tomorrow will be a long day without water.

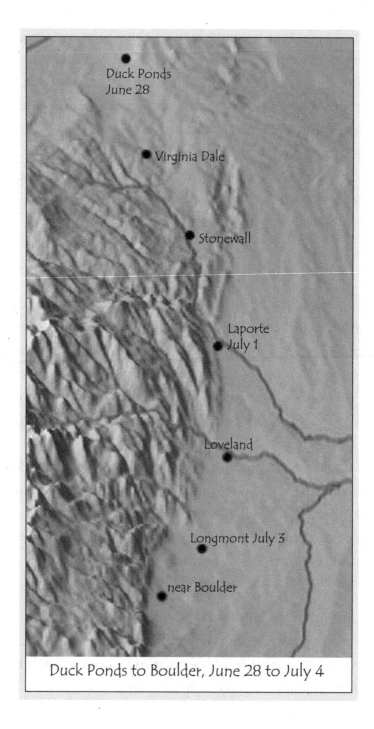

Duck Ponds
June 28

Virginia Dale

Stonewall

Laporte
July 1

Loveland

Longmont July 3

near Boulder

Duck Ponds to Boulder, June 28 to July 4

June 29, Virginia Dale

We did find water today, and lunched by a boggy meadow while our animals grazed. After nooning we ascended a long grade, and could see mountains about five miles ahead, through which we traveled the rest of the day. We are camped at the Dale, where there is a lively Inn and Trading Post. The innkeeper demanded to be paid in money. Brother Levin removed one of the diamond rings from his ear and negotiated a sale, but I do not think he got a very good exchange, being given only a pile of notes in various denominations marked "Collins."

This country is unlike any we have seen, being mountainous and broken and rocky and supporting timber. Hunters here have rifles and travel into the mountains where they shoot the big horned sheep.

June 30, Stonewall

We are camped again by ourselves at a small stream, after a short day. Jasmin took our bucket and walked to a nearby farm and returned with milk, which we will drink as soon as it cools.

July 1, Laporte

Today we passed through a great cut in the mountains, made by Precles, and traveled through a long narrow valley with mountains on both sides. We are camped on a small river near the community of Laporte, where the people are farmers and craftsmen and are organized into collectives. They were glad to receive our Collins scrip and we now have a supply of cheese and bulgur.

There are many farms and stockades in all of this country. We are still three days from Boulder and may miss the celebration. Skopie and Jasmin have become fast friends and Skopie seems to have fully recovered her English.

July 2, Loveland

Today we passed through Fort Collins, a Free City and the great rival of Boulder. Much of the country is forested with pines and broad-leaved trees, the forest being broken by many clearings where there are farms or buildings or shops. Many Precle buildings are in use, and the city seems quite populous. We nooned by the river they call Da Powder, at a factory where they make pumps for windmills, using Precle parts and casting those they lack with brass and finishing them on lathes. They have a strong militia here with which they defend themselves from the nomadic tribes of the deserts to the east.

We continued on a number of miles and are camped on a small river in the community of Loveland. These people are vassals of Fort Collins, paying them tribute each year, but claim that it is a good alliance. The young people here hunt lions, and both the young men and the young women are expected to kill a lion to become a full member of the community.

July 3, Longmont

We are camped on a small creek at a place called Longmont. There are many groups of people camped here, and all the talk is of the Rendezvous, which is only half a day from here, and at which there is said to be a great deal of trouble from large tribes of nomads that everyone calls "The Barbarians."

The largest group here is from the Republic of Ohio, who say they are remaining here where they are until the troubles are over. These people are all dressed in cloth, which they say is made on great looms powered by water. They say that they traveled here by water on six boats, coming up the Missouri and the Platte, and that in Ohio they have small railroad cars that they pull with oxen.

July 5, near Boulder

Yesterday at the Rendezvous there was a bloody melee. Some say that the trouble began between the Barbarians themselves; others say that one of the Barbarian chieftains felt that he had been insulted by the people of Boulder. The Boulder militia formed to meet the Barbarians but were unable to defend the city. The Barbarians set fires and captured the store of rockets that were to be set off for the climax of the celebration and turned them against the city, starting yet more fires. We spent all night fighting the fires, choking in the smoke with rockets shooting at us and powder magazines exploding. Most of Boulder has been burned, and we are camped on the river on the outskirts of the city. The fires are still burning today.

The Ohioans are worried about their boats, which they left at the fort at Greeley, and are returning there tomorrow. We hear that a large army of militia is moving south from Fort Collins to chase off the Barbarians, though their true objective, according to some, is the conquest of Boulder. Jasmin has joined a group of her neighbors from Medicine Bow who are camped in the hills, and Skopie and Raj are with her. We plan to meet up tomorrow or the day after. Brother Levin and I are attempting to find the Buddhists, but there is much confusion.

December 31, Boulder

This is Brother Levin writing in the journal of Solomon the Monk. I am staying here in Boulder with the Buddhists until spring, when I will join the other Californians who are returning to the Great Bay and will deliver this journal to the Green Rock Temple at Clear Lake. We will take the southern route, through Santa Fe. I have received no news of Captain Vallejo or the others of our party from whom we parted in Nevada. I assume that they were defeated by the desert and hope that they were able to return to the Great Bay without mishap.

On July 6, Solomon and I were captured by Barbarians who were going to throw us both into a large bonfire. Solomon told the Barbarian chieftain that he didn't wish for him to be burdened with his murder, and walked into the fire and burned to death without uttering a scream, his eyes fixed on the Barbarian chieftain. I was released and the Barbarians rode away quickly. The chieftain, whose name is Attal, has recently joined us here and is exceedingly diligent in his practice of Buddhism.

I never reunited with Skopie, but a merchant who visited here in the fall brought me a pair of beaded moccasins that she made for me, with news that she is well, with a husband in Medicine Bow, and is pregnant with a child.

The Fourth
and the Fifth Centuries
2321–2520

The earth had entered a Pliocene climate in half a millennium. Rainfall was heavy in far northern and southern latitudes, but the sub-tropics were deserts. Vegetation zones shifted too quickly for many plants and trees or the creatures who depended upon them to follow. About two thirds of the world's plant and animal species died out.

Gaia sought to cool herself with ice wherever she could find it, which was mostly in Antarctica. Warm currents pounded against the continent from every direction. Hardy mosses, ferns, and liverworts hastened the melting, and the more the ice melted, the faster the shrinking glaciers poured into the oceans. Huge cascades and roaring waterfalls dotted the landscape. Pockets of brown earth appeared, which then turned green. Winter was still winter, but every summer was an explosion of cracking, grinding, and roaring. Immense rivers flowed beneath the glaciers, and the glaciers sprinted toward the sea.

Around the world the oceans moved inland. Coastal dwellers who lived to be old could float in boats three fathoms above where they had played as children. Villages that had been miles from the coast could be under ten feet of water in a single lifetime. People around the Great Bay built their houses on stilts and pilings. The California coastline became a series of deep fjords and rias, often extending inland ten or twenty miles. San Francisco became a city of islands. All of Market Street was underwater. The sea covered half of Golden Gate Park, and lapped up against the Island of the Presidio. The Mission District was entirely submerged. There were docks and moorings on the edges of Haight-Ashbury.

Almost all of the Iberian Peninsula was desert, resembling the Sahara. The zone of aridity stretched around the Mediterranean north to the Alps and to the foothills of the Balkans. Thorny desert plants were all that grew on south-facing slopes, or none at all. People moved north to escape the heat and the drought, to be pushed back by the advancing North Sea.

Decade after decade of drought settled over the Central Plains. Desert sand dunes blew all the way up to the Front Range in Colorado, burying the nascent civilizations at their base. Erosion from spring floods washed much of the soil of the deforested Rocky Mountains down the canyons.

In California, young forests of bay laurel or tan oak covered the mountains. Willows and cottonwoods spread from the riverbanks. Reefs formed along the coasts. Crabs and other crustaceans found the submerged ruins to their liking. Clams and oysters ringed the Great Bay. Komodo dragons, escaped from some reserve, found the warm lagoons in Baja to their liking.

The crustal plates colliding under California continued to make adjustments. Earthquakes in the Sierras created new volcanoes at both ends of the range. Mt. Shasta exploded in a spectacular way, spewing six feet of ash across the whole Modoc

Plateau. There was a huge earthquake between Palm Springs and Lancaster, ripping apart the roads at Cajon Pass and leveling anything that was still standing in Riverside and San Bernardino, which wasn't a lot. Vertical slip became as important as strike slip. The Central Valley kept sinking; the Sierras were uplifting all along their eastern edge. New hot springs appeared from the Owens Valley to Carson City.

No one held a rendezvous for the year 300, and there was little long distance travel—people focused on trying to eat and stay alive. Large scale organization almost disappeared. Huge increases in insect populations made the growing of crops, even where the climate was favorable, less and less productive. Disease was common everywhere, and human populations around the world struggled to maintain themselves, and often did not.

Legacy materials and tools were more and more scarce. Few structures of reinforced concrete were intact—most were piles of rubble. The ruins of the ancient cities were either underwater, overgrown with vegetation, or covered in sand. Almost nobody was making any black powder; people hunted with snares, nets, bow and arrow, or the atlatl. An older man who was sharpening his steel knife on a rock to skin out a deer found that his son had already knocked out two scrapers from an oblong piece of stone that was lying on the ground and had the animal half finished.

The oceans were at a critical tipping point. Fish stocks had plummeted. Immense dead zones appeared. Acidity had increased so much that plankton had difficulty in growing shells and fixing carbon. Any further decrease in the pH of the oceans would cause them to begin releasing carbon instead of absorbing it, which would cause further warming. Any further warming would cause explosive releases of methane, and the earth's atmosphere would warm by another five or ten degrees. Life on land would have to endure temperatures not seen since the Cretaceous. The reptiles were hoping for a second chance.

In the oceans, the drama was being played out by plants and creatures too small to see without a microscope. An obscure protozoan might flourish in great blooms in the new acidic waters, only to be decimated in another decade. Chaotic vagaries of current and eddy could shift the balance one way or the other. Dark pockets of cold water still rich in oxygen and life alternated with clear and sterile turquoise.

By the end of the fifth century N.C., the Great Bay of California was 240 miles long, 30 to 50 miles across, and 160 feet deep in the middle.

∾ ∾ ∾

Janisse

Salinas Bay
The Year 339 New Calendar
from The Peripatetics, *by Jae West-Wind,*
Library of the Order of Antiquities

Mandl Amandaclan, poet, and his young apprentice gazed at the cannibal fortress and the depopulated country around it from the deck of the boat. Salinas Bay was two and a half miles wide here, but the pilot, taking advantage of the ebb, was keeping close to the eastern shore. They could see the ruins clearly. Earthquakes had destroyed many of the buildings, but the fortress itself had stubbornly defied collapse. Scores of white skulls hung from the walls on ropes.

"They really are cannibals, I guess," Janisse said.

"So everyone says. I have no reason not to believe them."

Salinas Bay stretched thirty miles inland: the Port of Soledad was at its southern tip, protected by a massive stockade. South of the town were the rich farmlands of Greenfield and King City. North of Port Soledad, the eastern side of Salinas Bay was a no man's land all the way to the Gabilan Hills. The cannibal fortress itself was a mere four miles north of the port.

"What were all those buildings?" Janisse asked.

"A Precle prison," Mandl answered. "They held thousands of prisoners there, from what we can tell."

"I don't think I like the Precles. Why do we study them?"

"They knew many things."

"They couldn't have known very many things. They almost destroyed the world."

"Yes, that is true."

Another poet, Deetr, came forward and joined Mandl and Janisse on the bow. They had all been at the Harvest Festival at Port Soledad. Four poets and six apprentices had recited and sung. The celebration had lasted two days. Their mood was still festive, but the looming presence of the Fortress made them lower their voices.

"They have been very quiet lately," Deetr said softly. "If they don't attack us, we don't bother them."

"But where are they raiding then?" Mandl asked.

"Inland, from what I hear. Along the San Benito."

"And Port Soledad thinks it is safe behind its redwood stockade? That's crazy."

"Rubello is getting old," Deetr said. "We're hoping that things will change when he dies. 'King Rubello,' they call him."

Mandl shook his head. "They'll only get stronger," he said, "as they spread their terror. You Salinians need to stop them somehow."

"We destroyed all their boats," Deetr responded, "but what else can we do? The Fortress itself is too strong to attack."

"Maybe you should eat more flesh and less fish," Janisse stuck in.

"The stale cadaver blocks up the passage—the burial waits no longer."

Deetr looked over Mandl's new apprentice. She was a quick one, with a strong sonorous voice. He could see why Mandl had taken her in. His own two apprentices, Robert and Makr, were in the stern playing chess. Deetr added the next line:

"Allons! yet take warning!"

Janisse smiled. Poets' games. She loved this part of the fellowship.

"He traveling with me needs the best blood, thews, endurance,
None may come to the trial till he or she bring courage and health,
Come not here if you have already spent the best of yourself,"

"Excellent," Deetr said, "your mastery grows apace."

Janisse thanked him. "Do the cannibals keep slaves in the Fortress?"

"Yes, like slaves," Deetr said, "they keep their workers locked up and they work in chains. Sometimes they make them fight, or they use them as human shields."

They were silent for a while.

"Foule thyrldome," Mandl said.

"What's that?" Deetr asked.

Mandl began reciting:

A! Fredome is a noble thing!
Fredome mays man to haiff liking;
Fredome all solace to man giffis,
He levys at ese that freely levys!

"That's Middle English!" Deetr said. "Where did you learn that?"

"It was one of my teacher's favorites," Mandl said. "She said it was from eight hundred years before the Collapse. The poet's name was John Barbour."

"Would you teach it me?" Deetr asked. "I can trade you something. I don't think you know my Coleridge."

Mandl recited the syllables of the first line of the poem, and Deetr repeated them. Then Mandl recited the second line and Deetr echoed it back, beginning again with the first line. In an hour he could recite all eighteen lines.

∾ ∾ ∾

Toward evening the pilot crossed over to the west shore and tied up at the piers at El Toro Inlet. No one camped on the east side, at least not south of Crazy Horse Canyon. El Toro Inlet was the best harbor in Salinas Bay and the busiest port north of Soledad. In the morning Mandl and Janisse were able to find another boat that would ferry them the twelve miles across the Bay to the Prunedale bluffs. Deetr's boat was going on to Monterey, and they said goodbye.

From Prunedale, Mandl and Janisse followed trails east to Crazy Horse Canyon, then turned north to meet the old Precle highway,

193

or what was left of it, at the quarry. The entire country around was so densely forested with giant redwoods that it was almost impossible to walk cross-country because of down trees. The Precle highway, even broken up and flooded at places by the Bay, was still the easiest way to go north.

They had a long day's hike. They were headed for the house of a ferryman and his family, where the ocean snaked through the narrow straits at Pajaro Gap to enter the broad Gilroy Slough.

The road was rough and they walked together. Janisse spoke first.

"There is a line in the Coleridge that you are learning,

And fruits, and foliage, not my own, seemed mine.

that makes me think of the lines I'm learning:

To see no possession but you may possess it, enjoying all without labor or purchase . . .

Do they mean the same thing?"

"Yes, in a way," Mandl answered, "though the Coleridge has more to do with private property."

"What is 'private property'?"

"A form of coercion."

"It is the things one owns?"

"No, those are your belongings. Private property had to do with wealth. The Precles would pretend that it was the same thing as your house, or your tools, but it actually had to do with paper certificates, saying that such and such was part of your wealth."

"It was just a game?"

"No, or yes, but a deadly game. They would kill to protect their wealth, and there were large armies to protect property."

"Do you mean land?"

"Land was only one kind of property, called 'real' property."

"How can anyone own the earth?"

"We would consider it an affront to the gods, would we not? They would pretend that they owned the earth—whole mountains even. They would hire mercenaries to keep others off the land. That's why they built the Fortress."

"What do you mean?"

"They would draw a line in the dirt somewhere and kill or imprison anyone who crossed it. Or they would destroy the land, to prove that they owned it."

"Is that how they almost destroyed the earth?"

"Yes. I think so. They set the earth on fire and then the floods came."

"Is that why we leave offerings to the sea, so that the fires won't come back?"

Mandl smiled. She had given him a set-up and she knew it.

"No. We leave offerings because the sea is beautiful. And because it helps to feed us. And because it is blue."

They could have continued east, through San Juan Bautista and Hollister, then up through Pacheco Pass to meet the Great Bay at San Luis, but Mandl wanted to visit friends in Morgan Hill, and then go on up the Santa Clara Valley.

As they neared the Gilroy Slough and Lomerias Muertas Island in the afternoon, the road was better and they separated. Mandl kept reciting the lines he had learned from Deetr, sometimes from the beginning, sometimes from the middle, to fix them well in his memory.

For not to think of what I needs must feel,
But to be still and patient, all I can;

And haply by abstruse research to steal
From my own nature all the natural man—

He'd heard other Coleridge. That poet from Santa Barbara knew "The Rime of the Ancient Mariner," but Mandl liked these lines better. They expressed the method of their work, the divination they practiced.

He walked slowly, stretching each pentameter over three paces. Iambs were easy, that way. Free verse was more difficult. He could hear Janisse behind him with her Whitman:

From this hour I ordain myself loos'd of limits and imaginary lines,
Going where I list, my own master total and absolute,
Listening to others, considering well what they say,
Pausing, searching, receiving, contemplating,
Gently, but with undeniable will, divesting myself of the holds that
would hold me.

Whitman required a more vigorous pace, and Janisse would soon pass him and take the lead on the trail. That was fine. This was how they worked. And she did pass him, smiling as she went by:

All seems beautiful to me,
I can repeat over to men and women You have done such good to me
I would do the same to you,
I will recruit for myself and you as I go,
I will scatter myself among men and women as I go,
I will toss a new gladness and roughness among them,

When the road turned west again along the Crittenden Straits, and they neared the ferry, Mandl caught up with her again.

"So when we leave offerings at a pass, do you really believe there is a spirit there?" Janisse asked him.

"Of course."

"But, what is the spirit like then? Does it have a form?"

"Yes, it has a form."

"Why can't we see it?"

"We do see it."

"But, if the spirit is the pass itself, what need does it have of corn-meal, or tobacco, or another stone being placed on the cairn?"

"It has no need, but it is appropriate for us to lay such an offering. It will help something good to happen, or stop something bad from happening, somewhere, sometime."

Janisse pressed him: "But you don't really believe in the spirits."

"I do believe in the spirits, and I believe that all actions have consequences. Laying an offering is an action, therefore it must have consequences. On the other hand, taking the pass for granted is also an action, and that must also have consequences."

"You are saying that it is *as if* it were real, but that it's not really real. Like we give offerings to the dead, but we know that they don't really eat them."

"That would still be in error. How do you know that the dead don't eat the offerings?"

"But we're taught that there is nothing permanent, nothing eternal, so how could there be a soul that lives on after death?"

"We know there are the dead. That is why we wash their bodies and offer them food."

"But why do we do it if it's not really true?" Janisse asked again.

"We don't know whether or not it's really true, or even what 'really true' signifies. You don't know that, nor do I. You have to realize your own nature first, and how it is 'really true' and not 'really true.'"

Janisse could tell that the conversation was over. She wanted to press him more, to needle him, to trap him into saying something ostentatious or presumptuous. He could be trapped by his pride, she knew that well. She addressed him formally.

"How many poems do you know, Teacher?"

"I know about a hundred. I learned all of the poems my teacher Miria knew, which was about sixty, and I have collected the rest from other poets. There are still many more for you to learn, before you begin singing your own songs."

"I already sing my own songs."

"Of course. I meant in performance."

"But all the old poems are in Precle, and people can barely understand it."

Mandl didn't answer but went on walking. When they emerged onto a meadow Janisse asked another question.

"Why don't we write down our songs?"

"Because our songs, which are really new poems, are still living. They belong to whoever sings them and they keep changing. You remember at the boat launching in Monterey, when Deetr sang the Wind Song? Some of those verses were from my song, the Sailing Song, except that he used them in a new way, in his own song, and changed the wording of a couple of lines."

"Do you think Deetr was right? Changing the lines?"

"I didn't think so right off, but most say he was right. It is an honor among us to have our words used by another poet. What other stature can we have?"

ɷɷɷ

They reached Rudy the Ferryman's small ranch at dusk. Rudy was an old friend of Mandl's. He operated a rope ferry across the narrows and lived with his wife in a small house above the inlet. Both of his sons were grown and were away helping with the cotton harvest on Panoche Creek, by the Great Bay.

The poets were fed and after visiting and much exchange of news bedded themselves down in the stable, which they shared with Rudy's mule. They made a soft bed in the straw and made love and lay in each other's arms.

"Were you and Miria lovers?" Janisse asked.

"That's a very personal question, but understandable. No, we weren't. Though we often slept together. It was a spiritual relationship. It drove me a little crazy sometimes."

"What makes it spiritual?"

"As opposed to carnal, of the flesh."

"Isn't our relationship spiritual?"

"Yes, I think so. If you say so. I hope it is. But it's also carnal, which I like."

They talked about other poets and their apprentices, of Andrea and Arno and their terrible break-up, of who were lovers and who were not, and of those of whom they were not sure.

"Makr told me that one shouldn't sleep with one's Teacher."

"That's probably because Makr wants to get into your pants."

Janisse smiled. "I think that part is true."

"Some do say that, about sleeping with teachers. That's because of teachers like Biksall, who opened whole schools, where it became a scandal. You don't feel that way, do you?"

"No, of course not. It's different with us." She rubbed her hand over his belly.

"What about Dyrsus?" she asked. "He never learned all of his teacher's poems."

"Some condemn him. I do not."

"But he performs."

"Yes. I like his songs, and he came and learned several poems from me."

A bird called from the forest, a long high-pitched whistle. Neither of them knew what bird it was.

"I'm ready for the last stanza of the Song of the Open Road," Janisse said.

"Ahh, yes you are." Mandl turned onto his side so that he could hold her. He put a hand on Janisse's breast and spoke softly into her ear.

Camerado, I give you my hand!
I give you my love more precious than money,
I give you myself before preaching or law;
Will you give me yourself? will you come travel with me?
Shall we stick by each other as long as we live?

Janisse spooned back against him and held his arms against her tightly. She had known the lines already.

∽∽∽

It took them two days to reach the southern extremity of San Francisco Bay, traveling up through Gilroy and the Coyote Valley. Unusually dense groves of valley oak made the walking easy and along the streams there were sycamores. Five miles north of Coyote they began to see the vast tidal flats of San Francisco Bay west of the old highway. The old Precle grid was still visible, marked by colors and changes of vegetation, forming a cross-hatch pattern that stretched for miles ahead and around them. They skirted the edge of the Bay, crawling over fallen slabs of concrete and lichen-covered columns. A corroded Precle sign in a grove of tamarisk said "Capitol Expy." There were boats moored around a tree-covered island that poked out of the Bay about half a mile from them.

Ruins of the old city were apparent all around them, if hidden by vegetation. Thousands of sea birds—rails, stilts, mergansers—waded and floated around the edges of the Bay, and even more circled above the water in great flocks. The huge, square-shaped ruins protruded from the water for as far as they could see.

"Which city was this?" Janisse asked.

"It was called San Jose."

"What happened to it?"

Mandl recited:

The earth, in her childlike prophetic sleep,
Keeps dreaming of the bath of a storm that prepares up the long coast
Of the future to scour more than her sea-lines:
The cities gone down, the people fewer and the hawks more numerous,
The rivers mouth to source pure; when the two-footed
Mammal, being someways one of the nobler animals, regains
The dignity of room, the value of rareness.

"Deetr knows a lot of Jeffers's poems," Janisse said. "I'd like to learn them from him."

Mandl looked at her a long time.

"Of course," he said.

One of the boats on the island had seen them, and was headed toward them.

201

❧ ❧ ❧

The Dragon Slayer

San Diego
The Year 471 New Calendar
Library of the Order of Antiquities

The Capistrano Mission stood on the bluffs above San Juan Cove, where the Camino Costa made one of its long incursions inland away from the many coastal rias. Ruins of a broad Precle highway led off inland on the bluffs to the north. The mission was a rectangular adobe hut, distinguishable from the dozen other huts of the village only by its slightly larger size and the tarnished bronze cross mounted on the roof above the door. The mission was divided into two rooms: a simple chapel with an altar, rough wooden benches, and several straw mattresses on the floor for travelers, and the friar's quarters, consisting of a bunk, a small hearth for cooking, and a pantry. These particular quarters were occupied not by a friar, but by Layman Peter Kilpatrick, who had inherited their stewardship from his confessor, an ordained friar of the Reformed Sect. Layman Peter wore his hair tonsured, wore friar's robes, but had never taken the Holy Orders. His explanation to his confessor, who had raised him there at the mission, had always been that it was a decision he wanted to make when he was older. After his thirtieth birthday, his confessor had stopped asking. On Peter's fortieth birthday, his confessor, who was dying, gave Peter permission to serve Mass and to hear confession. At fifty, after having been the sole representative of the Church at Capistrano for ten years, Peter was ready to take vows, but there was no one to administer them. There was a bishop in San Diego, a cardinal, in fact, but the cardinal was Catholic. Not that it really mattered to Peter, but it was a long way to San Diego, and there was no one else to keep the mission, even though, as Peter often admitted to himself, the mission was really just an inn. The mission offered hospitality and a bed to anyone traveling the Camino Costa, and one of these appeared every week or two.

Layman Peter was also a linguist, and enjoyed collecting and classifying the dialects spoken by his guests. His confessor had owned a copy of the Book of Psalms in Precle, and had translated it into their own Cappish. Peter followed his confessor's direction, and would translate a psalm or the Lord's Prayer or whatever other scraps of Scripture he possessed, such as the Beatitudes, into such dialects as he was able to pick up from his guests. Peter's own first language had been Baysigns—he had been dumb since childhood. Of all languages, Baysigns was perhaps the best to know, as sign language served as the lingua franca of the whole western coast, at least as far north as Monterey. Beyond Monterey Peter didn't know. He had never met anyone who had visited regions that distant.

Peter was so proficient in signing that he pretended to be deaf as well as dumb. Peter excused this subterfuge with the rationalization that it simplified his communication with his guests, as well as allowing him to eavesdrop on their conversations. His neighbors, the other townspeople of Capistrano, of course knew his secret, but it was a secret they kept.

In the fall of the year 471 northbound travelers brought news of a dragon in San Diego. The first discovery had been the regurgitated body of a child, only partially digested. After that the victims were mostly adults. The bodies were found strangled, the heads crushed to a pulp, and with puncture wounds all over their bodies. It was thought that the dragon would grab a man by the head and swing him around until he was dead. Most recently the dragon had taken to burning hamlets along the frontier between the king's lands and the lands of the church.

In late October, an "unbound swordsman" knocked at the door of the mission. Peter knew that he was unbound because he carried no sword. By fief law, a swordsman without a patron was forbidden to travel armed. But this man had announced his approach by blowing his horn, as honest men did. The swordsman was quite short, hardly over three cubits in height. Peter recognized his dialect immediately as from the pirate island of Palos Verdes, fifty miles to the north. No one else lowered the back vowels quite so much, and the central liquid had disappeared entirely except at the beginning of a word, when it was faintly trilled. The swordsman pronounced "sir" as "suh."

Peter admitted the man and prepared a supper of tamales with raisins and rabbit meat in a reduced tomato sauce. After dinner the swordsman signed that his name was Ruda, and that his patron had been killed in a night raid, and that therefore he owed a debt of vengeance on the killers of his patron. But Ruda had not wished to carry out this vengeance, as he believed that his patron had been in the wrong, which is why he was "unbound." Ruda was on his way to San Diego to slay the dragon, in hopes that the king there would then pay off his binding.

Layman Peter believed that his diminutive guest must be particularly adept and dangerous, but he liked him. His deaf act hadn't fooled the swordsman a bit—some minute disjunction of his timing, beginning to sign too quickly, or perhaps over-compensating, had given him away on the first exchange. But the swordsman was far too well-

mannered, or too wily a warrior, to make any show of his knowledge by a wink or even a smile, and they had continued conversing
in Baysigns. Peter wasn't sure he believed in dragons—his confessor
had said that though there were dragons in the Bible, they were mythical, or symbols—a coded language for feudal power, or to the rebels
who would overthrow it—but this counsel Peter kept to himself.

The swordsman stayed for a week, helping the villagers with whatever tasks they had at hand. Peter was making paper in preparation
for his next Scriptural translations, and Ruda helped with that. At
the end of a week the swordsman asked Peter if he could have the
bronze cross mounted on the mission to cast a sword and, though
it was in clear violation of fief law, Peter agreed. They worked
together to build the forge and the clay molds. It was a short sword,
leaf-shaped, and there was enough bronze for a small mace also, a
hammer-like implement with seven sharp spikes radiating from a
heavy ball at the end. The swordsman worked with stones to balance and sharpen the weapons. After dinner at the end of the second week the swordsman spoke aloud when Peter's back was turned,
telling him that he was leaving in the morning but that Peter was
welcome to accompany him. Peter was ready at first light and they
set off in a dense fog.

Peter and Ruda traveled inland, following San Juan Creek to Elsi-
nore, to avoid the long rias at Santa Margarita and San Luis Rey.
They turned south through Temecula and Escondido, and entered
San Diego through Miramar. A hundred years of El Niño rains had
transformed San Diego into the most populous country north of
Acapulco. Towns and hamlets dotted the islands and bluffs and
lagoons. Northbound currents kept ocean temperatures in the seventies year-round. Coral reefs grew in the clear aqua waters, and

mangrove swamps formed a labyrinth of inlets and bays. Oaks and twisty pines covered the higher ground. The peasants grew maize, melons, two kinds of bean, and a variety of peppers. These crops, along with fish and conch, some goat milk, and the occasional meat, provided an ample diet. But for the ravages of malaria and other tropical fevers, the population might have been twice what it was.

ରୋ ରୋ ରୋ

Former master swordsman Ruda, now outlaw swordsman Ruda, sat in the white sand with his legs folded beneath him. A lanky black man in a skimpy loin cloth crouched on his haunches beside him, alternately flattening and then again channeling the dry sand in front of him, as if he were trying to decide how to draw a map. Behind them were a dozen thatched huts, built on high stilts, surrounded by mangroves. In front of them were the crystalline waters of Tecolote Lagoon. Pink birds with spoon-shaped bills roosted in a nearby tree. In the distance, breakers crested over the reefs in Mission Bay. A day had passed since Ruda and Peter had split up at Linda Vista. Layman Peter had found a ferryman to row him across the mile wide inlet of the San Diego Ria, so that he could make his way to the king's palace on the Mission Hills peninsula. Ruda and Peter had agreed to meet there on the beach in three days.

Neither Ruda nor the man on his haunches were in any hurry. They were appraising each other and such things take time. A manta ray leapt in the bay and crashed back into the water with a great splash. Ruda's sword was hidden in his robes, but perhaps his companion suspected that. Also, the growing heat of the afternoon and the humidity and the man beside him were making Ruda feel overdressed. He opened his robes, exposing the short sword, and then removed them, folding them and placing them on the sand and laying the sword on top of them. He took the mace from out of his bundle and placed that beside the sword and settled back into the sand.

Another ray, or perhaps the same one, leapt again from the water and crashed again to the bay.

"Ey no draygon, mon, ta lizzid," the man said.

Ruda sat silently for a while, then asked if a lizard could eat a man.

The man nodded. "Dees a big lizzid, mon, bigger eniy gator. Eat a chile. Kill a mon, yes, eat a mon, I dunno. Try meybe. Eat ded men, though, alla time. Dig 'em up." The man made a digging motion with his hands.

Ruda considered this. But lizards didn't fire huts. Men did. Trouble was brewing and Ruda hoped that Peter's meeting with the cardinal would be as private as possible, that he would receive his ordination, and quickly take his leave.

"Can you show me one of these lizards?"

"Shur mon, I tekka you. We tekka canoe."

❧ ❧ ❧

Layman Peter was at that moment engaged in a game of knuckle-bones in the courtyard of the king's palace. The king's palace was situated atop the bluffs above the San Diego Ria, with views of the Loma Islands to the south and La Jolla Mesa five miles to the north. The grounds around the palace had been cleared of vegetation. That, and the position of the palace on the bluffs where it caught the sea breezes, helped to discourage mosquitoes. The palace was part adobe, but also part stone, with white plastered walls painted with black and ocher trim. Peter was on the ground by the doors of the great hall. The courtiers had seen him watching the games in the courtyard, and, assuming that he was a simpleton, had tossed a handful of silver coins at his feet, telling him to play a game. Peter actually knew the game, quite well. He often played knucklebones with his guests at the mission to see who would empty the chamber pots and clean the outhouse, but Peter played to his new role. As a simpleton, he had a certain advantage and he had quickly won three games, betting his whole stake every time. After his third game, Cardinal Wallas, who had been watching, bet a sack of gold oros on Peter, and challenged the king's brother, Prince Nobles, to bet against him. The prince at first refused to roll against a commoner, but the cardinal teased him, suggesting that maybe he was afraid to play a simpleton, or that perhaps the stakes were too high, and the prince had rolled the dice. The pot was raised several times, and Peter won the game with a bluff. He knew he wouldn't get away with that a second time.

The prince, having just lost more than a month's income from his entire estate, pressed the cardinal for a second game. The cardinal accepted. The ante was a small fortune, four bags of oros. The prince set his hole die and covered it with a coconut shell. Peter set his hole die to a five and did the same. The prince shook up three more dice and rolled them onto the floor: a four, a five, and a six. Peter rolled a five and two threes. If the prince's hole die were a six—and why wouldn't it be—that gave him a high pair. But it was Peter's pair of threes that led the table so it was Peter's bet. Peter acted excited and pushed in his silver, which made everyone laugh. But when the cardinal bet two hundred oros everyone stopped laughing. Assuming that Peter had hidden a six, and why shouldn't he have, the prince had better than three to one chances of winning. The prince matched the cardinal's bet and raised. The cardinal matched in turn. The cardinal hadn't seen Peter's hidden bone, but maybe he sensed that Peter knew his own odds of winning were two to one.

Prince Nobles rolled his last die and rolled a six. He looked pleased. Peter rolled another three. That gave him three of a kind on the table and Peter acted as if he had already won and reached for the stakes. The prince had to stop him. The cardinal laughed and made a comment about the prince's delusions, and the prince had fired back that if the cardinal were so sure of himself, why didn't he bet his San Clemente Hills on that. With the San Clemente Hills, the prince would have all the land north of the Ria, up to the narrow isthmus of La Jolla Mesa. The cardinal accepted the challenge, saying that he would wager the Hills against the prince's Tecolote Highlands. The king had now joined the onlookers and Cardinal Wallas asked the king if he would prepare the deeds. Papers were written and signed. Peter tried to look confused. With his hidden five he had a full house: there was no way the prince could win.

The disputed Tecolote Highlands, the area being ravaged by the dragon, were loyal to the cardinal but were part of the prince's domain. In his eavesdropping on court gossip, Peter had also learned that the king had been using Cardinal Wallas to contain the ambitions of his younger brother, but that the prince had lately sown doubt in the king's mind, hinting that the cardinal was out to get the whole kingdom for himself. All sides had spies, and all sides were quick to use torture to extract information if loyalty or persuasion failed. Or just to be sure.

As the deeds were being signed Peter got up, looking dejected, as if he had lost, and began to walk away. The cardinal caught him and brought him back and motioned to him to sit back down. The prince exposed his hidden six and folded his arms. Peter lifted his shell and then it was the prince's turn to stare. The cardinal's men quickly collected the gold and the deeds, and the cardinal said his goodnights to the king, bowing. Peter didn't think that the king looked pleased. The cardinal motioned for Peter to follow him and Peter did so.

At the harbor they boarded the cardinal's barge, with a square-rigged sail and waiting oarsmen, and headed for the cardinal's palace in La Jolla.

∾ ∾ ∾

Ruda and Lagosh threaded their way through the mangroves in a tiny dugout. They passed an alligator, which Lagosh pointed out, but kept silent. As the canoe approached a beach, Lagosh pointed to a large oak tree, half fallen over, with long branches that dipped in and out of the sand. Ruda had to stare at the tree for a long time before he saw the lizard. It was much bigger than he had expected and its skin was so dark that it looked like a second trunk of the tree. Its skin was beaded and it almost looked as if it were wearing mail. Maybe the lizard couldn't swallow a large man, but it could certainly swallow Ruda, whole. His sword suddenly seemed very short. A spear would be a better weapon, or a battle axe. Yet what would be the point in killing a lizard? He had come to slay a dragon.

"Drums, mon, gotta go," Lagosh whispered.

Ruda couldn't hear anything, but they paddled quickly back

through the swamp. When they reached the Raj village a large bon-fire was burning and the men were painting themselves.

"War-men comin. We gotta fite."

❧ ❧ ❧

Cardinal Wallas's palace was much finer than the king's. It was larger, the stone work of the bearing walls was better, the roof and much of the interior were of wood, and there were frescoes on the walls of scenes from the Bible. There was a haunting painting of the Savior at the well with the Samaritan woman. And there was another paint-ing of David slaying Goliath. Peter thought that the giant looked a lit-tle like the king. The cardinal brought Peter into his private quarters and closed the wooden door. On one of those walls was a painting of a dragon, a splendid dragon with stars in its crown. An exceedingly voluptuous woman was embracing the dragon, caressing its head while standing on a crescent moon.

"You like that?" the cardinal asked.

The question took Peter by surprise. He'd been too absorbed in the painting to be on his guard and he jerked his head before catching himself.

"I never thought you were deaf," the cardinal said. "What brought you to San Diego? You look like a member of the heretic church."

Peter signed his assent, and the cardinal signed in kind. When Cardinal Wallas learned that Peter had come to take vows, he laughed at the irony and signed that he would be glad to ordain him as both Catholic and heretic and that they would do that in the morning. He made Peter a gift of a Precle Bible, very rare, and bade him goodnight.

The attack came in the middle of the night. Layman Peter, in the guest quarters, had just extinguished his taper, which was down to a stub, after staying up late to study the pages of his new treasure. He heard men rushing through the passageways, and shouts and screams. Some were shouting "Dragon! Dragon!"

Outside, the granary had been fired, and there was smoke inside also, in the corridors. Peter made his way to the cardinal's bedroom. Cardinal Wallas was hanging from the centerpost, garroted. More men were approaching and Peter escaped by climbing into the latrine and closing the flap over him. That's how he survived the fire. All night he could hear the screams of men being tortured. The attackers had been the prince's soldiers.

In the morning, when he was sure that everyone was gone, he made his way down to the San Clemente Lagoon and washed himself and washed his clothes again and again, but he couldn't seem to remove the smell. He waded and swam across the lagoon at a narrows, and started making his way south. He was afraid to walk on the roads so he waded into Tecolote Swamp, hoping to find the swordsman Ruda at the place where they had separated. He had nothing with him—both his silver and the Bible were lost.

∾∾∾

It was foggy in the morning. They didn't see the ships approaching but they knew they were coming. Boat after boat pulled onto the gravelly shore and the knights and retainers of the prince's army formed in a line on the beach. The swordsmen wore armor of wood and hardened leather, with pieces of iron attached. The Raj were at the edge of the forest about fifty yards away, standing in the shade of the trees, armed with spears and atlatl. Ruda had asked Lagosh to paint him and he looked like the others, if dwarfish. As the line of swordsmen and axemen advanced toward them, Ruda stepped forward. Ruda didn't think their armor looked very good. Wrought iron, and no match for his bronze mace. A knight with a dragon painted on his breastplate rushed toward him. Ruda dodged his blow and thrust his sword through the man's neck. The man fell and Ruda swirled his mace above his head from a heavy leather thong. The Raj were cheering. There were shouts from the rear of the prince's army and the soldiers were retreating to their boats. The fog had lifted and a new flotilla was visible a hundred yards offshore—the king's army—maybe forty boats. The Raj didn't wait to see the outcome. They ran back through their village to their canoes, and Ruda ran with them. They would move into the swamp. Maybe they would be left alone. White men couldn't live in the swamp; they got malaria or yellow fever and died.

The Raj built their new village on the island of the lizards, and learned to hunt them. When winter came Ruda returned to Capistrano and reopened the inn. It wasn't a bad place to live, and the people were honest. Two of the Raj went with him, saying that they wanted to see the world. Peter was never found, nor any trace of him, though Ruda and the Raj had searched for a week. All assumed that he had been eaten by a dragon.

PANOPTIC

The Sixth
Through the Tenth Centuries
2521–3020

For reasons more like fortuitous luck than deterministic physics, warm currents in the ocean veered slightly away from the poles, and the stalemate between green and white shifted slightly back to white. By very small amounts each year, the remnants of polar glaciers began to grow, and each year a little more heat was reflected back into space. A certain diatom proliferated, particularly adept at dropping lime into the deep oceans, and seawater pH rose slightly toward the alkaline. There were several large volcanic eruptions.

Basically, the earth had little carbon in stored biomass left to emit, and creatures great and small began the slow process of recovery. It was perhaps immeasurable within the yearly fluctuations of the climate, but the earth was cooling, if only slightly. Ocean currents gradually stabilized into a new configuration, and snow began to fall in the northern and southern latitudes. Sea levels stabilized at 160 feet.

In numbers, human populations around the world resembled those of the Bronze Age, and bronze was again a favored metal, if usually alloyed with arsenic rather than tin.

In the Great Basin, Lake Lahontan filled and expanded, gradually becoming a patchwork across the whole western half of Nevada. Big horn sheep proliferated, along with kudus, elands, and ibex. Leopards competed with mountain lion to cull the herds of pastoralists, and people had to keep their animals within stockades at night. Cheetahs on the high prairies chased down pronghorn, and there were tigers along the Ohio.

In the California grasslands groups of people hunted with long nets set up with poles. Near settled communities, where people planted kasha and wild buckwheat, small groups of herders followed their sheep or cattle and traded with the farmers. More and more, though, hunting and gathering became the primary mode of subsistence around the Great Bay. Shell mounds began to accumulate along the coasts. People hunted with bolas and slings and collected wild honey and termites and yellow jacket larvae. Ducks and geese returned in huge numbers to the bays, and sea lions—a great source of blubber—were numerous enough to be aggressive.

Literacy was maintained only by a few religious or druidical orders. Languages began diversifying, and people often had trouble understanding the speech of those who lived on the other side of a mountain pass. Sign language was the lingua franca. Around the Great Bay grizzly bears waded in the sloughs. It had taken the grizzlies five hundred years to work their way down to California—the grizzlies hadn't been in any hurry, but they liked what they found. There were stories that people had seen grizzly bears take off their skins and that humans had climbed out from inside who were sorcerers and killed people or made children sick.

"Winter plague" was common wherever people built permanent towns.

In the year 699 a large meteor burned across the sky and buried itself in the earth north of the Niobrara River. Local herdsmen dug up pieces of metal, one of which was impressed with Precle glyphs, sparking a belief that the Precles lived in the stars and that their return to earth was imminent.

ॐ ॐ ॐ

The World Map

In the Yucatán only a few mountains remained dry land. In Colombia the Magdalena was an estuary for 250 miles, to the center of the country. The Orinoco Estuary cut Venezuela in half, still five miles wide at Puerto Carreño on the Colombian border. The great river of the Amazons was sea level a thousand miles inland.

The Paranás was a salty bay twenty miles wide at Corrientes, over five hundred miles inland from the submerged ruins of Buenos Aires. The coastline moved a hundred miles into the pampas.

England was an island of hills, ridges, and inlets. London was deeply submerged, and had been for three hundred years. The Thames Inlet was over a mile wide at Reading, and extended to Abingdon. Most of Essex, Suffolk, and Norfolk were underwater. Cambridge and Bedford were underwater. The coastline of The Wash extended into Northamptonshire. Lincoln was underwater, and half of Nottinghamshire.

The mouth of the Humber extended to Leeds, forming a broad bay a hundred miles wide: submerging York, Worksop, Doncaster, Rotherham, and Ripon.

In the north, the Tweed Inlet was a mile wide at Kelso, twenty miles inland. The Firth of Forth was a salt water inlet to Dalmary, twenty miles west of Stirling. The Firth of Clyde submerged Glasgow, and extended another twenty miles east. The Solway Firth covered Carlisle, and was still a mile wide at Brampton. Western Lancashire was below water. The Mersey Inlet covered half of Manchester, separated from the North Sea at Leeds by only thirty-five miles of hills. The Bristol Channel covered both Bristol and Bath, and followed the Avon five miles past Stratford, where it was still over a mile wide.

Across the Channel the coastline began in the hills ten miles southeast of Calais, ran east to Brussels, then snaked north and south all the way to Düsseldorf, under thirty feet of ocean. The Rhine entered the North Sea between Köln and Bonn, both of which would flood at high tides.

Denmark, the Netherlands, and northern Germany were entirely submerged but for a few storm-wracked island hills. Berlin was under salt water. The coast was about twenty miles south of Potsdam, near Luckenwalde. Hanover was a port. An inlet of the Baltic Sea separated Germany and Poland for over a hundred miles, the Oder emptying into a broad bay, six miles wide, where the river turned east at Neissemünde.

Tallinn was submerged, leaving Estonia a country of islands. Riga and the Latvian lowlands were submerged. At Helsinki, the Finnish coastline moved inland over ten miles. At Stockholm, the sea marched in seventy miles. In Russia, St. Petersburg was submerged beneath one hundred feet of ocean, and an inlet of the Gulf of Finland was thirty miles wide at Novgorod. The Volga Inlet was twenty miles wide at Samara, five hundred miles from the Caspian Sea, and extended another two hundred miles to Kazan. The Caspian itself was connected to the Black Sea through an inlet of the Sea of Azov, and thus was a brackish backwater of the Mediterranean.

In France, inlets of the Atlantic Ocean followed the Gironde, split Aquitaine in half, and submerged Bordeaux and the surrounding farmlands. The Loire was brackish at Tours. Amiens was a seaport, and the Somme was sea level at Brie. The Seine was salty at Montereau, and much of the ruins of Paris were submerged.

An inlet followed the Guadalquivir inland ninety miles, completely submersing Seville. Most of Rome was beneath the Mediterranean, including St. Peter's Basilica.

Twenty and thirty mile long inlets cut the Japanese Islands. Tokyo had been underwater for half a century and the bay came in over sixty miles. Waves battered Kyoto. Hokkaido was cut in half: Sapporo was under eighty feet of ocean. Both Korean capitals were beneath the Yellow Sea.

Salt water followed the channel of the Brahmaputra deep into Assam. The Bay of the Ganges was a hundred miles wide in Bihar. The Indus was a salty bay for almost two hundred miles.

In Southeast Asia, the new coastline was forty miles north of Ho Chi Minh City, and extended northwesterly to a point a hundred miles north of Phnom Penh. The Gulf of Thailand moved north two hundred miles. Bangkok had disappeared three centuries earlier. In Australia, Sydney was submerged, and most of Melbourne. The sea came in to Garfield.

The sorrow of China, the Yellow River, moved its mouth 250 miles west. Breakers covered the Forbidden City. In the south, Guangzhou was submersed, and all of the area around it. All of Kowloon was underwater, and most of Hong Kong.

The Yangtze was a salty bay a hundred miles wide on a line between Shashi and Shayang, five hundred miles from the old coastline. Wuhan, Nanchang, and Changsha were below water. Shangshui, in Henan, was on the coast, surrounded by hundreds of miles of tidal flats.

The Nile entered the sea near Asyüt, three hundred miles south of Alexandria, and two hundred miles south of Cairo. The entire Nile Valley was brackish, and the Nile Inlet was ten miles wide at Malawi, and still eight miles wide at Manfalut.

The Suez Canal south of Great Bitter Lake was a deep channel ten miles wide. Karachi was below water. Ahmadabad was a coastal port. The Persian Gulf pushed north four hundred miles to Ar Ramadi. Baghdad was under forty feet of water. Tel Aviv was under sixty feet of water.

Great bays and inlets cut hundreds of miles into Siberia. The Ob was brackish for a thousand miles. Surgut was under thirty feet of water, and the river flooded at high tide at Parabel, in Tomsk. Near Kuskatcha the bay was a hundred miles wide. Huge swathes of Khantia-Mansia and Tyumen were submerged.

The Yenisey Inlet was over fifty miles wide at Yartsevo, in the middle of Krasnoyarsk. The Lena was salt for six hundred miles. The Amur was a sixty mile wide bay in eastern Manchuria.

New England was technically an island: sea level followed

the Hudson north past Fort Edward and Fort Ann to Whitehall, covering Crown Point and Lake Champlain, and thence down to Montreal, where the bay was fifty miles wide. Nova Scotia was an island.

Houston was under a hundred feet of water and over twenty miles from any dry land. The Rio Grande was an estuary four miles wide at Rio Grande City.

The Mississippi was tidal to Helena, Arkansas, and the delta country below Friars Point was a shallow brackish bay over seventy miles wide, all the way to Pea Ridge. Augusta was a salt water port. The coastline moved inland eighty miles in the Carolinas.

The Bay of the Columbia was ten miles wide near Portland, and covered much of the city.

In California, the Klamath met the sea six miles below Weitchpec, emptying into a narrow twisting fjord thirty-five miles from open ocean. The South Fork of the Eel met salt water at Myers Flat, forming an inlet over thirty miles long. The Mattole Fjord came in ten miles, covering Petrolia with forty feet of water. Cape Mendocino was a long peninsula.

Southern Sonoma County and Marin were both islands: a salt water channel connected the Russian River and the Petaluma, covering the cities of Petaluma, Sebastopol, Guerneville, Healdsburg, and half of Santa Rosa. South of where Cotati had been, at the extreme headwaters of Stemple Creek, there was a narrow isthmus a hundred yards wide connecting the two islands. Waves broke across it during storms and at high tide. The Napa Valley was a salt water inlet to within a few miles of St. Helena.

Oakland was submerged, along with most of the East Bay, except for the hills. All of Palo Alto was submerged, including Stanford University. Waves crashed against San Francisco State. San Jose State was seventy feet underwater.

The ocean came in over twenty-five miles at Watsonville, spilling through the Pajaro Gap and forming an inland bay that covered Highway 101 south of Gilroy and stretched all the way to Pacheco Creek. The Salinas River emptied into the Pacific near Soledad. Monterey was virtually an isolated port. Herds of mustangs somehow flourished in the rolling hills near Pacheco Pass.

San Luis Obispo was an ocean port, fronting a broad bay. The Santa Maria Inlet came in fifteen miles. The Santa Ynez met the sea above Lompoc, which was underwater. Oxnard and most of Camarillo were underwater from the inlet at Calleguas Creek.

Most of Orange County and half of Los Angeles were underwater. Irvine, and the university, were underwater. Whittier and East Los Angeles had an ocean view, as did Beverly Hills. Palos Verdes was an island, almost as far from the mainland as from Catalina. The Santa Monica Freeway emerged from the ocean at Crenshaw. Beach Boulevard was underwater all the way to Rosecrans. In Newport Beach waves splashed against the bluffs below the ruins of Fashion Island.

Storm waves destroyed the mission at San Juan Capistrano. San Luis Rey was under a hundred feet of water. The Coast Highway only emerged from the water at a few places, such as Dana Point and the hills of San Clemente. Laguna Canyon was salt for two miles. Bays at Solano Beach and Del Mar extended inland seven miles.

The harbor at San Diego was so completely exposed from the south that it was useless as a port for half the year. The inlet at Mission Valley came in twelve miles, all the way to San Diego State College and La Mesa. The Sweetwater River was salt all the way past Chula Vista to the dam.

The Tijuana River met the sea in Mexico, thirty miles southeast of the submerged city of San Ysidro.

Palm Springs was almost oceanfront: tidal flats fronted Thousand Palms. Ocotillo Wells became a fishing town. Indio was under 160 feet of ocean.

Roseville was underwater; the edge of the Bay was halfway to Rocklin. The Yuba was sea level near Brown's Valley. The Great Bay reached to Folsom. The Feather River entered the Bay at Oroville, and tidal waters reached the outskirts of Chico. Merced was a port. The San Joaquin River emptied into the Great Bay near the town of Tranquillity, which became a trading center.

Currents in the Great Bay formed large whirlpools near the Carquinez Strait, and sometimes emitted a humming sound that could be heard for miles.

ⱸ ⱸ ⱸ

Clear Cloud

Putah Creek
750 years after the Collapse
Library of the Order of Antiquities

Clear Cloud had disembarked from the ferry near Cache Creek. He followed an overgrown trail along the creek for two days until he reached the pass near the hot springs. A woman with a shaved head was camped by the river. Intrigued, Clear Cloud walked into her camp and asked her if she were a Buddhist.

"I'm not sure what that means," the woman answered. "Why do you ask?"

"I saw your shaved head. My name is Clear Cloud. I am the abbot of the temple at Lower Lake."

"Ah, yes," she said. "I've heard of you. What do you study there at the temple?"

"We practice meditation and we study the koans."

"Which koans do you study?"

There were only a handful. Once, he knew, in Precle times, the Zen sect had hundreds of koans, each one carefully nurtured and passed on to the next generation. Now there were only half a dozen. In some ways, one koan was enough. How could it be exhausted? And a good teacher could improvise variations as checking questions.

"We have the koan of 'Mu' and the koan of 'The One Hand,'" Clear Cloud said. "And four others. The rest are lost."

"Ah," the woman said. "And how is it with Mu?"

Why was she asking questions like that? There was something disturbing about the way she laughed as she asked her question. Clear Cloud answered that his teacher had delivered several wonderful lectures on the koan and the importance of spontaneity. He himself had found the ideogram for "mu" and had lectured on its probable meaning in terms of the transmigration of souls, that since 'mu' meant 'no,' the koan meant that all things arise from emptiness.

"Ah," the woman said. Then she asked him if he would like some yaupon tea, to which Clear Cloud assented.

"In my travels far to the north, up on the Columbia, I heard a koan from a teacher there on the river," the woman said. "Would you like to hear it? Maybe you could tell me what its answer is?"

Clear Cloud responded that he would very much like to hear it, and that indeed he might be able to expound an answer for her.

"Long ago," she said, "an ancient Buddha asked, 'All things arise from emptiness. From where does the emptiness arise?'"

Clear Cloud responded immediately, knowing that an enlightened master should never hesitate before giving an answer. "From the Buddha!"

"Ah," the woman said, "can you show me that?"

Show? How could such a thing be shown?

"How would you answer that?" Clear Cloud asked, slightly annoyed.

The woman didn't answer, but refilled Clear Cloud's tea cup.

Clear Cloud started explaining to her how she needed to understand that the Buddha represented emptiness, and was therefore present in everything, but the woman quickly changed the subject and began asking him about his travels and about life around the temple at Lower Lake. When they finished their tea, she wiped out the two cups, packed up her gear, and made ready to continue her journey east. As she left she asked, "'From where does the emptiness arise?' I leave you with this koan." Then she had bowed and walked away, adjusting her bundle and the tumpline around her forehead.

Clear Cloud was bothered. How did he know that was a real koan?

A good teacher, of course, could come up with new koans. But the new koans never seemed as good as those of the ancient masters. Chao-chou! Invisible but with the power to darken the sun.

Mumon! With a giggle that still resounded after a thousand years. And the words of the golden-faced one himself.

Still, he was disturbed. Surely the koan had been corrupted. It made no sense. It seemed to have no point. Clear Cloud was disappointed. The woman hadn't known the answer either. Another lost koan. If it were a real koan.

It bothered him though. There was something troubling about it. What if it really were from the ancients? Another part of the great dharma treasure? What was it she was really asking him? How could emptiness come from anything? What *was* emptiness?

When he came to Putah Creek, Clear Cloud sat down on a rock to take off his robe and his moccasins to ford the creek. He walked along the bank looking for a good crossing point. As he was about to put his foot in the water he thought again of the strange woman's smile. She had a grin that laughed. What had her eyes been trying to tell him?

Suddenly the surface of the water stopped moving. His foot hung motionless in the air and then it was his foot, or the reflections of his foot, that were bouncing across the still surface of the stream. How could he have been so blind?

He sat down on the sand and pebbles of the bank and put his hands into the river and laughed. How could he apologize to his students?

He bent his face down to the water and took a long drink. He felt giddy but he put his moccasins back on. If he hurried he still might be able to overtake her. At least to make a bow, and to present his answer. And maybe she knew another koan.

~ ~ ~

Seruh

Lompoc Bay
850 years after the Collapse
Library of the Order of Antiquities

The drought was in its tenth year. There was so much smoke that people had trouble sleeping. In Lockwood Valley you couldn't see the mountains. No one knew where the fires were, though they seemed to be to the south and east, in the San Bernardino range, or in the Angeles. Some thought the fires were closer—right in the Tehachapis, or in the Padres.

When the First World had burned, according to the stories, there had been so much smoke that the people had all turned dark—not on the outside, but on the inside—so that their dreams were dark. And because their dreams were dark they couldn't find any dream helpers and everyone starved. Seruh thought that maybe the smoke was making everyone cross and short-tempered. The cattle seemed confused and weren't eating.

That night Seruh did dream, and she dreamt again of Lompoc Bay. She was on the bluffs where her people liked to camp in the spring, and she could see a man in a tule canoe paddling toward her.

During the eighth century after the Collapse, Lompoc Bay was ten miles long and four miles wide, opening onto the Pacific through a narrow inlet between high bluffs. At the beginning of spring, and again at the beginning of autumn, the sun would set directly between the bluffs at the end of the bay and the Clam People, Seruh's village, would hold a Big Time and everyone would dance in hopes of getting good dreams. The old city of Lompoc was completely submerged, and a narrow estuary followed the twisting course of the Santa Ynez River for another six miles east beyond the extremity of the bay.

Seruh hadn't seen any of her relatives in two years, since she had been captured by the Cowboys who took her to Lockwood Valley. "Cowboys" was what they called themselves, but everyone else called them the Blood Drinkers, because they kept cattle and bled them. Seruh's people had been gathering pinyon nuts in the San Rafaels when she had been captured by the Cowboy named Bobber. Bobber had raped her and then had sold her to his brother for two burros and six cattle. That had been a good price and maybe that was some of why the other women resented her.

In Seruh's dream the man in the canoe turned out to be Haenk and the dream became erotic. That annoyed Seruh. She was hoping for a dream of power. Her milk had failed and she could feel the dismissive gazes of the other women and none of them offered to suckle her child.

There was cow's milk, of course, and sometimes there was blood, and soon there would be acorn mush, but still. Among her own people the other women would have suckled her baby from the beginning, as a matter of course, just as with any other baby—that all the children be of one milk. Among the Cowboys only cow's milk was shared, and that was by the men.

The next day Seruh tried to avoid Haenk, not only because of the dream but because she thought that her husband was watching her especially closely. The acorns were dropping early that summer and though most of them were wormy, Seruh moved off in the opposite direction of where Haenk had his hut and was able to fill one basket. They were live oak acorns and would require a lot of leaching and Seruh split the shells and spread the nuts out to dry in the sun. If anything, the other women were even more stand-offish than they had been. Mersen's first wife, Beye, never particularly friendly, ignored her completely.

As Seruh was sitting on the ground with her acorns she felt an itching on her pubis and scratched and pulled loose a tiny crab louse with her fingernails. She moved off by herself to the edge of the camp where the other women wouldn't see her and searched herself for lice. Her heart sank when she saw that there were already nits. Mersen had slept with her as soon as her milk had failed and if she had passed the lice to Mersen there would be trouble. Mersen would know. Then Seruh thought that Mersen probably already knew, and that she should warn Haenk. Mersen would kill him and nobody would care.

Haenk was a sin-eater, an undertaker, one of the wind shamans who touched and disposed of the bodies of the dead, and he lived by himself away from the rest of the village. Seruh tied her baby into the cradle basket she had made and circled to the north and then backtracked and followed a trail along the ridge of a line of low hills, trying to move quietly, as the hunters did. Haenk found her on the trail a half mile from his hut. He'd been watching for her. When Seruh told him about the lice Haenk understood immediately. "Ah, that is why Mersen and his brother are at my hut."

Seruh told Haenk that she had had a dream and that she was going back to her people, on the coast, and why didn't Haenk go with her? They left with what they carried, but instead of going west, toward the Cuyama River, which is what everyone would expect, they headed south along San Guillermo Creek through the mountains.

Near the headwaters of the creek a condor led them to a dead cow. It had not been a good year for the cows. The cattle were weak but the men bled them anyway and now even the cougars were taking them down.

The meat was too putrid to eat but there were lots of maggots and they ate them. They hiked on another three miles in the twilight to the forks of the Piru where they dug a pit in the wash to collect some water and camped.

They left at first light and moved east again. The Cowboys didn't have horses but they had burros—burros could feed themselves even in the summer—and might try to follow them. The next night they camped on the Sespe below the hot springs near Devil's Heart Peak and were able to catch some crayfish and some insect larvae that hid beneath the rocks.

The next day they turned west and covered nearly eighteen miles, sometimes walking in the creek to avoid the brush. The following day Seruh wanted to rest but Haenk said no and they hiked south through Wheeler Gorge and made a camp on Matilija Creek at Rattlesnake Canyon. There were some black oaks there and they collected a few acorns. Seruh ground them without waiting for them to dry and just rinsed them in her loin cloth to have some pablum for the baby.

They traveled for four more days before they neared the village of the River People at Solvang. They had made the steep climb up Murrietta Canyon to the Divide and found chia seeds and had camped on Juncul Creek. They camped at Gilbraltar Swamp by Devil's Canyon on the upper reaches of the Santa Ynez, and then they had camped at the remnants of Lake Cachuma, which was mostly a boggy meadow.

Seruh wanted to visit the River People at Solvang, some of whom she knew, but Haenk was afraid. He was a Blood Drinker and they might not welcome him. And times were hard because of the drought and people were doing bad things and sometimes villages that had once been friendly no longer were. So they detoured south into the hills, avoiding the village, and didn't return to the river until they were three miles below Solvang at Nojoqui Creek.

They made the long journey down the Santa Ynez Valley in a single day by leaving at dawn and walking until dark. When they reached the beginnings of the estuary where her people liked to camp in the summer there was nobody there and no dogs barked. Grizzly bear scat was everywhere and all the huts were ripped apart. Tule rushes were scattered around the camp along with the remnants of baskets. They also saw some bones and Seruh said that they should leave the camp. There were mussel shells on the midden and Seruh wondered why they had been eating mussels in the summertime when it was so dangerous. It must have been a hard time. Haenk had a different idea of what had happened but he didn't say anything to Seruh. Some of the bones were burned and some of them were crushed to remove the marrow.

Seruh and Haenk climbed a hill north of the estuary and camped in the open about half a mile from the ruins of the village. They didn't build a fire. When they woke up in the morning the fog had come in and they were both wet and cold. In the daylight the devastation at the village was even worse than it had seemed the night before. Bones and broken pieces of skull were scattered around the grounds and more were in the bushes. Haenk gathered enough of the bones for a ceremony and wrapped them in a torn deerskin. The rest he piled in the center of the village and covered them with the willow ribs from the huts and whatever other wood he could find around. Seruh collected the baskets and the other personal possessions she could find and added them to the pyre, so that the souls of her friends and family would not be held back from find-ing their way to the Haven. She wanted the best for them. She was of their milk.

They lit the fire but they didn't wait for it to burn down. Haenk found a canoe on the banks above the bay and convinced Seruh that it was all right to use it. There was even a paddle. It was an old canoe and the tules were crushed but it still floated them, if barely. Half-submerged, water covering their legs, they pushed off into the estu-ary and took advantage of the ebb to float down the river and into the bay. They paddled to the middle of the bay and Seruh pointed to a canyon on the north shore and they made for that.

The sun was far to the west when they reached the mouth of Santa Lucia Creek, and then they had the flood tide to help them up the estuary. About a mile from the bay they beached the canoe at the mouth of a narrow side canyon that led off to the west. There was a grove of eucalyptus on the floor of the canyon and there wouldn't be many bugs. They cut tules for a bed and slept together for protection and to protect the baby but all they had to eat were cattail roots. The baby was hungry and cried and Seruh let it suck on her breasts hoping it would soothe him but it didn't and soon both of her nipples were sore. They were worried about the crying because of the grizzlies.

The next day they gathered tules and built a proper hut and gath-ered clams but didn't find many and Haenk didn't eat anyway. Haenk was going to bury the dead.

First he built a sweat lodge. It was small, with just enough room for himself. Then he selected stones that wouldn't explode when they were heated, and he sweated. When he couldn't stand the heat anymore he crawled out and dove into the river. Then he sweated again.

When he was thoroughly cleansed he took the bundle of bones he had kept and climbed the hills to the ridge. He ground off little bits of the bones, especially from the skulls, and made a drink with lemonade berry and datura root. He drank as soon as it was dark. As he opened his medicine bundle he said softly, "Now don't hurt anyone." Then he began to sing. He sang to the winds and he sang to the bones. He tried to talk to the souls of the dead ones but they attacked him. They cut him and they kicked him. He knew his face and arms were scratched and bleeding. He ground ocher from his medicine bundle and painted the Jesus Bird—the great condor who freed the souls of the dead—onto a rock. He wanted the Jesus Condor to bring the east wind from the interior that could blow the souls of the bones to the west, toward the ocean, which was their home, their milk.

Toward morning he felt the chill and began to shiver uncontrollably, but he forced himself to smash up the bones and grind them into a powder. The stars overhead were moving around in zigzags, which he knew was the way they really were, and he painted some of them on the rock next to the Jesus Bird. Just before dawn he felt a breeze stirring from the east and the shivering left him. He could smell smoke in the breeze. As the light built in the east the breeze picked up and he scattered the powdered bones into the air, telling them they could go home now. After that he slept.

That night Seruh let the baby suck again at her breasts and she thought she felt her milk dropping. She had a dream that some of her people were living on the south side of the bay near Lompoc Canyon. They would go to look for them when Haenk returned. And maybe the dream would be true and they would be reunited with her milk and then they would live.

The Second Thousand Years
3021–4020

When the Second Millennium dawned, very few people anywhere in the world were aware of it—almost all of them in some sort of religious order. One of them, living in a hermitage near Big Sur, even surmised that Bayspeak was related to the ancient Precle language of the texts she was studying.

Fewer and fewer traces of the old civilization remained at all, and they were explained by a wide variety of myths and stories. The knowledge and use of metals was local, but persistent. Copper, hardened by beating, was favored for needles. People made rope from horsehair; twine and thread from plant fibers; and wove woolen yarn. Fine hairs were felted. Beaver was esteemed, as was otter.

A colorful lichen had become common, which dissolved the lime of any exposed concrete with astonishing rapidity. Bacteria had long before eaten away any asphalt or oil-based pavement. A silvery white plant began colonizing the dry plains of the western interior, with short stinging hairs that captured any dew that might condense in the hours before dawn. There were shiny grasses and a sprawling prostrate vine with reflective waxy cells on its leaves. Wind pollinated plants were dominant.

In the southern plains kangaroo appeared, and no one knew

they were out of place. Jaguars moved up from Mexico, and competed with the lions that held the veldt to the north, where herds of wildebeest had pushed the bison toward Canada. White lichens covered Greenland, which encouraged the earth a little toward her recovery.

The Great Bay was enjoying a long summer. The occasional rains in July and August had given the bunchgrass a second chance. Purple needlegrass was reclaiming the valleys from the annuals, and providing year-round grazing. The Bay was blue and sparkling and settlements dotted its edges.

∾ ∾ ∾

Neska

The Feather River
1,200 years after the Collapse
from Legends of the Summer Age,
Institute of Medieval History

There was an otter girl named Neska who lived at the mouth of the Feather River.

While she had been raised in the Long House with her brothers, her true upbringing was in the countryside. She would go out early, while the dew was still on the grass, so that she could watch the forest animals performing their morning tasks. From her Fox Clan heritage, she would spend the afternoons riding, her brothers often joining her, exploring the rugged oak covered hilltops and passes. Her father's people had always been skilled with horses, and, indeed, all manner of woodland craft. Neska joined those upcountry people in gathering, collecting nuts and wild fruits, and learning the secrets of their ancient knowledge.

Following the ways of the Otter Clan, she went to sea, as did all of the people from her mother's side. Though Neska and her brothers were of noble blood, from the lodge of a chief, in this regard, going to sea, they were no different from any other of their people.

Neska dove for sponges about the jagged rocks and ruins that lifted from the sparkling bay beyond the harbor. Like all divers, she dove naked, and when she would break to the surface, a sponge in each hand, and climb aboard the boat, her brothers and their friends would trill and whistle. She was a big girl, as tall as her brothers, and they would kid her about that. Sometimes dolphins would sport and play about the boats, and Neska would laugh and play games, trying to throw necklaces of seaweed around their smooth snouts.

After diving, Neska would rest herself in the bow, letting the warm sun dry her skin. Ganyros, the old storyteller, claimed that he could see pictures in the white salt that dried on her body. When people asked him for a story he would laugh and call: "Neska, into the sea, bring me a new story from the gods of the waters."

Neska always complied—she loved the blue water and she loved his stories. She would lay on her back on the deck and let him gaze at her.

"Ah," he would say, "there are the magical twins, crawling on your belly—they are holding hands and are on their way to the World Tree."

Or he would laugh. "Neska! The Chimera, the wonderful phoenix, has landed on your breast. He has left the fire of your nipple and is taking wing from his nest on the mountain peak. He will fly off to meet Cinbys, the woodland girl whose wrists are plant stems and whose fingers are leaves. He will give her the gift of prophecy, and a charm of protection to help her survive her many adventures."

Neska turned over on her stomach. It was autumn but the sun was still hot and she wanted to dry her backside. Ganyros moved closer and sat by her hips. He stared at her buttocks and waited. Then he told a story.

∾ ∾ ∾

Long ago there was a woman named Redwood-Falling. She was called that because a large redwood tree had crashed to the ground during her birth. They had called that winter the Winter of Rain and Wind. Many trees fell that winter. Redwood-Falling was married to a smith who knew how to work metal, and had a son named Sparks-Fly. One day Redwood-Falling was out gathering in the forest and she met a man she did not know, or she thought he was a man. He was Loon, who lived far to the north, but he was walking around in the form of a man because he was looking for a woman. They talked and walked together and she decided to have intercourse with him.

When she gave birth to a daughter, they named her Bird-Song. That was because even when she was an infant her crying was high and musical. Bird-Song grew up to be tall and swift of foot. She could always beat the boys in races and then she would laugh and high singing would come from her mouth.

Bird-Song was still a gangly girl when Sparks-Fly matured into a skilled hunter. He was so beautiful that his parents were worried that the gods might be envious, and they sent him to live with the Sky People, in the land at the top of the World Tree. The Sky People liked Sparks-Fly and he began to dress himself and to wear his hair in their manner. Once in a while he would climb down the World Tree to visit with his father in the sweat house, or to take part in a men's circle, but always at night.

Redwood-Falling had eight more children, all of them boys.

Bird-Song matured into a strong and extremely independent young woman. She liked to wear fox skins on her braids or would tie them around her waist as her breechclout. She became a hunter herself, arising early, before dawn, to learn the ways of the animals. Bird-Song also liked to go out alone at night. She would slip out of her parents' lodge and move noiselessly along the forest paths she knew. Sometimes she would hide herself near the men's circle and eavesdrop on their songs and conversations. Most of all she liked to hide herself near the sweat lodge, so that she could watch the young men emerge naked from under the flap and dive into the pool on Mouse Creek.

Early one morning, just at dawn, a man came out of the sweat who was so handsome that Bird-Song said to herself, "That is the man I am going to marry."

She could tell by the way he moved, the way he jumped slightly from foot to foot, that he was as careful and skilled a hunter as she was herself. He had the sureness and agility that only comes from spending many days alone in the forest. He slipped into the water silently and swam.

When he returned to the sweat lodge, Bird-Song crept forward to look at his footprints. She saw a hair floating in the water and plucked it out. She would find him. Secretly, she collected hairs from all of the men in the village and from all of her younger brothers. None of them matched and she decided that the hair must be from her older brother, from Sparks-Fly.

∾∾∾

Neska shifted and turned onto her side. She turned her face away from Ganyros. "Tell a different story," she said. "I don't want to hear about the necklace of human hearts."

Ganyros was silent for a while. Finally he said, "You can't stop a story, dear Neska."

"I don't like this story. Tell something else."

"Then I will tell you about Tekmet and Chryswa, and Chryswa's secret lover, and how that caused the world to burn."

∾∾∾

As was the custom, before Tekmet and Chryswa were to be married, Chryswa went to spend a night in the shrine of the Goddess, so that she would never be owned. Before she left, Tekmet rubbed sage oil onto her breasts and olive oil around her pubis and on the lips of her vulva. Then he retired to his hut to await her return in the morning. Unlike many young women, who make arrangements with an old lover or friend to sleep with them, Chryswa hadn't told anyone in particular to visit her. In fact, she hadn't told any of her friends what she was doing. This was the old way, and she thought it would be most pleasing to the Goddess. And besides, it was just better that way.

She lit a candle in the hut and set a lantern outside the door. Her first visitor was a boy from Red Town who worked in the hemp fields. She knew that he was really too young to be there at all but she let him in anyway. He was over-excited and finished almost before he started so that it made Chryswa laugh. He left quickly, after presenting her with a coil of rope, which Chryswa placed at the side of the hut.

Her second visitor was old Crook-Spear, from the shanties by the Bay. He was old and fat but energetic in bed and gave her quite a ride. The night was late when he took his leave. He gave her one of his steatite carvings, this one of a doe giving birth, with her front legs folded and with her neck bent around so that she could see her fawn emerging from her body. It was strikingly beautiful and Chryswa thanked him with a deep kiss. The deep kiss re-inspired Crook-Spear and they returned to the bed.

Chryswa was ready to sleep after that. She blew out her candle and brought in the lantern. Her body had been touched. It had been good and she could bring the Goddess's blessings—her pleasure, her freedom, and her excitement—back to Tekmet in the morning.

She dozed off and was half dreaming when she knew there was another man outside the hut. She wasn't required to answer his call but she did, with a whisper. He lay down in the darkness beside her and began stroking her body, his hands moving down her arms and then along her flanks and down her legs and then up over her belly to her breasts. His fingers were long and slender; Chryswa thought they were like feathers, they were so long and soft and sensitive. His hands circled around her cheekbones and across her forehead and around her ears and he kissed her face and then her lips. She felt the fire move through her and met his passion with her own, her tongue meeting his and her own hands moving down his back and buttocks and reaching around to his groin. She rolled onto him and pulled him inside as easily as practiced lovers who know all the moves and angles of each other's bodies.

He let her have her way, until she pulsed and moaned, then he rolled her onto her back and explored her more. Chryswa felt herself being touched in new places that she had either not known about or had forgotten. He seemed to be mapping her, seeking out some new position and sensation, a new texture, and then he would stop or stay there until her body acknowledged his discovery. Or he would twist his hips and then the same place would be different again. Or he would press into her deeply, letting her pleasures return to her clitoris, until with his urgings and extra proddings she would convulse again, choking back her moans from shame.

When she woke up the sun was high and it was already warming. She didn't remember falling asleep, but she must have. She looked around the hut but there was no gift. Why was that? For THAT, for what they'd done! She felt light-headed. She should already have returned to Tekmet, he would be waiting, but how could she go like this? This was not supposed to happen here. It was supposed to be sexy and lusty, hot and licentious and abandoned, but not like this. This was madness. Who had he been?

She put her face to her pillow to smell where he had been. She found a hair. She held it against one of her own hairs and while it was of a darker color it was the same length. She rolled the hair into a tiny coil, tore a small piece of cloth from the hem of her skirt, and wrapped the hair in the cloth. Then she straightened the pillow and found the pearl. It was not a large pearl, and not quite round, but it had been drilled and a piece of gold had been hammered into a wire and pressed through the hole and then the ends had been hammered and chased around the sides of the pearl into two scallop shells that formed a clasp. It was stunningly fine and beautiful work and she wrapped it up in her cloth with the hair.

It was time to return to Tekmet, if she was still going to do that. She had to offer herself to him and see if he would take her, just as she was, touched and lusty.

Tekmet was at his workbench, working on a silver bracelet with a small rounded hammer. He looked up at her expectantly and Chryswa broke into a large smile.

"Look," she said, "I bring gifts." She gave Tekmet the coil of rope and showed him the carving, saying that she thought she would keep that one for herself.

"Two gifts!" Tekmet exclaimed. "However did you come by those?"

He was playing with her. Chryswa moved up to the back of his chair and put her arms around him. "Admirers, I guess," she laughed.

"Who did that carving?" Tekmet asked.

"Pan." Chryswa giggled. "It is always Pan who visits the Goddess." She knew that Tekmet would guess that the carver was Crook-Spear, but the Goddess preferred anonymity, and Tekmet was too well-mannered to ever call the carver anyone but Pan. And Crook-Spear was too well-mannered to ever claim differently, or, indeed, to make any reference or allusion to their tryst at all. That was the way it was done. To do otherwise would be an affront to the gods.

She pressed her breasts into Tekmet's back. "But I'm tired now and need to rest. Come to bed with me."

She told him about her night and her pleasures. They made up their love in the bed and shared all their thoughts and fears and hopes and loved each other until late in the afternoon. Somehow she never told him about her third visitor, and then it seemed like it would be awkward to tell him, and then it seemed like it was too late. So she didn't.

∾∾∾

Tekmet and Chryswa were married, and when a daughter was born nine months later they named her Aldora, as she had been a gift of

Pan. Chryswa noticed the long fingers right away, fingers so slender it was as if they were reaching out to become wings. Two years after that Chryswa gave birth to twins, both boys. The girl grew up to be tall and beautiful and headstrong. All the young men were crazy for her. Maybe it was her bearing, or her proud breasts, or just being tall, but everywhere she went the men fell in love with her and everywhere she went she left broken hearts.

Her parents despaired of her ever falling in love and finding a mate, and she had caused so much trouble in the village that they sent her to Feather Falls to live with Tekmet's relatives. They were all the more surprised when word came back that she had fallen in love with a man on the river and was living with him. He was an older man, and somehow had been able to tame the girl. One of Tekmet's cousins said that the couple was planning to come downriver to the Bay at the time of the big circles to meet the family, after the man, whose name was Sukol, had sent gifts.

Chryswa and Tekmet made their own preparations. There would be a feast. They would offer a deer and bake salmon loaves and fry the light wafer cakes made from poppy seeds and amaranth.

It had hardly rained all spring. A day before the solstice circles were to begin Sukol's brother paid the customary visit to Chryswa's lodge to present Sukol's gifts and to formally request that his brother be admitted to the house. He was a pleasant man named Kalish, was respectful to Chryswa and Tekmet, and joked good-naturedly with the twins. After dinner he presented the gifts he had brought from Sukol. Tekmet was given a steel file, extremely rare, wrapped in leather. Chryswa's package contained a set of carved horn combs wrapped in elk skin. They were quite beautiful, but Chryswa's eyes were fixed on the leather cord that had been wrapped around the package. There was an azurite bead on the cord that had been drilled and had a needle of gold through the hole. The ends of the gold needle had been hammered against the bead into two perfect tiny scallops.

"The combs are beautiful," she said. "He must be a fine artist."

"Yes," Kalish answered, "and that gold work is his specialty."

When Kalish was ready to take his leave in the morning, Chryswa slipped him a tiny packet, wrapped in cloth.

"Please give this to your brother," she said, "but only when he is alone."

಼಼಼

Sukol lay on his stomach. Aldora tried to turn him over but he wouldn't let her. He kept his legs and elbows spread out and she couldn't turn him.

"Is it my mother?" she asked. "I don't care whether or not she gives her permission."

"Just go to sleep, Aldora," Sukol kept answering.

Finally she settled down. "I will make some tea for us, then we will sleep," she said.

Aldora made a strong mint tea in the next room, but in Sukol's cup she steeped the datura root. She waited for the trance to take hold and then she turned him over and had her way with him for as long as she wanted. After that she searched through his clothes. She found the packet and the pearl with the gold scallop clasps and the hair. She didn't really understand. She thought that her mother was having an affair with Sukol, and that she was trying to take him away from her.

Sukol was in a deep sleep and Aldora dressed quickly and left. As she walked south she wondered over and over how they had been doing it, when, how long. She had ideas and then she had other ideas. When she reached the huts and lodges where her family lived she set fires in the brush all around them. The brush was very dry and a wind was blowing and none of them escaped and then the fire spread.

Aldora returned north quickly, but when she reached Sukol's hut he was gone, along with his pack goats and his best tools and his best clothes. Aldora set fire to the hut. Then she set more fires in the brush. She moved upriver to Feather Falls and there she set fires all around the encampments. She hiked east until she got to the World Tree and she set fire to that so that no one would escape. Then she hiked far up into the high country where the ground is granite. She built a small lean-to by the lake and lived with the loons. Below her the fires burned, and smoke hung over the Bay.

Neska kicked Ganyros with both her feet. "That was the same story," she choked. "You just made that up so that you could tell the same story."

She rolled off the deck, so that the story salts that had caked on her body and the new salts collecting on her cheeks could return to the sea.

The Snow Shepherd

Trinity Alps
1,900 years after the Collapse
from Legends of the Summer Age,
Institute of Medieval History

Odi was too dazed to move. He'd hit his head at least three times in the slide. It was a stupid fall. He should have known better than to trust his weakened arm. Now he just had to rest for a few minutes before dropping down to the North Fork. Not too long, though. It was snowing heavily. And even if he reached the river he might not make it out. It was snowing pretty hard. He'd have to make a camp and build a fire. And rest. He needed rest. And then maybe cut some skis, if the snow didn't melt. Who would have thought that it would snow so early? Skis would be best. Snowshoes were called "man-killers," and now he knew why. Skis would take more time. He'd have to chop down a pine. Or, better, a cedar, if he could find one. He knew there were weeping spruce below Bear Wallow. They would do. He'd have to make it to Cold Spring, but that wasn't far.

Odi remembered the first time he had seen that grove of weeping spruce, twenty years before. He was looking for a lost sheep. He'd had a girl with him that summer. Minka. How had that happened? A girl for him. His first. She'd been Kelta's sister. Kelta, Larko's wife. Larko, his friend, the shepherd Larko. They'd seen a lot, he and Larko. Larko was older, and was shepherding on the East Branch. And had built that cozy hut above the river. They'd stayed late that year, into November. And Minka had come to his camp, which was just across the river. Had they been drinking? Odi couldn't remember.

He didn't think so. How had he approached her? Maybe he didn't. Maybe she had come over to his camp just to visit. Or to bring a message from Larko and Kelta.

Odi and Larko had had some wild times. Like their trip over to the Great Bay that summer when they had been captured by vaqueros in Redding and sold to one of the longboats as oarsmen. They'd circled the entire Bay, rowed through the Straits and the West Bay and out the Golden Gate to the open sea and to Santa Cruz and farther, all the way to Soledad. All and all, their captivity hadn't been so bad. They talked and laughed about it afterwards. They'd escaped while in port in Vacaville on the way back, and had hired on as rowers on another boat that was headed for Redding. The whole trip had been less than a year. When spring came and the snows melted, Larko and Kelta had taken a flock up country to the mountain pastures where it was cooler and the grass stayed green longer. Larko was New River people. They were famous for their sheep. But maybe Odi was the first to bring them over to the high pastures of the North Fork. Not the first, no. That was silly. But the first in a while. There were stories. And he'd found old huts. And there was that old shepherd on Rattlesnake Creek who had a real cabin and had served him lima bean soup. And there was that miner who lived alone and saw things. The old man didn't really do any mining in those days; he caught fish and he hunted and he talked to spirits. But once he had been a miner.

And that's why Odi had gone over east to the copper works at French Gulch. He thought he'd learn smelting and that he would mine copper but that it would be good to learn smelting first and somehow he'd lost Minka. Her family didn't really approve of him and Minka's relatives had taken her home to Hoopa where they dried salmon and they were going to meet up later and get back together and get married but somehow it never happened and Odi had worked as a smelter at West Shasta where there was a dig. There was lots of glass in that dig, Odi remembered that, and they melted glass also, but everyone had glass. Iron also. There was iron in the dig. But smelting iron took a lot of charcoal and they mostly dug for copper. Copper axes were the best. One could fell a tree with a good copper axe, and chop it into firewood to melt copper to make axes to fell more trees. Odi laughed at that. Kort would think that was funny. Or he would have, if he were still alive. Kort was probably a teenager now, in a new body, and maybe he would be remembering his previous life. Kort was very advanced. Or maybe one of the other Magicians would find him in a divination and recognize him. His good teacher, Kort. His bad teacher, Kort. It had been on a copper trading trip to the Bay. Kort was looking for tin. Sometimes they had found a little tin, but not that time. And Kort had approached him and told him that he had the Mark, and asked him if he knew what that meant. Which Odi didn't, really, though he thought he did.

It was a kindness, in a way, Kort's invitation. Odi was young and very full of himself, but then Kort had his own reasons also. Most of the Order lived near Shasta, on the edges of the lava field, where they used the metals to refine the colors of their spirit seed. What if he'd stayed with the Order? His life would have been different. He could have become a Mage. Maybe he could have had a temple. He'd learned a little and then he had shown off. He'd used his powers with Bedera, or that's what he thought. But maybe it had been Bedera who had been seducing him the whole time. Then he had lived with Bedera and her people and thought maybe he could be a Mage on his own. And Bedera's people had welcomed him. Honored him even. He'd been a hard worker, and had shared it all with the Clan and his voice had been welcome in the councils and how many years had passed there raising his children and nursing Bedera and working their barley fields and making that good beer that he drank too much of and the training for the ceremonies and the good parties.

And then there was Frida, who had told him about the loom-work going on in the Petaluma country. And just from her descriptions he could see new possibilities, new ways to set patterns, and maybe the patterns could even be used in the Work. Yes, he still thought so. And Frida had also had a loom between her legs, and then he'd had to leave, so he went to the Petaluma. He helped the Brotherhood building looms that could weave a pattern from cards and he'd lived in the trance of the patterns, Odi admitted that, and he had designed one himself—with a golden eagle in it. Or maybe it was a firebird, Odi was never sure, a phoenix, it must have been a phoenix. And there were designs in the belt that pointed to portals in the mountains, in the high country, where one could talk to spirits, and the spirits of the metals were hidden in the designs and ornaments also. Thinking of the secrets of the Metal Work made him think of the seed power, and holding it back, reserving it and building it up and the color change and that depended a lot on the woman one worked with and then for a while Odi felt very sexual.

Odi just stayed in that—a vaguely good feeling that brought energy to his spine. Odi remembered that there had been a spirit that he wanted to talk to. He'd called it with that belt design and then he'd woven the belt and kept it and that had woken up the spirit and the spirit lived in the Trinities and so he'd left the loom-workers and come back to the Trinity River. He had a good coat and a bearskin cap and his copper axe and he camped on Rattlesnake Creek where there was a grove of yew trees and he'd cut himself a bow that he was going to finish when he made camp at Cold Spring. He could see the canyons of the Salmon from the divide where New River and the Trinity looked north toward Cecil. He'd never been down there and those people had soapstone and he wanted some to make a pipe. Then he could smoke the cherry leaves and make peace with the spirit he'd aroused.

Why had that man shot him with an arrow? Maybe he owned the quarry. Odi didn't know. Maybe he thought he was someone else—someone who was fucking his woman. But Odi had escaped and now he was close to his spirit. It was a bad wound, though, in his shoulder. He had bled a lot. That's why his arm was weak and that's why he fell. And that's why he needed rest. And sleep. To get his strength back. And to talk to his spirit. And there was something else but Odi couldn't remember. Odi felt a warm glow growing all around him, and he could see the spirit, beckoning to him, from a great circle of light.

The Third
Through the Fifth Millennia
4021–7020

The climate of the northern latitudes varied between cold and mild, the cycles often stretching over five hundred years. Forest and tundra advanced and retreated, though by the year 5000 the tundra held a definite edge. Atolls grew around new volcanoes in the Pacific, and new island chains emerged.

Early in the Third Millennium a cache of "painted books" with strange pictures in them was discovered near the Santa Ana River, preserved in some buried ruins.

A tribe of agriculturalists southeast of the American River discovered that the huge hyperbolic towers on the edge of the Great Bay at Rancho Seco were aligned to the equinox. As the Bay began to recede, the people built a great replica of one of the towers out of adobe, hoping it would bring back the waters.

By the end of the Fifth Millennium sea levels had dropped fifty feet, leaving beach terraces ringing the hills, puzzling future generations who would wonder why there had been beaches in the desert.

Elephants were common all around the Great Bay, and ranged into the surrounding hills and mountains to browse the chaparral.

∾∾∾

Malik

Bear River
2,500 years after the Collapse
from Legends of the Summer Age,
Institute of Medieval History

Malik heard Heather singing as she came up from the spring. After that he didn't care as much about the mess his nets were in. The morning was already warm and she was wearing a short breechclout wrapped around her waist.

"Why are you singing?" he asked.

"I'm singing because I saw my husband in my dream last night and because I knew that you were up here mending your nets."

"You saw me in a dream?"

"Not you," she said. "My other husband."

"You saw Reyk?"

"No, silly. Crag, my dream helper."

When Malik didn't answer she added: "Reyk is not a husband, at least not yet. How would you feel about that?"

Malik shrugged. "He is always extremely gracious and respectful. I like him. He's trustworthy. He brings gifts. Do you want another husband?"

"I need someone to look after my mother's trees," Heather answered. "If I don't take care of them, they aren't mine anymore."

This was true. And Malik didn't want that job. He liked the boat. And there was already plenty enough work helping with his sister's trees.

"Why do you want them?" Malik asked.

"Because my mother took care of them," Heather answered simply.

She also knew that if she had another child, which was unlikely but not impossible, and if the child were a girl, she would need property. And as the youngest, she should receive the best piece, which would be the oak trees. That would be okay with her older daughter, who liked it on the Bear River.

They were quiet for a while and Heather laughed: "Don't worry, he won't live here."

Malik shrugged. "Whatever."

Heather was not fooled by his lie. She was wise. Gratitude came easily to her. She had asked Crag Bighorn, her dream helper, about bringing Reyk here to Bear River. And she thought how Malik had a lot of that ancient male lineage of ram wisdom in him, which was some of why it was so easy to love him. And she recognized that his pride and reserve were that of the bighorn, and she loved that too.

She'd asked her question to Crag in her dream, but as soon as she had asked him she knew the answer. It was completely clear. She'd have to build a new hut up country, near her mother's trees.

She stroked Malik's arm and back. "I am so blessed."

Malik smiled and went on with his mending.

"What about Abba?" Malik asked.

Heather laughed. "Abba would join the marriage also. Of course."

Heather picked up the water jar and rested it on her hip.

"I will make a magic for you today, for your nets, with my sister. You will catch a fish for us."

She sang this song:

To the water I go,
to the deep green Bay:
I call all good things for your nets.

To the dragonflies I go,
their wings bright in the sun:
I call their veined wings for your nets.

To the stones I go,
curved stones in the creek:
I go to find weights for your nets.

To my bean plants I go,
my tall twining beans:
I sing to find knots for your nets.

To my hair I call,
to my long flowing hair:
I give it to you for your nets.

Heather had one more medicine to prepare. She had already cut a bit of Malik's hair while he slept and had buried the tight black curls on the east side of the camp, by the cedar tree where she had seen the snake. Now she would be away for a week tending her mother's trees, and she needed someone to sing the fish into Malik's nets.

Malik was in the hammock when Heather returned to the hut. There was another young woman with her, a short woman like Heather, a dark-skinned woman. Malik raised his head. Both women were giggling.

"Malik," Heather said, "this is my Circle Sister Anandi. She'll be staying here while I'm away."

෴

Heather's young nephew Bobo arrived early to fish with Malik. Bobo was Oak Clan, Heather's clan. Malik's boat was larger than those of many of his friends. It could carry a crew of three or four, but Bobo was nimble and the two of them could easily handle the boat. Great masses of tule rushes, bundled and woven, formed the long hull. Malik had added outriggers for balance. There was a single mast and a square-rigged tule mat sail. Extra poles laid across the hull formed a half-deck, upon which Malik had constructed a shade cabin from willow saplings. With a good breeze it could fly. He'd always win races.

Today Malik wanted a big fish. It was too early for steelhead or salmon. Malik would try the bottom. Maybe he could find a sturgeon. What had Anandi meant by all of her talk about circles? She had woven words and stories around him, and he was still spinning from her songs and her body. Strong, she was strong. Why did he feel like he was turning over? If he wasn't careful, he'd be girl-crazy. He was singing as they set their first net.

The first net was just a sampling, to test the temperature and salt of the Bay. He pulled in a few smelt and splittails. He'd have to sail out to find the saltier water. Which was okay, since then he could check his crab traps at the Buttes. What had Anandi meant that he'd be the father of a new lineage? Why had she been singing all those salmon songs? Funny girl, that Anandi, so plucky.

When they sailed into the deep inlet on the west side of the Buttes there was another boat pulling traps. It was Josh and Rose, Salmon Clan people like Anandi. They both called Malik "brother" instead of "cousin," but in a joking way. Or it seemed like a joking way.

"Traps are full, my brother," Josh called to him, grinning.

Grazing on the abundant tiny thin-shelled clams of the Bay, the crab population had exploded. Malik and Bobo pulled their traps, stowed a dozen large crabs in a basket, and rebaited the traps with the splittails.

The crabs ensured that there was plenty of food. There was no need to pull in more small fish. Malik wanted to sail farther west, where there might be deep salty currents carrying flounder. And if the water were less brackish there might be a sturgeon. They could well use the oil from one of those fish. What was that oil that Anandi had put on him? He could still smell it if he rubbed his skin. It was sweet and spicy and evoked a feeling of deep comfort and peace, like the smell of the feet of new-born pups.

"Starboard!" Bobo called.

Malik pushed the tiller and they narrowly missed beaching themselves on the rocks of the point. What had gotten into him?

As they neared the western edge of the Bay Malik tied the sharpened spindle-shaped gorge to his largest smelt with two thin pieces of straw line, so that it would break loose if the line were pulled hard. He let out twenty fathoms of his best line and tied it to a stout pole, then tied it again to one of the outriggers—just in case. Then they drifted.

"How's that Anandi girl?" Bobo asked him.

Malik smiled. "She's good."

Seagulls, terns, and mergansers were already circling and landing around the boat. Scaups were paddling out toward them. The sun was high in the blue sky and they took refuge under the canopy.

"There's going to be a big party with the Salmon Clan when the run comes up," Bobo said. "Everyone's talking about it."

Malik was wondering why he hadn't heard about the party when the coil of line was pulled sharply out of his hands. He grabbed the pole and braced himself. When the line pulled taut the pole bent over and snapped. The whole boat shuddered as the power of the fish fell onto the outrigger. Bobo quickly brought another pole. Now all they needed was some slack. The boat was being pulled southwards, against the wind.

"Gotcha," Malik thought.

It took all afternoon to wear the fish out, playing the slack between two poles, gradually bringing the fish to the surface, then letting more line out when the great sturgeon dove. It took a long time to land the fish. It thrashed and the line cut Malik's hands deeply. It spooked when they tried to club it and dove again.

Finally they wore it out and it floated beside them belly up. Bobo tried to hold it by putting his hands in the fish's gills but it thrashed one last time and sent Bobo flying into the water. Malik tossed a net and with Bobo in the water they were able to get the net around the fish.

The fish was too big to pull on board. It must have been as long as both of them put together. They lashed the net to the outrigger and Bobo ripped out the gills. It must have weighed eight hundred pounds. It was dark when they got back to the camp on the Bear River. Anandi was all prepared: she had a fire built and all of her knives out.

When Malik asked her how she had known they had caught a sturgeon, she stared at him in disbelief, her eyes big and her mouth open. "I sent it to you," she whispered.

Malik wasn't sure about that. One couldn't give orders to a fish, not even shamans. Fish had to be entreated. Or fooled.

"It's huge," Malik said.

Anandi smiled. "They get bigger every year," she said. "Be sure to leave some out for the birds, for my sisters."

Malik nodded.

"Oh, and she's full of eggs," Anandi added. "Those are for us."

That night Malik dreamed that the great fish had swallowed him. And that Heather had sent diving birds to peck the fish open to release him.

The Sixth
Through the Tenth Millennia
7021–12020

In far parts of the world several civilizations rose to prominence and then disappeared—the lifespans of large-scale societies had shortened. A chain of city-states on the Deseado in Argentina developed a pictographic writing system, and took advantage of their long inlet to become traders, sometimes sailing as far north as the Paraná. As the green belt in the Sahara expanded and the lakes filled, a dynasty of matrilineal kings emerged in Chad and Libya that claimed descent from the Pharaohs who had built the pyramids. For three hundred years there were great bazaars on the Yenisey River in Siberia, caravans coming from as far as the rich uplands of Tibet. Cities seemed to rise and fall in Mexico on a thousand year cycle.

Several times boats arrived on the coasts of North America, by accident rather than by design, carrying strange and exotic people. Around most of the world, however, people stayed where they were and kept spread out. Cities were where people got sick.

In California, autumn tended to come early and to persist into December or even into January, with the days pleasant and the nights cool. The broad-leaved trees took on colors by turns, the yellows of the various oaks finally giving way to the reds of the maples.

Global sea levels continued dropping for five thousand years. Deep sea deposition of carbonate increased. Greenland, once again, was covered with ice. A star in Cepheus marked the North Pole.

High erosion rates in the mountains had deposited thirty feet of sediment on the floor of the Great Bay, covering whatever was there before like a blanket of new fallen snow. By the end of the Eighth Millennium, the Great Bay had receded nearly to the Carquinez Strait. Grasses flourished in the new valley, and during the winter months tens of thousands of sand hill cranes filled the meadows and wetlands. People imitated their dances.

ω ω ω

The Sand Listeners

Mojave River
six thousand years after the Collapse
from History of the Kingdom of Kuxlaven, Guererreo

They heard the camels long before the caravan arrived.

After the envoys had washed and eaten, and the gifts were arranged, Old Sesqua came out of her wickiup and met the envoys in the shade of the cottonwoods.

The envoys were dressed in short sarongs, dyed a deep turquoise blue, wore finely woven sandals, and both had thin light capes tied around their necks. Neither were strangers to diplomacy, and through a series of two interpreters, greeted Sesqua and her people and presented their gifts.

There were bundles of dried dates, as well as bundles of many other dried fruits, all exotic and from the deep lands of Mexico. There were rolls of fine cotton cloth, in many colors. There were copper axes and knives. There were wheels and axles that could be assembled into small carts.

When all of the gifts had been presented, the envoys explained the purpose of their mission, and the questions of their lord. They moved knotted strings through their hands and read from a long belt woven of dyed quills and tiny shells. They told how they had traveled by boat northward for many days to arrive at the port at Thousand Palms. They told how they had traveled northward through the mountains and the desert to finally reach the home of the Sand Listeners on the Mojave River, and how they hoped that their request would be granted.

Old Sesqua pondered their questions for a long time and no one spoke. Finally she agreed to go on a listening, but warned the envoys that no one knew if and when the sands would speak, and made arrangements to travel to the dunes the next morning. The dunes had been moving nearer to them every year but they were still two days' journey away. Sesqua took three apprentices and they set out just after dawn, on foot.

The first night they camped at the last springs, on the edge of the Devils Playground, and refilled their goatskins. There were other great dunes to the north of them, but these dunes never sang and they called them the Quiet Ones.

When they reached the sand the girls made camp at the foot of the highest and steepest ridge of dunes. They had carried some dried food but while they were at the dunes they only ate the sand food, pulling up the tubers and eating them raw. On the third day the dunes began to sing.

The deep voice of the Patriarch boomed and moaned like a bullfrog might if a bullfrog were a thousand feet high. But there were other voices. The Wife sang entreaties and sang of great loss. The Wife sang tears and panther songs. She sang the orange of the dawn.

And there was a third voice, a voice the listeners had never heard before. It was a young voice, an icy voice that creaked and punctuated the sand from everywhere at once. It sang of snow and of ten thousand miles of glistening crystals. It sang of rain and of animals that died too young. It sang of time longer than any of them knew.

The women climbed the dunes following the ridges and the sun was high before they reached the top. They had let Sesqua lead and the girls were spread out behind her but they all saw her suddenly sink into the sand like a rock into a pool.

Deep beneath the sand Sesqua visited the Lord of the Envoys in his distant palace. She saw the armies that had formed to the east and the south of him and she saw him cutting the skin of his arms and his breasts and his penis and she knew that none of it would help him.

The singing of the sand had now formed into words. The Patriarch and the Wife greeted her and told stories and she saw great elephants in snow and she knew that the Child was trying to give birth but that one of them, either the Mother or the Child, would die.

She saw the springs of her people where the bighorns came down to drink and she saw the screwbean and the desert willow. She saw the Mojave River twisting across the desert like a sidewinder, rising up from the sand and then disappearing again into the sand. She saw great Soda Lake fill and then dry, and then there were large metal insects made of iron and steel crawling on the ground and belching blue smoke and then there were soldiers in blue coats and then the lake again filled, and she wondered if she were back in her own time.

Sesqua dropped again, deeper into the center of the dune, and entered a great room, a great hall in which a land of grass and prairie stretched out of sight into the distance. There were winding rivers here broader than any she had ever seen and she saw people floating on the river in boats of skin. The singing of the voices would harmonize and there would be drum beats and then again there would be weeping.

Sesqua waved to the people in the boats but they were too far away to see her. She entered a copse of trees and followed a path through a forest and then saw mountain ranges before her that stretched as far as she could see. It was too far to walk so Sesqua floated and passed a land where people had fish's heads and then she found a green land where the plants could speak.

The voices of the plants mixed with the singing of the sand and Sesqua knew that they must tell the envoys that their lord and all of his family and clan would have to leave the place where they lived and find a new home in the mountains, where there were trees and where snow fell.

Sesqua fell again and was again in a dry land where a great sand dune was moving toward her like a huge wave approaching the shore. She was lying on her stomach with her head toward the dune and the sand began to wash over her. When the sand had completely covered her down to her legs she began to swim, deeper into the sand, and found herself at the camp where the girls were waiting for her.

The Far Millennia

BEGINNING TEN THOUSAND YEARS
AFTER THE COLLAPSE

It may have been the shortest interglacial in geological history. It went off like a flashbulb, did its work, and was over. The earth was a poorer place, but it could have been worse. Thousands of species of plants and animals, large and small, vanished forever, but it could have been worse, much worse.

Cleansing ice began creeping down from the north. Winters were long and often severe. Passes in the Sierras rarely opened until the middle of summer, if at all, and snowfall became common and heavy in the mountains all the way to the Santa Ana range in Southern California. It was getting cold, and very quickly.

People on the Modoc Plateau painted the animals they saw on the walls of caves and on the rock faces along the edges of their lake. They painted elephants and bears, the big horned sheep and the long horned antelopes, the lions and the panthers, but compared to the art of the Upper Paleolithic the painting had a chastened quality. Humans were always depicted with the animals, often in scenes of great pathos, and plants and trees were painted in fantastically elaborated branchings. The paintings were elegant, but lacked the magical optimism and the sense of unlimited power that had characterized the paintings of their predecessors forty and fifty thousand years before them. Class *Mammalia* had dodged a bullet and everyone knew it.

At the beginning of the Eleventh Millennium, sea levels had dropped to their lowest point in twenty thousand years.

After miles of meanderings across the broad Central Valley and the flats of Suisun and San Pablo, the Sacramento River flowed swiftly through the Golden Gate, then flattened out and meandered another ten miles across a gently sloping coastal plain to finally empty into the Pacific Ocean in a lazy delta a third of the way to the Farallones.

By the Fourteenth Millennium the Farallones were part of the mainland and sea level would still drop another 120 feet. Monterey Bay disappeared, the Pajaro emptying into a deep canyon with a spectacular falls. Point Reyes was over twenty miles inland from the coast. The Channel Islands were a single land mass, five times their previous size and separated from the mainland only by a two mile channel of treacherous water at Point Mugu.

It was going to be cold for a long time. The earth seemed to crave a long winter. When spring at last reawakened and the ice again retreated, the earth would still be a poorer place. There would be no surface deposits of ores or minerals, no underground reserves of energy, and far less resilience in the biosphere. So the earth settled into her cold slumber. She was in no hurry to wake up.

ॐ ॐ ॐ

The Caribou Hunters

Pit River
sixteen thousand years after the Collapse
from Myths and Legends, *Archives of the Colleagues*
of Thermocene Studies

Sengimet, Ridiwyn, and Jennith lived on the Pit River on the Modoc Plateau. When their friends moved south to follow the elephants down to the valleys they decided to stay.

It was a hard winter. It was dark and they lost their shadows. It was dark so the light of their dreams was as bright as the sunlight and sometimes they were confused. It was a hard winter and cold and sometimes bad feelings came in and sometimes they were hungry and there were bad feelings between the women and the man felt bad.

They were eating lichen like the reindeer but they couldn't find any reindeer, which is how the young one got the idea. They were all pretty hungry. The women were fighting and the man couldn't hunt or he would hunt but he couldn't find any deer.

The nights were long but not always happy the way nights should be and not always restful. He left early with his arrows and the young one painted a reindeer on the rock and sang to it until it was ready to come alive and then she climbed through the rock.

It was already dusk when Sengimet saw the deer. It was a young female and he thanked his luck. He thought it was an ordinary reindeer. He didn't know that it was his younger wife who was out looking for the deer herd. Sengimet aimed and his first arrow went through her heart.

Out of her love Jennith tried to stay in her deer body but she couldn't and when Sengimet saw what he had done—that it was the younger of his two wives that he had killed—he was overcome with grief. He began wailing loudly and crying out and all the snow began dropping from the tree branches in great clumps. Maybe a wind had sprung up.

Now Jennith appeared as a deer spirit—she looked like a real caribou standing there in the snow by the body of the girl but Sengimet recognized her voice and she talked to him. For a while they talked like lovers and then Jennith told him that he must take her body back to the shelter and eat it. Then she wandered into the forest.

Sengimet was crying the whole time but he dragged and carried the body back to the shelter and even Ridiwyn cried some. They butchered the body and carried the entrails out to some rocks for the wolves to eat.

After that Sengimet spent more time in the forest. He was hoping that he would see her again because he was still in love with her and he was grieving. He would hide in glades along the river and chew tobacco and sing calling songs. Or he would walk across the ice when the river was frozen and search for her tracks.

Sengimet and Ridiwyn never had any children. When they grew old the gods took pity on them and changed both of them into reindeer so that they could go on searching for Jennith. They wandered far to the north to the frozen country and then they climbed into the sky, and that's where they still are—those three bright stars, Vega, Deneb, and Thuban, that circle around the pole, chasing each other and marking the way north.

Afterword

This is a work of fiction, and for purposes of the story I have used accelerated rising of sea levels beyond that of current projections. And yet, such rises are not impossible. At the end of the Pleistocene, sea level rose 120 feet in twelve thousand years, and that without the unprecedented human-generated changes to the atmosphere of today. Carbon dioxide levels in the atmosphere are already thirty percent higher than during any of the warm interglacials of the last million years, and probably higher than at any time in the last twenty million years, and show no signs of abating. Quite the contrary.

New studies of global climate change and the dynamics involved, based on ice cores or subtle isotope ratios, continue to appear every several months in *Nature* and *Science*, almost all of them increasing the severity of current predictions. Meanwhile, little is being done to change the course of industrial development. The quality of life on earth is not a corporate concern, even if it happens to be for some members of the boards.

And it is unlikely that an apocalypse will save us. Much more likely is a gradual degradation of the quality of life, and, for many species, of their habitat and their chances for survival. In late Roman times, in the European provinces, where aristocratic estates shared the valleys with the estates of the Barbarians, citizens complained about the interruptions of the mail service, but went on writing poems in the latest styles. On the other hand, a storyteller has a certain license, and there is a mural in the British Museum depicting Canterbury in the seventh century: Saxon hovels set amid the ruins of the fine Roman buildings; sheep and cattle grazing the overgrown markets.

ACKNOWLEDGEMENTS

Thanks are due to Jeremy Bigalke, who was driving me hundreds of miles to a book signing in Portland as I wrote the first chapter of this story, and who kept quiet and let me write.

A number of people listened to the stories, and encouraged me with their attention, including Gwyllm and Mary Llydd, and members of my extended family: Howard, Pat, and Coral Pendell, my daughter Marici Pendell, and my mother Carol Pendell.

Walter Mandell shared his own vision of an influenza outbreak on an online forum, which rang true. Joanna Reichhold provided muse-like inspirations more than once, with her own stories and questions. Erik Davis invited me to read at his book party for *The Visionary State* in San Francisco, where the public airing of the beginnings of the story encouraged me to continue. Philip Daughtry, Jeremy Bigalke, Gary Snyder, Thomas Christensen, Iven Lourie, Rob Matthews, and Richard Grossinger read the manuscript and offered feedback. Thanks to my editor, Jon Goodspeed, for patience and perspicacity. And thanks to the Buzzards, ever my support group, who created expansive vistas in which some of these stories could be visited on the wing.

And very special thanks to Laura Pendell, who carefully listened to the stories with her sharp and encouraging ear and accompanied me on road and trail trips to many of the locations described in the book.

About the Author

Poet DALE PENDELL was the author of the award-winning *Pharmako* trilogy, a literary history of psychoactive plants. His poetry is widely anthologized, most recently in *The Wisdom Book of American Buddhist Poetry* and *The Baby Beats and the 2nd San Francisco Renaissance*. Combining the teachings of poet Gary Snyder, Zen teacher Robert Aitken, and philosopher Norman O. Brown, Dale developed themes of "ancient wisdom / wild mind." Besides writing, Pendell was a consultant for herbal product development and botanical surveys as well as a computer scientist. He was the founding editor of *Kuksu: Journal of Backcountry Writing* and a cofounder of the Primitive Arts Institute. He died in 2018.

About North Atlantic Books

North Atlantic Books (NAB) is an independent, nonprofit publisher committed to a bold exploration of the relationships between mind, body, spirit, and nature. Founded in 1974, NAB aims to nurture a holistic view of the arts, sciences, humanities, and healing. To make a donation or to learn more about our books, authors, events, and newsletter, please visit www.northatlanticbooks.com.

North Atlantic Books is the publishing arm of the Society for the Study of Native Arts and Sciences, a 501(c)(3) nonprofit educational organization that promotes cross-cultural perspectives linking scientific, social, and artistic fields. To learn how you can support us, please visit our website.